A Burning Place.
A Screaming Place.
White heat blazing across searing land. Flaming reds. Vermilion reflections. Glowing orange embers. Caustic air, insufferable within parched mortal lungs. Cracked fissures scoring the dry earth. Redstone mesas towering up from a fractured landscape. A smoldering primordial place where a soulful requiem is sung. A place inhabited by none.
Molten. Glaring. Forbidding.
Know there is a Screaming, Burning Place Above.

A Sacred Place.
A Silent Place.
Vaulted ceilings of stone. Dark stillness. A living, breathing pulse of the Ancient Ones. Twisting shadowed chambers. A primitive Labyrinth. Maze of Magic. Cool catacombs where Truth reclines in timeless repose. The last sepulcher. A holy sanctuary. The deep inner sanctum where the slumbering Knowledge remains untouched. The hallowed Tomb of the Tabernacle where a song of life is sung. A place inhabited by the Ka. . . the Guardian Spirit.
Cool. Dark. Waiting.
Know there is a Silent, Sacred Place Below.

Books by Mary Summer Rain

Nonfiction

Spirit Song
Phoenix Rising
Dreamwalker
Phantoms Afoot
Earthway
Daybreak
Soul Sounds
Whispered Wisdom
Ancient Echoes
Bittersweet
The Visitation

Fiction

The Seventh Mesa

Children's

Mountains, Meadows and Moonbeams

With Alex Greystone

Mary Summer Rain on Dreams

Books on Tape

Spirit Song
Phoenix Rising
Dreamwalker
Phantoms Afoot
The Visitation

The Seventh Mesa

A Novel by

Mary Summer Rain

HAMPTON ROADS PUBLISHING COMPANY, INC.

For information write:

Hampton Roads Publishing Company, Inc.
134 Burgess Lane
Charlottesville, VA 22902

Or call: (804) 296-2772
FAX: (804) 296-5096

If you are unable to order this book from your local
bookseller, you may order directly from the publisher.
Quantity discounts for organizations are available.
Call 1-800-766-8009, toll-free.

ISBN 1-57174-061-9

Printed on acid-free paper in the United States of America

*To those readers who would perceive the gentle
Heartbeat of Truth that softly pulses beneath
the covering Shroud of Fiction.*

Contents

THE KA'S FOREWORD

No name have I, yet I have had many names. I possess no body, yet I have form. Untouchable am I, yet I have substance. I hear and see because I perceive. Naught can harm me, yet I retain formidable power. I live.

I am the eyes of the redstone monoliths that dwell upon the crematoria sands. My ears ride the scorching breath of inferno winds. My awareness of your stealthy approach is acute. I am changeable, yet have remained immutable through the ages. I am.

In your folly you have oft trespassed upon the Burning Place Above. In your ignorance you have ventured too near. In your simplistic curiosity you have passed into forbidden territory. Therefore, I am.

Would you believe that you would be allowed to trespass? To be permitted entry? Would you think that you would gain easy access? To see? Would you not consider dire consequences for removing the sacred objects of the Ancient Ones who set them there? Would you be so ignorant to believe a powerful safeguard had not been provided? Therefore, I am.

Some have foolishly called me Curse of the Pharaohs. Some call me a Haunting Thing. Vile. Specter of Death. Ghost. But those terms emit from the tongues of frightened mortals. I am none of those things.

I am The Preserver. The Living Protector of the Seal. The Watching Spirit. Guardian for the Ancient Ones. I am the Ka of the sacred Seventh Mesa. I am.

For eons have I existed here within the cool and dark recesses below the Burning Place Above. For eons have I existed for the sole purpose of preserving and protecting the sacredness that dwells here in the ancient Tabernacle of the earth.

My ears have heard. My eyes have seen. My heart has felt. Your loud footfalls through the Ages have been clumsy, your sight has been primitive and your deeds have been self-serving. Yet I await in patience for the light of true spirituality to ignite upon the horizon of the land.

Until mortals lay down their arms and recognize the Family of all Humankind. . .I am. Until the little children no longer hunger and their sweet mothers no longer weep. . .I am. Until mortals cease desecrating the benevolent Grandmother Earth and return to living the Way. . .I am. Until your eyes and ears and hearts are opened. . .I am.

Your warring, your immaturity and arrogance gives unto me the energy that feeds my purpose. I exist with power bestowed upon me so that, in your primitiveness, you cannot misuse the beautiful Secrets I protect, for truly, you are as careless children without understanding.

I am Wisdom. I am Love. I am pure Spirituality. Until you have gained a large measure of these things, you are not ready to tread the holy Corridors below. I do not malevolently bar your way, I simply await your enlightenment until you have proven to possess understanding and your spirits radiate spirituality and unconditional love that is inherent within the hearts of the children of the earth.

Until then. . .I am, for I am the Preserver. The Living Protector of the Seal. The Watching Spirit. Guardian for the Ancient Ones. The Ka of the Seventh Mesa.

I am. . .because you are not.

Part One
THE BECKONING

Twisting paths. Unexpected byways. Beckoning waysides.

The causal forces for man's ultimate pathway through life are not directly contingent upon the impetus of the individual's personal desires or decisions, but rather upon the beautiful and nebulous promptings of the wise Spirit within, which is ever acutely aware of its purpose.

We take subliminal notice of the whispered urgings. . .And we are restless beings until we act on the compelling directives within. We then move to the sweet sound of our own metered chanting. We drift along the warm current of our flowing spirits and, in gentle Acceptance, do we set foot upon the twisting paths, the unexpected byways and the beckoning waysides.

Michael

A living blackness. A breathing void. A silence that screamed.

The man listened.

His ears strained for sensory clues until they pounded with the forceful pain of it. No perceptual sound came through the deep, ebony surround of unearthly stillness. No sound emitted from within the thickly congealed blackness that now surrounded him like a great black hole in space. The total vacuum was a senseless thing, senseless except for the bone-chilling coldness beneath the man's trembling fingers that suctioned to the rough stone walls like clinging tentacles. Taut fingers anchored him to the only solitary reality there was—the singular solid reality that insured his hold on sanity in this underground place of nothingness.

Inching along the cold wall, his forward progress was agonizingly slow. The man's mind ached to force his body to speed forward, forward to discover and gain an exit out of this frigid, still place, but now that wasn't even an option for him.

His forward movement ceased. He needed to gather his rationality, his logic.

Mind probed the darkness.

Would his next step fail to connect with solid ground? Would he be suddenly pitched downward into an unseen abyss? The vivid vision of the possibility caused him to shudder. He clearly imagined his helpless body plummeting in the freefall, flailing limbs twirling like a child's pinwheel; pitching, spinning, downward through the consuming blackness, then finally hitting bottom—broken and lifeless—ending up no more of consequence than a misshapen doll, discarded and forgotten.

In the man's imagination, he clearly envisioned how this desolate, lightless place would then voraciously feed upon his shattered form, with nothing left but the unwanted whiteness of his fractured bones.

His mind tortured through the possible scenarios. Would the final impact of his body make a sound in this soundless place? Perhaps a splash? Were Stygian waters, foul and bottomless, awaiting him somewhere ahead? Below?

Renewed fear swelled within the man's active mind. Gleaming droplets of sweat beaded out from his every pore, his every cell. The wetness seeped out, soaking and gluing his clothes like a second skin.

He cautiously slid his leading foot forward another testing inch. By God, he silently avowed, he'd be damned if a careless mistake now was going to end his life in a fatal fall. He had a lot of living to do yet. He had important things to accomplish, landmark discoveries to make, great contributions that could alter history—especially if he ever made it out of this godforsaken place.

As the exploratory foot scraped forward, the noise of it was greatly magnified. The harsh sound of grating sand echoed through the oppressive stillness.

The man froze and listened again.

His mind raced through all he'd known of such underground caverns. There should be sounds. There damn well should be some sounds.

He strained to listen for the metered echo of mineral-rich water dripping off the end of hanging stalactites. He sought to hear some distant moaning or howling air movement through the stone configurations. He hoped to at least pick up the expected sound of rustling wings from disturbed bats. Some sound should be heard.

But there were none, nothing but those of his own solitary, lonely movements and labored breathing.

His scalp crawled. Terror gripped his spine. Tears stung his eyes.

Alone.

So alone.

The frightened man's searching fingers trembled along the cold wall. Now they were his eyes, his ears.

He concentrated.

Again the exploring foot inched forward into the blackness.

It struck a barrier.

A rock? Then, daring to take one anchored hand away from the comforting security of the stone wall, he raised it before his face and slowly extended it out over his leading foot, forward toward the unknown.

Fingertips immediately connected with another wall directly in front of him. Quickly he pulled the other hand over to it. A dead end? Was this what it had finally come to? His end? Was this to be the anticlimactic finale of his existence?

Curiously, the man's seeing fingers explored the angled stone that blocked his way. Confusion flooded his wildly racing mind while he frantically traced up and down the crevice of the stone junction. What his discovering fingers were conveying was not a comprehensible message. This ell-shaped turn of the cave was not at all like the others had been; this one was an acute right angle. And, with rising excitement now temporarily overshadowing his former fears, the experienced fingers desperately traced down the ruler-straight and smoothly-mitered corner. It had not been a random configuration of natural stone. It had not been a natural cave surface. It had been expertly *chiseled.* It had been *constructed*!

This discovery threw the man's logic into chaos. What did this mean? How could this even be?

He was a long way from the hidden entry opening and nearly a mile down into the black cavern. Yet someone had chiseled a plumbed corner and expertly constructed a smooth wall!

How?

Who?

What?

His mind was spinning with the discovery of the incredible feat. Thoughts racing with myriad speculations and probable ramifications of the enormity of the curious find, the man's breath came in clipped rushes.

Excitement began to build and, with a pounding heart, his trembling fingers dared to return to the glassy smoothness of the new wall before him. The mind found it hard to accept the fact that it felt like smooth marble.

Then, scurrying fingers suddenly halted their frenzied scrambling. Fingertips dipped into an indentation. Quickly now, worrying hands frantically worked over the cold wall. They raced over engravings—one after the other—until the man's arms stretched full out over the wall.

Yes! The entire *wall* was filled with engravings! One right after the other, up and down, across from end to end!

"Calm," he panted into the dark. "I need to calm down."

And consciously straining for controlled mastery over the irritating distraction of his erratic respiration, he forced himself to breathe at a slower, quieter rate.

He cursed the inky surround. What he wouldn't have given then for a flashlight. Angrily he berated himself for his earlier stupidity. Never before had he ventured into a cavern without first placing fresh batteries in his lantern. He thought about the useless piece of equipment he had abandoned some time ago. How long had it been since then anyway? Hours? Now he suffered the consequences of that singular oversight. He silently cursed as he thought about what he would give for just one quick look at the thing that towered before him now.

Concentrating intently, his eyes automatically squinted with the effort of choosing a singular engraving to center his mind on. Experienced fingerpads attempted to transfer the image to the man's mind's eye for identification. Over and over the excited digits traced the sharp indentation of the ancient configuration.

The man's skin prickled with rising goosebumps. He frowned in frustration as impossible hypotheses gathered form. Could he be wrong?

Again he concentrated on the detailed carving. Yet, as amazing as it seemed, all his extensive experience said that it was so. He shook his head in disbelief.

"What?" he whispered. "What? How can this be? This is impossible!"

Again. Again. And once more just to be certain, he retraced over the symbol chiseled in the smooth stone. His finely-tuned mind was computing but not believing in the impression.

"What the hell is an ancient Egyptian cartouche doing in a cavern deep beneath the American southwest desert?"

Knowledgeably he inched his anxious fingers down to the engraved character directly below the pharaoh's name. The man's heavy brows knitted tightly together in consternation.

"Oh shit! What's this?" he flared with growing excitement.

More intimately now, he cautiously felt over the new carving that was more complex than the deciphered one above. Meticulously did his mind interpret what his fingerpads saw for him. And suddenly, shockingly, all the experienced man's years of accumulated knowledge, judgments and conclusions were shattered. What he had been touching just could *not be*! It was absolutely unheard of. No! Undeniably impossible! Yet. . .here, in solid carved-in-stone relief was evidence of a hugh thunderbird—an American Indian thunderbird—intermixed with ancient Egyptian hieroglyphs!

What was this place?

What incredible place had he inadvertently stumbled into?

How could such a find be classified? There just was no such place on the face of the earth that displayed Egyptian symbols *with* American Indian petroglyphs! Yet. . .

Quickly forgetting all his former fears of the place, the man became totally absorbed with the mysterious wall. Wholeheartedly pouring all his concentration into the strange and baffling enigma before him, he meticulously centered his attention on yet another engraved character. Like a sightless person intent on reading Braille, exploring fingers carefully examined the new carving. Up, down and around went the sensitive fingertips. The intricate computer within his mind searched relentlessly for the connecting information that would validate the findings.

Searching.

Searching.

Finally his mental screen flashed two concluding words.

ORIGIN UNKNOWN.

Greatly frustrated, the man swiped at the sweat that dripped from his brow. And, like a nervous safecracker, he ran his damp palms down his pant legs and again touched the object of his attention.

Over and over he intently retraced the unfamiliar rune. Over and over he studiously followed the outline of the curious symbol. And drawing from his expansive experience with disintegrating papyri, ancient tablets and complex Babylonian and Persian cuneiforms, his mind-based calculations continued to spew forth the identical conclusion as before.

ORIGIN UNKNOWN.

The inexplicable options were mind-boggling. They were far beyond any comprehension the human mind was capable of.

The man in the depths of the dark cavern had thoroughly studied the major civilizations throughout time. He was at least subliminally familiar with the basic generalities of their written language—their symbols. But this, this was unlike anything he had ever seen or felt. What unknown race was this engraved character from? And what did it mean? Why was it here among Egyptian and Native American symbols?

Again anxious hands felt the cold wall. Arms splayed out to stretch wide. Yes! The entire wall was full!

On tiptoes now, the man reached with straining fingertips high above his head. How far did the writings reach? To the top of the wall? And how high was that? Being hopelessly unable to accurately determine—or even hazard an educated guess without the flashlight—he again returned his attention to the individual engravings. Quickly he took a sampling survey of one chosen portion of the cryptic monolith. Fingers traced over and into the perfect indentations.

Excitement grew to a fevered pitch as he identified each source in turn.

EGYPTIAN. . .EGYPTIAN. . .UNKNOWN. . .AMERICAN INDIAN. . .UNKNOWN. . .AMERICAN INDIAN. . .EGYPTIAN. . .UNKNOWN. . .UNKNOWN. . .UNKNOWN. . . .

"Shit!" he cried. "What the hell have I got here?"

Nowhere on earth had such diverse cultures intermingled their language. Nowhere had such evidence been discovered recorded in hieroglyph and petroglyphs in stone! Nowhere, just *nowhere* had there been evidence unearthed that would even begin to substantiate that such a mixing was remotely possible.

Searching fingers locked onto an UNKNOWN character while the man intently concentrated.

It was then the sound came.

It was then it speared through his consciousness.

If the young scientist hadn't been so intent, he would've heard it long before now—he would've heard it begin the very moment his searching fingertips first touched the smooth engraved wall. But now, now it had grown in volume enough to cause a diversion of thought. Though it was yet merely a nebulous and muted background sound, it had greatly intensified from its beginning volume, and eerily, its cadence began to meld with the man's own pounding heartbeats. This rhythmic drumming of another heartsound became increasingly louder and louder from somewhere deep within the thick blackness beyond him.

The man held his breath while straining to hear.

He cocked his head to listen.

Scalp crawling, he shakily called out into the palpitating void, only to hear his own cracked voice echo throughout the twisted tunnels of the cavern. The sound of it shattered the stillness, yet when the last reverberation died out, the ominously metered heartbeat remained strong. It had gained strength. Clearly its source was closer. Closer. Its approaching presence stirred the air over the man's damp face and he convulsed in a sudden shiver that racked his bones.

Louder.

Louder, more powerful beats drummed and echoed from the blackness and the Thing's breathing was heard whooshing in and out of unseen lungs. Huge lungs.

Heartbeats, thundering now, throbbed through the man's head until he feared it'd explode with the deafening vibration of it.

A powerful force of breath then blustered through the stone corridors. The man slapped his hands over his ears as he desperately tried to soften the roar of the frightening sound.

Then. . .silence.

Nothing.

Nothing but the sudden appearance of a pair of shining eyes. Glaring, brilliant blue eyes floated around the cavern bend. They neared the man.

They hovered unblinking. Glowing.

And slowly, ever so slowly, did they float forward.

Michael Greystone screamed.

He screamed and screamed and screamed.

The young man's throat burned raw from the emitted force of his night terror. Slowly, he glanced about as his sharpening consciousness dispelled the vision. Blinking, he discovered himself on the floor of his own bedroom. He was wrapped in a rumpled tangle of damp sheets and twisted blankets. Body, sweat soaked. Pajamas, plastered like wallpaper, stuck solidly to the clammy skin. He trembled as convulsive shudders ripped through his body.

"Oh God," he moaned through chattering teeth, "not again. Oh dear God, not again."

Michael sighed heavily as he allowed himself to crumple back onto the receiving pile of covers that'd been wrapped like a barrier cocoon around him, as if he'd frantically attempted to return to the warm and safe womb waters.

Breathing easier, his gaze swept the familiar room and stopped at the closed French doors. The daybreak light lazily wafted through.

Golden. Warm.

Songbirds noisily chirped in the century-old maple branches that reached their gnarled limbs out to scrape against the second floor of the brick colonial. It was a beautifully bright New England morn. Cheeriness poured into the small room. It poured into the man's mind.

Reality solidified.

The pitiful figure that had been curled in the fetal position groaned, while long limbs painfully inched away from the central core of security they had so desperately sought out. They ached sharply as tense and constricted muscles stretched to unfold. Joints cracked as they straightened full out.

How long had it been this time?

How long had his limbs retracted tight like some threatened hedgehog?

How long had he been subjected to the dream terror that forced him into the excruciating, self-imposed position?

How long? It felt like an eternity.

Now he listened to the common bird sounds. Sweet reality. Now he could safely relax without fear of an unknown terror snapping at his exposed extremities. And once calmed, he remained on the floor to think about what could be happening to him.

Considerable time was spent on musing the occurrence over. He recalled that even as a young boy he had never experienced any traumatically restless nights. At least he couldn't remember any. If they'd been anything like these most recent nightmares, he was certain he'd have recalled them—vividly. Then again, if they'd been so terribly horrifying, perhaps his immature mind would've protected him by effectively blocking them out. No, that wasn't a valid excuse. His mother had always been the sort of person who would've insisted he talk out his night terrors. Besides, as a youngster he hadn't been one to believe in grotesquely deformed, foot-dragging bogeymen or slimy, slavering monsters that crouched beneath his bed waiting to grab at his bare ankles. No, he never had the usual childhood imaginings of untold horrors living and waiting just behind his clothes in the closet. No, he never recoiled in bed to stare in a terrorized state from the edges of the covers at the frozen eyes of his toys that stared back at him in the dark. Never. No, never. Not once.

Thinking back on those earlier years, a soft smile tipped the corners of his mouth. Even his wildly imaginative adolescent fascinations with the mysterious Egyptian curses, rotting mummy wrappings and the oddly-shaped mythical characters of that ancient time never elicited any devastating nightmares within the colorful scenes of his childhood dreamscapes. Yes, he now underscored with confidence, his developing young mind had indeed taken all his intriguing fascinations in stride. He'd kept reality in check.

Michael's thoughts trailed up through time. Even after his appointment as Assistant Curator of Antiquities of the Boston Museum, when he'd been exposed to the most frightening artifacts of ancient human remnants, he'd never dreamed of the hideous things—not once. So, he wondered, why now? Why start getting spooked now? And why dream of such a phantasmic dark place interring such an impossible hodgepodge of cultures mixed together? Why dream of a breathless place, a place where some thing breathed? A place far below the earth that was naturally constructed by the birth throes of the planet, yet held precise architecturally engineered sections?

In the light of day Michael sighed and recalled the dream. It had seemed so real. . . so vividly real. He remembered his utter amazement to discover the smooth wall with the engravings. And what really confounded him were the symbols he couldn't classify. . .the Unknown ones. Now he could clearly envision the outlines his dream fingers had traced. And he wondered if he would ever come across anything like it in his lifetime. The entire dreamscape scenario was a baffling enigma of contrasts and contradictions.

The young anthropology professor sighed again as he subliminally watched the random dust motes aimlessly float upon the sunbeam that speared the bedroom carpet. His wandering eyes shifted upward to focus on the various plaques and masks that adorned every available inch of his walls. It was an innocent enough collection. Authentic souvenirs of his years of field study hung as daily reminders of his extensive research and exhaustive expeditions into the interiors of exotic places. He thoughtfully looked from one to the other.

Ebony wooden voodoo faces stared back.

Colorful Toltec masks hung mute.

A woven grass Masai ceremonial face had sightless eyes.

Photographs of the wide-eyed Haitian medicine man looked out with a wild expression.

The rare Egyptian amulets.

The turquoise scarab mounted on the black velvet plaque.

As a bonded unit, all their empty eye sockets gaped to stare at the man on the floor. The masks—a dozen pair of accusing eyes—looked out from a joined consciousness. They looked down upon the one who had removed them from their sacred soils.

Upon the glass coffee table, the obsidian statuette faced the man expectantly. The pointed ears were alert. The sharply extended snout tested the air in its stately frozen stance. Anxiously, Anubis watched. Patiently did it observe through slitted eyes of golden topaz.

Upon the cluttered desk, an elaborately-carved kachina doll stood among the stacks of research papers, scientific reports, and anthropology magazines. In the still room, its feathers fluttered.

The man slowly sat up.

Hypnotically he looked back and forth from one collected artifact to the other.

The room felt electrified. Alive.

Goosebumps quivered over the chilling surface of the man's skin. A living power was growing. He could feel it. His psyche prickled to the force that was slowly beginning to swirl about the room.

Michael's attention was riveted to the sacred scarab. Its delicate shell shimmered with sparkling iridescence. Eyes, beady and gleaming, appeared to flare with life.

His attention shot over to the black voodoo mask. Spirit eyes seemed to glimmer behind the empty sockets.

A subliminal movement caught his attention and he shuddered at the sight of the kachina feathers wafting, quivering again.

The man's neck hairs stiffened.

Something palpable was happening.

Slowly, his eyes met those of each mask. He stared at the voodoo mask.

"You know something, don't you."

Next he peered over at the empty sockets of the Masai warrior.

"And you know about the dreams."

Then his gaze shifted to the native American medicine man's photograph. He stared into the wise one's eyes.

"And you know what it all means. You're trying to tell me something important, aren't you old man." Michael leaned forward. His eyes locked on those of the photograph. "What is it that I need to know? These dreams have some grave essence that's pulling me in." Michael lowered his head and a tear fell along his cheek.

"Yes, Old One, I know what you'd say," he whispered. "You'd say that I'd know the meaning of all this if I was in touch with my heritage."

Then, Michael Greystone, intelligent thinker and experienced anthropologist, shook his head. He attempted to shake off the irrational thoughts. Nervously, he ran trembling hands over his face and raked his fingers through tousled hair. After all these years had he finally reached the crisis point? Had he finally lost the edge? After all these years was he finally falling victim to the folktales, the cultural horror stories and fabled curses? The Evil Eye? The mumbo-jumbo? No, just not possible, not even probable. Not him.

Michael disgustedly mumbled as he collected the nest of blankets and threw them onto the bed. Striding into the small bathroom, he paused before the mirror to examine his reflection. He half expected to see the image of a man going mad looking back. But no, Michael saw Michael. The reflection was unchanged. Who he saw was a tall and lean man of ruddy complexion. Eyes so dark they resembled coal. Strong cheek bones framed by thick, blue-black hair. This was not the face of a madman. Then, in an effort to distract himself from the destructive thoughts, he leaned over and angrily spun the shower faucet. He desperately needed to clear his head. And once exposed to the reviving spray of stinging pellets, his foggy mind began to sharpen by degrees. Now, with his mental faculties stimulated into clarity, he began to reason with the analytical mind he'd been trained to utilize.

The massaging pulse of streaming water worked to soothe the tense neck muscles and, standing beneath the steaming waters, he began thinking back to the time three years ago when a colleague had left reality and sanity behind. Michael sighed and shook his head at the vivid memory of it.

Clifton Westlake had been a brilliant young anthropologist. His future had been so much more than merely promising, for he was clearly headed toward obtaining the honored distinction of becoming the most respected and ambitious man in his field.

Working in tandem with a renowned archeologist, Cliff had broken through the complex coding of several important petroglyphs discovered on tablets unearthed from Mayan digs. Before that he'd meticulously pieced together nearly undecipherable remnants of symbols on a preserved buffalo hide found in a cache buried beneath the Colorado plains.

Michael recalled the telephone conversation with Clifton just before his breakdown. The man had appeared wildly ecstatic over a mysterious find somewhere in the general vicinity of the American Southwest. The excited man was going to have to regroup, he'd said. Yet now Michael remembered how cryptic Cliff had been about it all. He recalled asking Cliff what he thought he'd had and his friend completely avoided the question—didn't even want to voice a hint as to what it was about, only that he was soon going to present to the world the greatest discovery of all time. It was going to shock the entire world.

Then, Michael recalled, several months had gone by without further communication between them before Clifton Westlake hit the headlines—he'd killed himself. And, upon further investigation, the authorities had found his apartment cluttered with crosses and all manner of protective amulets. The authorities had searched extensively for some type of personal journal that'd possibly give them leads to what the bright young researcher had been working on. They'd searched for whatever caused the man's sudden fear and ultimate suicide. Nothing had been uncovered to shed any light on the situation.

Now Michael Greystone seriously contemplated the complex puzzle. What were the causal factors that drove his good friend over the sheer precipice into the dark depths of insanity? What mysterious project had he been involved in? Were there others or was he working alone this time? And, if there were others, were they too driven to self-destruct or are they now too frightened to come forward? No one had ever come forward.

Michael worked the shampoo into an overflowing mass of

lather. His mind hadn't been on the simple task at hand. The unceasing flow of thoughts coursed rapidly through his head like the high mountain river waters surging downstream.

Had Clifton experienced vivid nightmares that terrorized his nights leaving him a sweating and bumbling mass in the mornings? Had he awakened screaming too? Is that what marks the beginning of the end?

Stepping out of the shower and grabbing a towel, he berated himself again for his negative thinking. Everyone knew that anthropologists had to be level-headed. They couldn't delve so deeply into the mystical aspects of obscure cultures and be so taken in to the point of losing their handle on reality. Imaginations had to be reined in, contained. The intelligent and logically reasoning mind couldn't be allowed any extra length to conjure up specters in one's bedroom.

Michael quickly dressed, shoved his papers into the worn briefcase and stood beside his desk to study the old kachina. He gently touched the decorated figure.

"You don't know a damn thing, do you. You're just wood."

The man turned to eye the masks on the wall. They were all just lifeless effigies.

"You're all just stone, some wood, grass and feathers. You're nothing more than simple inanimate objects." He then chuckled under his breath, shook his head and strode out the door.

Out on the bright, tree-lined street of Chestnut Drive, Michael crawled into his old Volkswagen Beetle and started up the engine. Looking up through the shadow-laced windshield, he watched the leaves of oak and maple as they shimmered in the light morning breeze. Down the street, branches gracefully arced over the road, creating a living archway of greenery. He appreciated the beautiful reality and solidness of life.

Michael's attention was drawn back to the brick colonial. The elderly widower had been kind to rent him a room in the large, private house. Reasonable rental rates were few and far between, especially so near the cultural hub of Boston.

Now, gazing up at his bedroom window, he envisioned the personal collection of figures that shared his room. They certainly were nothing more than crude carvings and he was embarrassed to recall his former state of lapsed logic.

The shift lever was forcefully shoved in gear. The little Bug jerked forward and sped down the lane with the green and living ceiling, but the driver wondered if, back up in the solitary stillness of his room, feathers were fluttering.

The pleasant route to the Boston Museum wove through stately neighborhoods that the old city families called home. Traditionally, the proud stone structures hidden behind yawning yards of perfectly trimmed hedges and towering oaks housed the descendants of most of the Founding Fathers. The smell of old money permeated the area. And although the young professor could never hope to attain the social status of those dwelling behind the manicured estates, he still gained some enjoyment from passing through and seeing the grandeur of the solidly constructed symbols of opulence that represented a way of life long abandoned. Now the wave of the rich appeared to be toward Carribean condos and private islands.

The little VW noisily puttered through the quiet streets until the cultural center came into view. The vehicle deftly swung into its reserved parking slot of the large lot. It sighed as the engine was cut. Although the car was old and somewhat battered on the outside, it'd been a loyal and reliable friend to the young man who'd bravely guided it into dry and dusty deserts and over high, twisting mountain ranges of the Pacific Northwest. Other than a few coughs now and again, the little Bug had dutifully served its owner well.

Michael Greystone entered the imposing building that dominated the center of the cultural district. Cavernous corridors stood empty before him. The immense floor-to-ceiling curtainless windows took in the bright sunlight and splashed it down onto the marble floor creating a distorted chessboard splayed across the interior walkway. As the man made his way along the warming corridor, footsteps echoed against the massive walls and, coming up to an unimpressive oaken door, he went through to the Acquisitions Department.

Now, within a windowless stairwell, he descended the three flights of narrow metal stairs that led to his private domain and came out at one of the sub-basement levels. Here there were no sunsplashed floors, no bright windows, just the dreariness of business.

Upstairs there'd soon be a commotion of human activity going on; docents reciting their memorized spiels to enthralled visitors, hoards of semi-controlled school children being herded through the many exhibits and cash registers ringing up continual sales in the retail shop—but here, down here within the deep subterranean levels of the famed museum, there were poorly-lit mazes of corridors linking the offices of the various department heads and their respective secretaries with those darkly mysterious rooms that were no more than holding chambers for acquired antiquities not yet examined, catalogued and tagged.

Footsteps echoed along the narrow corridor until the metered sound stopped at their destination. Painted boldly upon the frosted glass set in the door was the pronouncement that this tiny cubicle belonged solely to Michael Greystone, Anthropologist, Acquisitions Assistant, Boston Museum Department of Antiquities.

The man went in and tossed his briefcase on the desk. Immediately he flipped on the ventilation switch. It got insufferably stuffy down here, he thought as he did every morning upon entering.

Just next door, within an even more confining space, his secretary worked with devoted efficiency.

Michael pressed the intercom button.

"Anything pressing this morning, Ashley?"

The activated intercom rasped with static, yet the sultry voice drifted back through the machine.

"Good morning, Dr. Greystone. As a matter of fact, there is. Doctor Neusome wants to see you right away. He said to go to his office as soon as you got in this morning."

Michael wasn't up to facing the department head so early. He never was, but today he was even more reluctant because the old man could always tell whenever Michael had had one of his recurrent nightmares again.

"I'll give him a call."

The voice on the other end hesitated. "Ahh, I don't think that'd be a good idea, Dr. Greystone. He specifically said that I should tell you that he wanted to see you in his office first thing."

Dr. Greystone sighed. "He say what it's about?"

"Well no, but he seemed real chipper this morning," came the amused tone.

"Ashley, Neusome's never chipper. Anything else for me?"

"Oh, just the usual public inquiries. I'm working on clearing those up now." Ashley paused long enough to spark Michael's psyche.

"What else, Ashley?" he pushed.

"Well," she hedged, "there was a call for you earlier. In fact, the phone was ringing when I came in. It was a Dr. Theodore Weatherbee. He's a professor from some university out west. Let's see. . . where's that memo. Oh yes, he was calling from Boulder, Colorado. He wanted to talk to you and he sounded like it was real urgent."

"Boulder, Colorado. You sure of that?"

"Yes, it's right here in front of me."

Michael frowned. "I don't know anyone out there. What'd he want?"

"Well, I never got that far actually. When he found out you weren't in yet, well, he just mumbled something about the nice hours you kept and then asked for the department head. I patched him right through to Neusome and they talked for quite a long time. Then Neusome left that message for you."

Michael knew his secretary was holding back. "Ashley?"

"Yes, Dr. Greystone?"

"Ah, you didn't by chance overhear anything you could tell me about, did you?"

"Why, Dr. Greystone! Are you insinuating that I listened in?"

Silence.

"Are you, Dr. Greystone?"

Waiting.

A heavy sigh was heard over the intercom. "Well," the secretary finally admitted, "maybe it's about some sort of short-term transfer."

Dr. Greystone was stunned. "For me?"

"Yes," came the immediate reply, "out to Colorado."

"What for? In what capacity?"

"Well, I really couldn't. . ."

Michael was losing patience. "Ashley!"

"To teach, Dr. Greystone."

"Teach!"

"Well something like that. It's just for a little while."

"Thank you, Ashley. Oh, and by the way, you can cut the Dr. Greystone bit. That's always a sure sign you're hiding something."

He disconnected the line and wondered what the old man was up to now. Boulder, Colorado? Why the hell should he go all the way out there? Wasn't he doing a good job right here in Boston? Well, he decided, he'd never know what's going on if he didn't hightail it down the hall to Neusome's office. Dammit, as if he

didn't have enough to worry about, now Neusome had to complicate his life with disruptions.

Michael rapped softly on the department head's door.

"Come in! Come in," came the gruff bark.

Doesn't sound so chipper to me, the younger man thought as
he opened the door and peeked around it.

"Ah, Michael! Just the young man I wanted to see. Sit down,
sit down, my boy."

The visitor did as bid and suspiciously eyed the elderly man
behind the cluttered desk. He didn't have to wait a moment longer
for the mystery to unravel. The portly gentleman wasted no time in
getting down to the heart of the matter as he peered over his glasses.

"How much do you know?" he asked, leaning forward and
squinting knowingly at the younger man.

"Know? All I know is that Ashley said you wanted to see me
right away."

A disappointed look of incredulity washed over Dr. Neusome's
face.

"Oh come, come now. Do you actually think I'm some ig-
noramus? I know how she hangs on that phone. . .been doing it for
years now."

"Who?" Michael asked.

"You know damned well who. She spill the beans? What'd she
tell you?"

Michael grinned to think of Ashley's discovered eavesdropping
habit.

"She said it was something about me being temporarily trans-
ferred out to Colorado."

Dr. Neusome said gruffly, "And did she also say why?"

"To teach," came the reply.

The department head humorously shook his head.

"That busybody's in the wrong position. She's working for the
wrong people. That little informer should be working for the CIA!"

Michael blushed. Had he informed on the woman? Had he just
provided the verification for Neusome's suspicions?

"Oh well," the elder waved him off uncaringly. "I suppose it's
naturally inherent for the woman to feel compelled to snoop. No
harm done here though, thank God." Then he squared himself in
the leather chair and looked hard and long into the younger man's
eyes.

"The call I received this morning was from Dr. Theodore Weatherbee. Known the man for years, we go way back. He desired to speak to you direct, of course, but since you weren't available he decided to connect with me to clear it and get my thinking on it."

"It?" Michael repeated.

"Don't be impudent. I'm getting to all that. Give an old man time to straighten out his thoughts."

Michael smothered a grin while the elder cleared his throat and began to explain.

"Now, Dr. Weatherbee has been head of the Anthropology Department at the University of Colorado for seventeen years. He's highly respected among his peers and runs a tight ship out there in Boulder. From what I've also heard, the students think the world of him. They look up to him like some sort of all-knowing, all-wise sacred guru or something like that.

"Anyway, putting aside his mystical image, the good doctor seems that he's suddenly found himself in a situation of some desperation. He's unexpectedly shorthanded for a particular course. His bright anthropology professor got himself into a serious automobile accident and, at this moment, he's comatose." Dr. Neusome sadly shook his head. "Pitiful, just pitiful," he mumbled to himself before again addressing Michael. "And, they'll just have to wait it out to see what the final prognosis is going to be. Of course the man may yet come out of it, but for now, Boulder's without a much- needed professor to carry on."

The younger man frowned, "I don't get it. Why can't this Weatherbee fill in himself?"

"Too busy, Michael, he's much too busy with having his hands full of other departmental matters, you know; administrative duties, budget and such. Besides, his students wouldn't want to hear anything from him but all the hoodoo mysticism stuff. Tarnation, they'd never get anything worthwhile accomplished. They need someone, Michael."

Dr. Greystone winced. "And you want me to be this someone to fill in for him."

The old gentleman frowned. "No, not me. I want you right where you are. God knows how much I need you here. You're a damned good assistant. No, it's Weatherbee who wants you."

"I haven't taught in years," Michael said.

"Doesn't matter. You and I both know how easily you slip into lectures and how quickly your excitement builds when you're talking about your work. No, that doesn't matter a whit."

"Dr. Neusome, just how did Dr. Weatherbee hear about me, anyway?"

The department head blushed a bit and lowered his gaze. When he looked at Michael again he was sheepishly grinning.

"I suppose I bragged a little too much about my new assistant when he first came to me. Old Theodore never forgot those things I said about you."

Now it was Michael's turn to grin. "Like what things?"

"Oh now, now, we don't want to get sidetracked, Dr. Greystone. Let's keep to the issue at hand, shall we?"

Michael could clearly see that the man was embarrassed so he let the question go unanswered. He turned his thoughts over to the situation at hand.

"So? What's the consensus? Do I just pick up and head for the hills or am I permitted the luxury of deciding for myself?"

"Of course you have input, son, of course you make the final decision. What are your thoughts on it?"

"I haven't had any time for thoughts. I've never been out to Colorado. I've lived in New England all my life. I don't even know what it's like or if I'll like it there."

The elder man shook his head with remembered journeys out west.

"Beautiful place, Michael. I must, in all honesty, say it's magnificent country, magnificent country. Clean air, painted sunsets, high mountains, turquoise skies, congenial people, relaxed atmosphere. . . "

"You sound like a starving travel agent hurting for business," Michael cut in.

"Well," Dr. Neusome sighed, "guess I do at that. But you might also keep in mind that Boulder's got plenty of free-thinkers," he added with a twinkle in his eye.

The young man's eyes twinkled back. "You mean radicals like me."

Dr. Neusome shrugged. "That's not necessarily what I meant, Michael. I simply meant that Boston can be a bit stuffy for a young man like yourself with such wide vision. Perhaps a time among more open-minded peers would do you a world of good. Remember, it's not a permanent move, just a temporary position to give him assistance, just until Weatherbee sees his way clear, sees what's what. There's not a whole lot going on here just now, nothing pressing, so perhaps a change of scene would be beneficial."

Michael smirked. "You hinting at opportunity again?"

"Well, certainly you must admit that this new turn of events could quite possibly open something up for you. You of all people know about those possibilities as well as I do."

Then the elder man rested back in his chair. The leather creaked as he became reminiscent.

"I certainly don't want to bore you with an old man's melancholia, but there were opportunities placed in my path years ago that I wish I'd taken then. I was too hellbent on one singular goal to see how anything else could've widened my horizons, expanded my own field of vision, so to speak. Now that I'm old, I'm too set in my ways, too feeble and brittle of bone to take hold of new opportunities even if they did present themselves at this late date." Dr. Neusome eyed the younger man. "Some things are meant to be, son," he whispered cryptically.

Dr. Greystone remained deep in thought while his eyes scanned his boss's office. Awards hung proudly displayed along the walls. Testimonials to the elder's achievements and contributions to their chosen branch of research. Proof of the dedicated man's years of exhaustive labor in the name of knowledge and science.

As Michael panned the cluttered room, he realized that here was the man's final reward, a small office in the dank and dark sub-basement of a moldy museum. Would the old man be stuck here if he'd taken those veering opportunities he pined about? If the man had ventured forth into the exciting unknown, would his name merely be listed as one of the museum's directors or would it have been renowned worldwide, emblazoned in history forever? Was this underground realm his own future if he stayed? And would a change of scenery finally put a rest to his own horrifying nightmares of late?

"Well, Michael?" came the gentle words from behind the desk.

Michael sighed.

The elder prompted, "As much as I hate to force a quick decision, Dr. Weatherbee does need an immediate response with this. If you should choose to decline, he needs time to make other contacts although you are his first choice."

Would the nightmares really stop? Had the confines of this dark labyrinth day in and day out been mutated into representative dream symbols of a future that was ultimately going nowhere? Dead-ending? Then visions of clear mountain streams filled the screen of his mind's eye. Michael smiled.

"As long as it's temporary," he finally said. "I'll go as long as you hold my position here at the museum."

Dr. Neusome beamed with satisfaction and deep relief.

"That's my boy! Of course you'll still have your position to return to. You've chosen wisely, Michael. You're going to love Colorado."

Michael avoided a response to that last comment. Instead he addressed the timing.

"How soon does this Weatherbee need me?"

Dr. Neusome's bushy brows knitted. "Day before yesterday, son, day before yesterday."

After the young Dr. Greystone had left his office, the elder man swiveled his chair to face a photograph he'd taken of a native American shaman he'd come to know well. The doctor's thoughts drifted. They were drawn into the photograph. Yes, Michael had experienced another dream. Michael was a chosen one. He would not be able to resist the return to his native heritage, for there, there he would find more than himself. Oh yes, it was there he would find his destiny.

The following two days were a blur of hectic activity. Michael had hurriedly finalized the necessary arrangements for travel. His kindly landlord had understood the unexpected situation and had promised to hold the young doctor's room. No, he certainly wouldn't remove any of the wall hangings or vacate the collection of odd artifacts; they'd remain untouched and be there when the doctor returned.

To be absolutely truthful, although the older gentleman knew the grotesque articles were evidence of his boarder's unusual profession, he had no personal desire to see nor to touch them. Oh no, indeed, when the young man left, he'd avoid the eerie room like the plague. He never had let on, but the hideous faces hanging about the walls scared him to death and, now as he watched the little Volkswagen pull away, he silently prayed that the young man's terrifying nightmares would finally be over. As the widower stood out and waved a last farewell, he had a deep inner knowing that there was a powerful force at work in the young man's life. He'd pray hard that Dr. Greystone would be strong enough to meet the force that was now in control of his future.

Emmy

T he cloudless sky was painted with a lapis blue pigment. The gilded arms of Ra were blazing down over the little adobe community. Though it was only early morning, already the old buildings were quickly absorbing the permeating heat. For early autumn it had remained unusually warm. It was going to be a hot fall season. The woman sitting on the tiny shaded porch knew so, not because of the unseasonable heat, but because all the other nature signs said so, had all pointed to a time of prolonged heat.

Ramona Winter was fifty-eight, yet appeared much older. Her difficult life had taken an unkind toll on her features. The pain and suffering of daily living was clearly evident on her countenance. Deep crow's feet had gradually worked their way out from the corners of the dark eyes. Worry lines now creased the once smooth brow. Wrinkles marred the thin skin just below high cheek bones, and her dark hair, still long to her waist, had begun to intermingle with silvered strands.

Yet Mrs. Winter, for all the obvious signs of age, still presented a striking veneer. Her back, ever straight as an arrow, made her look proud and filled with an inner dignity she couldn't hide. Hair, always perfectly parted down the center and neatly braided, fell in a thick rope down her back to below the waist. Brightly-colored skirts, clean and gay, were never without their silver conch belts. Peasant blouses with intricately embroidered flowers were worn modestly over the ample breasts. Delicate turquoise earrings decorated the small ears, bestowing a splash of brilliant color to the clear complexion. But the woman's most attractive attributes were her dancing eyes and genuine smile. These two shining characteristics were by far what folks remembered most about Ramona Winter.

Now, like clockwork, she positioned herself on the step of the porch where she dutifully took up her watch for the postman. . .waiting. . .watching.

The sun beat down. Ramona dabbed at the dampness between her breasts. No amount of discomfort could be too unbearable to keep her away from her morning vigil on the steps. She was waiting for a very important letter to arrive. She'd been waiting every day for weeks now—it had to come soon. The longer it took the more anxious she grew because she knew that truly, it had to be any day now.

Local folks passed and stopped to chat with the woman. All the while, without appearing too obvious, Ramona would let her eyes gaze up the narrow street. She'd have to keep checking for the first sign of the mailman. People understood her anxiety, they knew what she was waiting for and each one would express their own hopes that, when the letter finally arrived, it'd be good news. And yes, wasn't it a terrible shame they made her wait so long for word of their decision?

Alone again, Ramona's mind drifted back over her life. It hadn't been all that wonderful, but when she reviewed it, she also had to admit that it hadn't been all that bad either. A gentle smile tipped the corners of her full mouth when she thought about her own childhood.

It was so happy, having been spent within the circle of the close-knit family. In those early days, they didn't have much, but what they did have, everyone treasured and shared equally—selflessly.

Recalling those times, she remembered evenings when the entire family gathered around the old, battered wooden table and, when the bowls had been passed around, there hadn't been enough in them to cover the bottom, yet the smiling faces and good humor persisted. The shared optimism had lightened the heavy burden of the leaner times and brought love and warm companionship into the family unit.

Now that she had grown and was still raising her own family, those wonderful attributes remained to soften the hardships of the present. Life went on, yet through the various adversities, state of mind made all the difference between fatalism and optimism.

Mrs. Winter's heart pounded faster now as she spied the uniform of the postman. Please dear God, she silently prayed, please let him bring it today. She stood to straighten her back.

An eternity of time passed as the jovial postal carrier made his way down the street. It was his habit to stop along the way to chat with this one and that one. Lately, Ramona wished the man wouldn't be so friendly with everyone he encountered along his route; it only prolonged the interminable agony of the waiting.

She wrung her hands as he drew closer and closer. To the excited woman on the porch it was like standing in a line waiting her turn for the Final Judgement.

Her heart gave an audible lunge as the postman drew up to the porch.

"Good day, Ramona. Here's today's pile." His smile hid the compassion he felt for her. He knew her expected letter wasn't in the stack.

"Good Morning, Christopher," she greeted back while nervously taking the mail. Then she patiently waited to go through it until the man had reached the next house.

Advertisements, bills, and flyers addressed to Occupant. One by one she flipped through the pile. She released a heavy drawn-out sigh and, refusing to admit to the tear of frustration that threatened to spill from her eye, she turned with a flurry of skirts.

"Mrs. Winter," called a strange voice from the dusty street.

She spun around. "Yes? I am Mrs. Winter."

The uniformed young man climbed out of the tiny vehicle and came up to the adobe.

"Mrs. Ramona Winter?"

She nodded.

"Then I guess this is for you," he smiled, holding out the special delivery letter. "You'll have to sign for it."

The woman frowned as she took the envelope. Eyes widened with bright joy as she read the return address. Shakily she scribbled out her name.

"Good day, ma'am," the man said, tipping his hat before returning to the vehicle.

Ramona stared down at the fancy envelope and, before she opened it, she clutched it to her chest, raised her misted eyes to the brilliance of the clear sky and prayed it'd be good news. Then, with hands shaking, she tore into the envelope.

Emmy Winter had a lilting laugh that had an infectious effect on everyone within earshot. Today the busy florist on Arroyo Street was full of customers placing last-minute orders and picking up bouquets for the upcoming festival. Although the place was brimming with people and business was more rushed than usual, the sound of the young woman's laughter brought smiles to the customers.

In the back room, six women were at work expertly creating the floral arrangements. They chatted and laughed at each other's jokes. And the sounds of their gaiety drifted out to the front of the shop.

Emmy Winter had been hired on as an apprentice arranger three years ago. She hadn't known anything about the business other than a love for working with growing things. That was all the prerequisite the owner needed, for he could immediately spot raw talent a mile away. Since then, Emmy had proven herself to be a quick learner and, within a year's time, she had been promoted to head designer. She had several awards for her exceptionally imaginative work when she designed centerpieces for special banquet dinners and once for a Presidential visit to the Governor's mansion. Now that the big Festival of Lights was upon them, she closely inspected the work of the other women and added a final touch here and there, all the while, talking and joining in with the open banter of her co-workers.

At twenty-five, Emmy Winter presented a striking image to the casual observer. Her deep, bronze skin had a richly-tanned tone that glowed with healthful vigor that naturally flushed the silkiness of her high cheekbones. Full lips were sensual. Large, slightly almond-shaped eyes framed the deep blueness that peered out with wide, childlike innocence. Hair black as a raven's wing fell long and lustrous to her small waist. Like her mother, she wore the feminine gauzy peasant blouses. Unlike her mother, she preferred jeans that accentuated the long, tapered legs. Through the delicate earlobes hung silver earrings shaped like two feathers. Around her neck was a beaded choker she had designed and handcrafted herself.

With all the beauty the young woman possessed, the owner of the busy shop had wished she was more visible to his customers. He figured such an attractive young lady would naturally generate additional business—not that he needed more—but he thought of her as a blossom among the flowers and had actually approached her about the matter of working the front counter. But the reluctant woman had no desire to handle the retail end of the business. All she wanted was to remain in the back room where she could concentrate on her floral creations—that was where she was happiest, she'd said.

Emmy had been grateful for the job because she needed to help out with the family's finances. She was glad things had worked out so well, but in the back of the shop was definitely where she felt she belonged.

As Emmy Winter was making some helpful suggestions to one of the workers, another tapped her on the shoulder.

"Em, you've got a visitor," she said, inclining her head toward the curtained doorway.

Emmy turned to see her mother standing there with a wide grin and brimming tears. Immediately the young woman knew why the elder had walked the distance to the shop. Immediately she knew it was all over—her dreams had finally been realized.

"The grant? It came through?" she blurted with wide eyes rounded with hope.

Ramona nodded as she held up the envelope. Daughter and mother hugged one another tightly. Tears flowed freely. The workers squealed with delight for the wonderful news, for they knew no one deserved the college money more than Emmy Winter did. And, although this meant they'd have to find a new floral designer and they'd miss their good-hearted friend, they were overjoyed in their hearts and wasted no time in rushing forward to congratulate the two.

Emmy, after gaining a measure of composure over her high excitement, removed the letter and nervously read the contents. The grant amount had been for more than what they'd initially applied for; the reason was fully explained as she read further. Tears again filled her eyes.

It appeared that the solitary application for the grant money was not all the organization had received. They'd gotten letters from Emmy's friends, coworkers, neighbors, and relatives—all sadly explaining her dire circumstances and how deserving she was. The total amount of the grant had included an anonymous donor check to be used for the purchase of a vehicle so she'd have the transportation required for her field work in anthropology.

One after the other, each worker in turn read the long-awaited letter and each shook their heads and smiled at their friend's good fortune. They teasingly speculated who the mysterious donor was and My! how they wished some stranger would send them checks like that!

The group grew silly with it all and they clicked their tongues with the playful bantering.

"Emmy's got a Sugar Daddy!" they sang. "C'mon, Em, tell us who he is."

"Em's got a secret admirer!"

"Maybe it's the governor!"

"No," said another, "it's that handsome man who has the stretch limo!"

The chorus rang on and on until they saw how they were embarrassing Emmy. The mother was clearly enjoying every minute of the friendly teasing, but the daughter was overly flustered with the entire thing.

One of the women extended out her arms. "Okay everybody, look what you're doing to poor Em. For heaven's sake, it's a mystery enough without a bunch of hens cackling over it."

With that sobering statement the ruckus settled down and each worker again sincerely congratulated the two women before sauntering back to their individual work stations.

Sanity had been restored.

The shop owner came in and, after offering his handshakes and hugs, wanted to give Emmy the rest of the day off. She would hear none of it though. There were still orders coming in and she felt obliged to remain responsible and even stay late if she had to in order to get them all filled.

Ramona hurried home to prepare a celebration dinner.

Business at the florist returned to normal.

Later that evening, after neighbors and friends had left the party in the Winter's home and Emmy had helped return the place to rights again, she held her mother and kissed her.

"Thank you for all you did today," she said.

"Honey, I would've invited the whole town if we'd had the room for them. Everybody is so happy for you."

The two held their embrace for a long while before Emmy whispered into her mother's ear. "I have to go out."

Their eyes met. Ramona looked deep into the blueness of her

daughter's. The unusual color spoke back. It reminded the elder that her daughter was chosen as the special one that was born to every third generation of their clan—one born with the stars in her eyes. And the elder knew her daughter's destiny was guided by a force other than her own. It was a force born of their ancient ancestors. . .the Starborn Tribe.

So now, hearing her daughter's words, Ramona simply nodded. She understood the younger's great need to be alone—to go seek the Silence That Speaks.

Ramona lovingly smoothed back a stray wisp of hair from her daughter's face and patted her cheek before placing a kiss on her forehead. No words passed between them. None were needed, for the two had a silent language—an ancient one.

Outside in the cooling darkness of the Taos night, Emmy Winter pulled her shawl over the narrow shoulders and looked down the street. Fingers gripped tighter around the straps of the rucksack she carried.

Ordinarily, as she passed the many lighted shops during an evening walk she'd stop to look in and window-shop, pausing now and again to take the time out to enter them and chat with the local keepers. But tonight was not intended to be a leisurely stroll down main street, nor was it a social excursion through town. Tonight was to be one of those special nights when she walked right out of town and into the dry plains where her special place of communion was located. Tonight was to be one of those sacred nights she wouldn't tell anyone about—not ever.

The city limits were behind her now. The harshness of the electric lights was merely a yellow glow that receded into the background with each forward step she took. If she kept walking straight ahead the town lights would never totally disappear from view, but soon she'd veer off around one of the distant buttes where the true color of the night would be absolute.

She walked on toward the thicker darkness that stretched out before her like an endless sea of black.

A light breeze lifted the end strands of her ebony hair.

New scents delicately wafted in the clear air. The sweet fragrance of western sage drifted lazily past and through her sensitive being. She inhaled deeply, bringing the welcomed essence of the beloved earth into her body, her mind, her receiving spirit.

Soon the towering butte sentinels loomed up before her and she never tired of their magnificent presence. At night they were especially impressive. The depth of darkness made them appear larger, taller somehow. Or perhaps it was during nightfall when they truly did grow and stretch themselves to the stars. She'd seen stranger things—things she'd learned from childhood to accept as natural.

Slowing her pace she cautiously picked her way around the wide base of one of the buttes. It had taken her a few more minutes to gain the dark side but she had come here alone many times before and could do it in her sleep, yet because the land was always changing—shifting—she still had to be careful not to stumble over a newly-fallen boulder.

When she finally reached the center of the far side, a total blackness engulfed her. The surround was no longer backlighted by the town's garish lighting.

The darkness was complete.

Now she was ready.

She waited for the proper mood to settle within her. She waited for the Peace Within to come to the forefront. And, when the first nebulous wave washed over her, she slowly removed her shawl and respectfully withdrew the sacred medicine items from the woven sack.

Gently pulling out the blanket serape, she lifted it up to the twinkling stars. Arms extended high, she whispered an old traditional prayer before lowering it over her head and letting it fall upon her shoulders. Covered now, she extracted cedar and sweetgrass from the bag. She knelt and ignited the mixture. To this she carefully added juniper and mesquite. Soon the embers glowed around the edges of the cedar. A curling wisp of smoke snaked up into the night. And, closing her eyes, a low chanting emitted from her heart as she rested back on her heels.

The cedar would burn. It would burn for as long as she needed it to.

The song would continue. It would continue for as long as needed—as long as it took.

This time it didn't take long. The familiar sensations began at her lower spine. It was like gentle fingers lightly touching her back. Slowly, ever so slowly, they worked their way up until her neck prickled, then the scalp tingled.

The familiar scent of the smoke swirled about her, but there was something different about it this time. A delicate new fragrance began to blend with the prepared mixture and she couldn't readily identify its source, yet experience told her that it was one that could manifest of its own accord.

Her eyes remained closed in order for her mind to see more clearly.

The haze of smoke shifted.

It shifted.

It drifted.

It slowly rose and then fell close to the ground. It circled her three times before rising once again into the night sky.

Something was joining her this night. Now she was no longer alone. She spoke without moving her lips.

"Who has come to my sacred ground?"

The wind gently whispered around the towering butte.

The young woman's hair stirred.

"What manner of spirit joins me this night?"Silence.

Her nostrils flared to take in the new, sweet fragrance.

"I know this essence. I wish to know it better, for it greatly appeals to me."

And the scent overpowered the cedar and sweetgrass.

Deep within the clarity behind her eyelids the woman saw a pinpoint of brilliant light. She watched the light in rapt wonder as a multitude of blinding rays began to spear out from it. As they slowly extended, they changed colors and undulated as if radiating from a powerful source. The central point grew in power. It expanded into altering forms.

Enthralled, the woman watched with held breath.

An eagle, wings spread wide, silently and gracefully wavered its wings in slow motion.

A dog, alert pointed ears, sniffed the air at her presence.

An animated kachina beckoned, its feathers wafting gently.

A regal buffalo raised its noble head to acknowledge her.

Fluidly did the perfect forms alter before her wondering eyes.

She dared to silently speak. "Are you the Shape Changer?" she inquired with deep respect.

Immediately the last form melded back into the pinpoint of light. It pulsed before her now like a beating heart.

And sound came into the vision.

A muted heartbeat grew in intensity until the vibrant sound

thundered and drummed through the dark night. The vibration of it moved her. It struck a sensitive chord within her soul and she wanted nothing more than to lose herself within it—swim within its warm current—return home to it.

A lone tear made its wandering way out from beneath the closed lid and coursed down her smooth cheek. She willed her being to join the intense beauty she felt moved to commune with. She willed her heart, mind, and spirit to touch.

Nothing happened.

Yet the beautiful brilliance remained strong. Like a pulsar it radiated love, wisdom, and deep compassion.

The heart beat on. Louder and louder did it beat until its echoes resounded against every standing butte for miles around.

The woman's spirit eyes watched in awe and listened.

She stopped the effort of willing and simply allowed her beingness to rest in the dazzling magnificence of the light and sound. It was then when she felt herself begin to near the essence and found that it had form—a form her soul memory related to—that of a tall, white being.

She lost herself within its comforting warmness, its rightness.

And they touched.

The crumpled woman twitched. She twitched again. Emmy Winter's shivering woke her.

It was black all around. The cedar embers were cold and so was she. How long had she been asleep? She sat up and, pulling her knees up to her chin, she leaned against the hard base of the stone butte.

A multitude of stars twinkled overhead. The moon was new.

Dark and hidden, it remained an ebony orb encircled by a faint aura of light reflected from the brilliance of its far side. And with the totality of its darkness, the surrounding firmament danced in glittering prismatic grandeur.

Blue starlets glistened. Green and red. Gold. White.

A vast canopy of shimmering jewels covered the barren and cold land below.

Not a breath of breeze stirred the tall sage or clumped mounds of desert brush. Not a single soft sigh could be heard soughing across the expansive plain. It was that special time of night, that silent time, when the Wind Spirit held its breath so that the stillness could surround Grandmother Earth. It was that holiest of holy hours when nothing stirred. Out of deep respect, all of nature bowed on bended knee. It was the Sacred Silence when Grandmother Earth prayed.

A shooting star arced in its short-lived descent before it was abruptly extinguished.

The lone woman sat up, crossed her legs and arranged the heavy blanket wrap about herself. The chilled trembling was lessened now. There were more important things to concentrate on.

The deep reverence of the high solemn moment of meditation had swept her up into its hushed sacredness. The power of Grandmother Earth's prayer permeated her entire being. Every fiber, every cell of her receiving body vibrated with the holy energy of that which she perceived.

Tingling now with the mystical force of it, the woman leaned far forward, stretched her arms out over the cool earth and completed her bond with the eternal Entity of the Earth's Spirit.

Knowing fingers gently moved slowly over the dry soil. Deft fingertips perceived the soft heartbeat of the living Earth Spirit.

Heartbeats, steady and sweet, pulsed evenly in time with her own. And the two became as one while the high firmament of stardust looked down, saw that it was good, and smiled.

When a soft caress of wind kissed Emmy's cheek, it served to break the deep meditative state. The time for prayer was drawing to a close.

She lifted her head and slowly straightened her back.

Standing now, the woman raised her arms to the sparkling firmament and keened a low chant. Her closing benediction was lilting and sweet. It had come from the heart and was accepted by the Great Spirit as the offering rose up on the wings of the Wind Spirit.

Silence pervaded the land once again.

Out on the lonely desert plain a solitary figure walked the shadows. Emmy had had an exceptional experience this night.

Since her girlhood, she'd been taught certain ceremonies and sacred ways. She'd been privileged to witness many mystical aspects of nature's finer realities and, when she had begun venturing out alone to make her private prayers, she'd often been rewarded with the beautiful visions the spirits saw fit to give her. But this time was different and it had meant something different too—something immensely important. These were natural. Tradition had taught that good people with pure hearts were bestowed with certain natural gifts of vision when their Prayer Smoke was offered up. There was nothing mysterious or supernatural about it—it was simply an expression of pure nature as experienced by the People for centuries past.

Ancestral tradition also cherished its secret. . .that of a filial bond with the stars. The People, throughout time, kept their beginnings a sacred thing.

Now, as the lone desert figure walked away from the sheltering sentinel and out toward the branched saguaros, her spine pricked as some ominous omen speared her sensitive psyche.

She slowly turned her head back toward the towering butte that still held the remains of her Prayer Smoke fire at its feet.

Nothing there but the butte called the Standing Stone.

Senses perked to acute awareness. She continued out through the desert brush. She was deeply lost in thought about her earlier vision and what it could possibly mean for her. Never before had she been visited by such an emotional symbol. The pulsing pinpoint of light had touched her very soul. It had called to her. But why did it alter forms like it had?

She began to go deeper into it when she felt a slight pressure on her back. It was as if someone's warm palm had gently touched her, yet it seemed like more of a pulling sensation.

Again she slowly turned to look behind her. She squinted and peered through the darkness.

Nothing but the Standing Stone.

Now she wasn't so anxious to turn around again to continue her walking. One incident could be mere coincidence—simply a false physical anomaly—but two were definitely intentional.

Her sharp eyes followed the rugged outline of the ancient butte. There was something mildly different about it. It was almost as if it had life—as if it were breathing.

She stared at its towering blackness.

In the distance, a pair of wizened eyes looked out over the vast desert expanse at its feet. A lone figure was out there staring back. The hulking mass of stone recognized the figure and it heaved a great breath, gathered powerful energy unto itself and expanded its size.

Wind beginning to gust now, the woman cleared the cloying hair from her face and stood mesmerized at the sight unfolding before her. It appeared that the butte had stretched and altered into a wide mesa of some sort. But that couldn't be possible, she told herself, it just couldn't be possible. Surely she was just tired from the exhausting night. Yes, that was it, she was overtired. Yet. . .

Unsettled with the simplicity of the quick rationalization, she began walking back toward her sacred prayer ground, all the while, keeping her eyes fixed on the unexplainable altered shape. The closer she got, the more drawn she felt to it. And when she came up to within arm's length, she slowly reached out her trembling hand and placed her palm gently upon the stone.

It was warm.

It should've been cold but it wasn't. It had an electrifying quality to it. A pulsating current could be clearly felt.

The woman raised her head and looked up toward the pinnacle.

"What are you?" she whispered.

And in a resonating yet gentle voice that only the soul could hear, it answered back.

"I am The Guardian. The Protector of the Sacred Keep of the Ancients."

The woman's body shuddered.

The throbbing of the stone felt like the coursing of blood through living veins. Strange as it was, she felt some ancient kinship with it.

"Why are you here?" she whispered.

The voice reverberated with power. "As long as greed dwells within the hearts of men, I live. As long as ignorance pervades mortal minds, I live. As long as the sighted remain blind, I live. Until the prescribed Time aligns in the Houses, I live. For it is because of all these things that I am."

"Why are you here now? Why are you telling me this thing?"

"Watch and listen. Listen and watch. You will know in your heart, for you are the designated one of your ancestral starborn people. You are being called. You are needed."

Then, beneath the woman's fingers, the pulsing slowed. It slowed and stopped.

The stone cooled to cold again. A whip of thunder cracked overhead.

And when the woman looked up into the sky of false dawn there were no clouds in the creeping predawn greyness that washed over the land.

Ramona was up and busily bustling about the kitchen when her daughter finally returned home. She went about the business of preparing the family breakfast, but being wise in the intricate aspects of The Way, she hadn't been too occupied not to notice her daughter's peculiar look as she hypnotically walked through the kitchen, entered her room and closed the door without saying a word of greeting to anyone.

This reaction in itself was normally expected after one spent a night keeping the Prayer Smoke of the Vision Way, for coming back into the mundane facets of daily life took some adjustment time. But it was that curious look the girl had had that concerned the elder woman most.

She passed the filled plates around and the sleepy younger children began digging into their food. Ramona's eyes locked onto the man's across from her. She knew he'd also taken note of his daughter's strange behavior.

"What do you think, Hawk?" she whispered to her husband.

He merely shrugged.

"You saw her expression too. I know you did. Tell me, what do you think happened last night?"

"Yes. I saw her eyes when she came in."

"Well?"

Emmy's father was reticent to voice more. He'd been deep in thought since his daughter walked through the door. A little fear and a lot of excitement gripped his heart. He was not eager to share his thoughts.

"Well, Hawk?" Ramona pushed.

The man's voice was barely above a whisper. "I have seen it on some before. That look."

"When? What does it mean?"

"It was a long time ago when old Redbird came back down from that mesa from his vision search."

The woman waited for the explanation that didn't seem to be soon forthcoming.

"So?" she said anxiously. "What does it mean?"

Again the man shrugged his wide shoulders.

"Hawk!" she pushed quietly so as not to bother Emmy, "you know and you will tell me. What does it mean?"

He shrugged once more. "Maybe it means some different thing

for different people. I don't know. I wasn't there last night so I can't say for sure what it means for our Em."

"Well what did it mean for Redbird?"

Silence.

"Hawk?"

"It made him crazy," he said coldly. "Redbird, he came down from that butte with that same look as Emmy had an' then all the time he went 'round mumbling 'bout some *thing* that lived there way under the stone. He. . ."

"What stone?" she interrupted.

"That mesa. That seventh mesa. Anyway, he swore on his medicine bundle that some terrible spirit scared him and chased him 'round tunnels under that mesa." Hawk Winter sadly shook his head. "Poor old man, he rambled on an' on about seein' some great treasure; gold, giant gems the size of women's baskets, a black wall with strange writings an' all kinds of other things. Wild things."

"Like what?"

"Oh, he said he saw the inside of a great pyramid way down in the center of Grandmother Earth beneath that old seventh mesa. He swore there was even some kind of burial ground there with a tomb. He claimed that some evil spirit guarded it. He said there was a light down there comin' from a big crystal stone too." Hawk's head swung back and forth. "Old man was never right in the head after that. He just never gave the story up. He talked 'bout it till the day he died."

"How did he die, Hawk?"

The man shrugged.

"Hawk! How did Redbird die?"

"He killed himself. He was always afraid that that bad spirit with the strange eyes would get him. Guess he figured he would be better off doing it himself instead of living in fear of that thing comin' to get him."

Eyes wide, Ramona wondered. "Could it be that he never gave it up because the story is true?"

The gentle man across the table sipped on his steaming coffee.

He gazed out the window at the first golden rays of sunlight that speared through the opening.

"There's been stories, Ramona. There has been tales of just such a place, but it is not a place for men to walk. They say it is a burning place that is heard to scream." He turned to look back at his wife. His eyes were cold.

"But Hawk, our Emmy couldn't have had the same vision," she softly said, placing her hand over his. "She did not go to this Redbird's place. She did not go to that seventh mesa place."

Her words were not consoling, for the man had a faraway look in his eyes.

"You know what they say, Ramona."

"You mean about the buttes? About those Standing Stones out there?"

He simply nodded.

"But that is only a story too, Hawk."

"Is it? Is it, Ramona?" he asked with a raised brow. "The old ways don't ever change, Ramona. The Ways always remain the same through time. They remain like stone. . .just as solid as those Standing Stones in the desert out there."

The woman stared at her husband. "Hawk, have *you* heard them speak? Have you?"

The man sighed deeply. "There have been times," he mused with the clear remembrance. "When I go out there late at night to make my prayers like Emmy did, when the darkness would be especially black. These times I thought I heard the buttes whisper to each other. Back and forth their words went. But with the wind also blowing it is sometimes difficult to tell—to say for sure—but yes, there have been times when I was sure I could hear them breathing, almost feel a heart beating out there somewhere. I think the story is not a story. I think it is true. I believe the buttes and mesas speak back and forth to each other on certain nights. . .special nights."

Ramona's eyes were wide. "But what did they say? And what could it mean?"

"I don't know what they say. I have never heard the words. Perhaps only a few can hear the spoken words. . .and only they can know what it means. . .only those who have heard."

"Do you think our Emmy heard last night?"

Silence.

"Hawk, do you think our baby heard?"

"I don't know. I just don't know. She is the chosen one of our clan so maybe it is so. That could explain her haunted look when she came in. And if she did hear the buttes and mesas speak there's a reason. If those Standing Stones out there spoke to her and she heard, there's a good reason. In her future, something is waiting for her. The ghosts of our ancestors are calling her. They will be guiding her feet."

The man's wife thought on what she had heard. After giving it all considerable time, she had one last question.

"What you said about Redbird and that thing that chased him. You said something about it having strange eyes. Did Redbird say what was so strange about them?"

Hawk glanced out the window again. He wished he could ignore his wife's question.

"Hawk? Did you hear me?"

"I heard."

"Well?"

"Redbird said the eyes were a strange color. Redbird said the eyes were blue. . .just like Emmy's."

A week later, Emmy Winter cashed her gift check and bought a secondhand Jeep. Three days after that she didn't head down to the University of New Mexico as planned, but headed north, north to Boulder, Colorado where the acceptance letter originated from.

Theodore

$\mathbf{T}$he animated figure paced back and forth in front of the desk while he talked. Occasionally he would squint his eyes to peer up into the entranced faces of the crowd that filled the semi-circle of graduated seating. Behind the top row of the lecture hall students had crammed the standing room to full capacity. Many of them weren't registered for this Anthropology III class, so either they had free time on their hands or they'd skipped their final class of the day to sneak in and catch this one, because it was a rare occasion when the head of the department lectured.

The over-flowing crowd was an expected event whenever Dr. Theodore Weatherbee took over a class. In truth, most of the students had hoped the replacement for their former professor would never be found because they dearly loved the old man now presiding. He had a magical way of holding his audience spellbound.

The portly instructor paced the wooden floor.

Golden rays of late afternoon sunlight speared down through the tall hall windows to highlight the man's thinning grey hair. It reflected now and again off the old-fashioned wire-rimmed spectacles that precariously rested low on the man's aquiline nose. Eyes resembling chocolate-colored marbles twinkled with the excitement of the lecture subject. And although his mode of dress was a bit outdated and a shade dishevelled, the shiny gold chain of the antique pocket watch was always visible. This was his pride and joy, an anniversary gift from the university directors, which commemorated outstanding work over the many years of his tenure.

This particular period of Anthropology III was the one he both enjoyed the most and also dreaded the most. He enjoyed it because

it consisted of those select students who appeared more inquisitive and eager to question. Their high level of exuberance
thrilled the instructor by rekindling his own interest in the
subject. Yet he dreaded the class for the very same reasons—
their endless curiosity and infernal questions always speared out
in myriad directions making it ultimately futile to maintain any
semblance of a lesson plan. The class invariably ran off course.
Berserk was closer to how he thought of it. Yet. . .weren't the
young minds refreshing!

A hand anxiously raised and waved wildly at him for immediate
attention.

"Yes?" the professor acknowledged.

"Dr. Weatherbee, what about the American Indians? Didn't
they coexist with the. . ."

"Young woman," he quickly cut off. "I may be old, but I can
keep a train of thought going. I believe we were discussing the
Aztecs."

"I know that, sir, but hasn't there been recent evidence of
American Indian beliefs that coincide with those of the Aztec
culture? And wouldn't that in turn support an actual time of
coexistence negating the alleged migratory theory presently believed in?"

The good doctor paused to sigh over the deep thinker's fine
logic. She'd skillfully sent the subject matter careening off in
another direction. But, as always, he never let an inquisitive
question pass unanswered.

"There have been no artifacts unearthed to support such a
coexistence as you speculate on."

Undaunted, the young student smiled at her mentor and responded to his statement.

"If a tree falls in the deep forest and nobody hears or sees it fall,
does that then mean it didn't actually fall?"

Snickers rippled throughout the student body.

Doctor Weatherbee lowered his head to peer over the top of his
glasses.

"Young lady, are you being flip?"

"No sir, not at all. My point being an underscoring of the
premise that if. . ."

"Yes, yes. Do you think I'm some feeble-minded imbecile
down here?" He loosely waved his hand through the air. "Your

point was indeed clear enough. What you are saying is this. Just because archaeologists have not uncovered Native American artifacts dating back to the time of the Aztec civilization does not necessarily prove they didn't or couldn't have existed at that time. All it means is that they've yet to discover the proof of it."

"Yes!" the student cried, beaming. "That's exactly what I mean. It seems to me that if two cultures believe the same things, there's an underlying basis there for further speculation and deeper thought. I don't know," she softened a bit nervously, "I just think the Indians were here a lot longer than the historians and anthropologists believe and longer than science has proven."

The pensive wise man thoughtfully rubbed his chin.

The student speaker sat down.

Professor Weatherbee flipped his hand like a fish fin. "Up. Up, up, young woman. We're not through with this line of thought yet. You haven't taken it far enough to leave it."

She hesitantly stood to await his further words.

He pensively considered her theory a few seconds longer then stared up at her. "Why?" was all he asked.

The woman stood mute and frowned. Then, "Why what, sir?"

The class snickered.

The seasoned professor didn't find anything humorous. He ignored the general twittering. "Why is it that you believe the Indians have lived here longer than science has substantiated?"

Obviously embarrassed, she merely shrugged. "Just feelings, I guess."

"Feelings? *Feelings*? You would have us going around writing the history books based on *feelings*? Can we *do* that?" The doctor shoved his hands deep in his pockets and peered up at the exposed student. "Where's the scientific verification? Where's the physical, carbon-dated artifacts to support your theory? Where are the years of laborious research? The meticulous recording of archaeological data? The digs? Would you truly make a monumental historic breakthrough by saying it's all in your head? Or heart? Or psyche? Just *feelings*?"

Amid the humorous grins of her classmates, the woman visibly blushed with humiliation.

The arena of students began to laugh at the woman's embarrassing situation.

A deafening crash came then.

The student body jumped in unison and spun their heads back to the direction of the sobering sound. The professor had slammed a pile of books onto the floor.

All eyes were wide and centered on the instructor. All was silent.

"Now that I seem to have your undivided attention," he softly said, "I think you all owe this young lady an apology for snickering at her honesty. Not only that," he added, "but you might just like to also know that she is not only openly forthright with her own thoughts on this subject but those same thoughts are indeed *shared* by more than a few of today's greatest thinkers!"

The arena silence became weighted and pressed over the lecture hall.

Heads turned from the man down on the floor up to the woman who slowly slunk back down into her seat. Some heads bowed with shame. Most eyes were locked on the professor as he continued to explain further.

"Just because I choose to challenge a student's private theory does not necessarily mean that I am personally in disagreement with it. Perhaps I wish to make you go deeper into it—unravel the tangle that your ideas are caught up in."

He pounded the desk with his fist.

"But yes! It is true!" he bellowed before lowering his tone again. "Although it has not come out officially yet, recent re-thinking appears to be shifting in this very direction! Lately, little bits of things keep cropping up here and there. Minute pieces of history's puzzle are no longer cut and dried as they once were. They refuse to fit neatly into the total picture we've already contrived. No matter how those pieces are turned and twisted about. . .they *do not fit!*

"My young friends," the professor sighed, "the renowned researchers, the experienced archeologists, the anthropologists and their knowledgeable peers are having *feelings*. They are now beginning to make new calculations, revised speculations that make the new puzzle pieces fit. Why do they fit? Because history is being rethought by the experts. And, because of this, a bright new picture is unfolding. That's why the pieces will fit where they rightfully belong."

Silence.

Then, a wave of hands shot up.

"Doctor?"

"Professor Weatherbee?"

"Doctor?"

The rotund gentleman laughed at his students' high level of energy and newly-sparked curiosity. Oh, how he loved the electrifying and reviving feel of the generated current. Being back in the living flow of the young minds again was a much needed shot in the arm for his fading interest—his recent stagnation.

Smiling, he pointed to a young man with long hair tied back at the nape of his neck.

"You there," he selected. "The one with the ponytail."

The man stood respectfully. "What're your feelings on this issue, Dr. Weatherbee? Do you have feelings that some of our thinking on history is in error and needs to be revised?"

"That goes without saying, young man," the instructor began. "Clearly we're learning new things all the time. With great strides and new advancements constantly being made in research technology, who can tell what we will come up with next.

"Take the method of carbon dating for instance. Just think how much we've learned from that one singular technique. The application of it has been invaluable. Now they've just come up with an even more sophisticated method of dating.

"Yet, as with all things, as time advances, so does the technology. Who's to say what our next resource tool will be? We're already utilizing lasers to visually bore through layers of rock and pyramid stone, perhaps some yet-undiscovered device even more potent and versatile will be able to penetrate the stratum layers like butter and reveal marvels that would've remained hidden— forever undiscovered. Perhaps that *proof* of the simultaneous civilizations we spoke about earlier will be evidenced within some rocks rather than being unearthed from layers and layers of discarded cultural rubble. Perhaps the ultimate verification will be found in an entirely unimagined place not yet considered or dreamed of. However, there are now certain experts who are compiling a remarkable amount of data that will most certainly substantiate the theory that Native Americans were indeed an *established* civilization on this soil *centuries* before the timetable presently touted. Does that answer your question, young man?"

Not wanting to appear disrespectful, the student hesitated. "Ahh, not exactly, Dr. Weatherbee. What I wanted to know was, what are *your* feelings about utilizing feelings as a means of scientific method?"

The elder down on the floor quickly responded.

"You're splitting hairs, my boy. You're attempting to peel the banana and throw away the fruit." The professor humorously mimed the action. He then narrowed his perceptive eyes and squinted back up at the student.

The student quickly responded. "I'm sorry, doctor, but I don't follow. Are you saying that feelings are an actual valid process to scientific method?"

"No! Feelings are the *prerequisite* to scientific method! Feelings are the generating factor that create a certain thought or a nebulous, yet unformed idea—the theory! Then, based upon the conditional feeling, action is taken—only after that does scientific method enter the process to bear out the validity of the feeling with its concrete finding. See? Sometimes the feeling comes before the formulation of the precise idea or theory and, sometimes the thought comes first and the feeling follows, but always, they are hand in hand. They are a marriage."

The professor began pacing the floor.

"Now, that young lady up there says she believes the Aztecs and the combined nations of the Native American people existed simultaneously on the ancient continent of what we now refer to as North America. She also admitted that she has no solid foundation for this belief. She has no carbon-dated artifacts to show us that would substantiate such a claim, yet she wholeheartedly believes this theory simply because of her strong inner feelings. Now, my question to this august group of fine minds is this. Is she wrong?"

A low murmur of speculation and quick consulting swept over the arena. Heads turned back and forth as the students deliberated among themselves.

A student finally stood.

Dr. Weatherbee nodded wisely. "Ah, it appears we have an appointed spokesman for the decided verdict. Well? What's the consensus?"

The young student glanced about his peers then straightened his back with confidence.

"She would not be wrong to formulate a new untried theory based solely on feelings."

The professor's brow jutted up. "And why not?"

The student cleared his throat and went for it. "Because feelings actually act as a motivational impetus toward instigating further research resulting in the culmination of the eventual discovery or experiment that would validate the theory one way or the other."

"Exactly! And I believe you all owe that young woman over there an apology for your earlier rudeness and skepticism."

The class as a whole grinned and apologized aloud.

The girl blushed and giggled.

"All right everybody, now that that's cleared up, we need to go deeper still into this entire issue of feelings. What instigates a feeling that diametrically counters the established and proven belief? What is it that makes one oppose and question that which has already been allegedly verified and universally accepted as fact?"

Silence.

"Mmmm?"

Frowning students faced the professor. They were mute.

"Oh come, come now. You are not first-year students here! Think!"

After a time, a small hand fluttered just above heads.

Dr. Weatherbee acknowledged the middle-aged woman who he remembered as always being painfully shy.

"Yes? Go ahead, dear. Let's hear it."

"Well," she softly said while rising from her seat. "Some folks just seem to know things. I mean, they have this strong inner sense that beeps whenever something doesn't sound right."

The group had been intently listening for the shy woman's answer and then they snickered. Not because of what she'd said, but because of how she worded it.

The woman grinned beneath flushed cheeks. "Well, it's kinda like that. Some people just seem to know things and they act on their strong feelings of what feels right to them. It doesn't matter to them if their feelings run radically in opposition to accepted thought or not because they believe in them. Then they go out to prove the feeling's correctness. Well, anyway, that's what I think," she added before self-consciously sitting back down.

The class nodded in agreement.

"So then. You all agree with that?" Dr. Weatherbee asked of the group.

Various acknowledgements of assent emitted from the arena.

"Good! Now we're finally getting somewhere. But!" he snapped, bringing up a pointed finger. "Where do these so-called inner senses come from? Mmmm? What is their prime source?"

A buzzer blared on the professor's desk.

He disappointedly flipped over his palms. "Sorry people, period's over."

A loud uproar of objections arose from the student body. Groans and curses muttered out their displeasure while hands frantically shot up in a last-ditch effort of squeezing in one or two last shots at extending the interesting discussion.

The little man down on the lecture floor grinned with pleasure, held up his hands to indicate it was over and strode from the hall.

Back in the relative quietness of his private office, Dr. Theodore Weatherbee mentally reviewed his last lecture of the day. The students' enthusiasm to continue was uplifting to say the least, but it was also draining for a man of seventy. He would've dearly loved to stay with them and talk long into the early evening as he used to be able to do, but now it was far too strenuous. He wondered how long he could maintain this straining pace.

As his gaze panned over the office, his eyes rested on the stacks of unanswered letters, unfinished reports, unread papers recently published by his colleagues and unattended departmental correspondence. What a mess. What a damned mess.

He sighed, then in irritation, grabbed for the phone and dialed Boston.

"Dr. Neusome, please. This is Weatherbee."

The woman on the other end of the line didn't need the gruff voice to identify itself. She'd heard it enough times over the last few days to know the caller was sitting in Boulder. And, stifling her urge to cut him off, she politely replied that Dr. Neusome would be right with him.

"Theo! How's the weather out there in the good ol' Rockies?" came the jovial voice.

"Don't you give me any of your claptrap small talk, Conrad. I've just finished up a grueling two-hour lecture and I don't know how much longer I can let my own work go. It's piled so high in here I can't see the clock on the wall."

Boston chuckled. "What's the matter, you getting too old and crotchety to be guru anymore?"

"Dammit, Neusome! Where's Greystone? Sightseeing?"

"Calm down before you blow a vessel, Theo. He just left two days ago, give him some safe travel time for God's sake. You can't expect him to drive straight through or you're going to end up with two professors in comas."

Weatherbee sighed. "I know. I know. It's just that I got me so damned much work stacked up here. I'm always trying to do ten things at once and there's just too many. . ."

"How are the kids, Theo?" came the gentle question.

"Oh God, Conrad, they're so full of youthful vigor and curiosity. I've nearly forgotten what a boost teaching them can be. If I weren't so far over the hill. . ."

"Yeah," Boston interrupted. "I know what you mean. Look at me. Here I sit, sequestered down in some godforsaken basement office all day pouring over reports, papers and requisitions for acquisitions. Then, when I do manage to leave the room it's to spend endless hours down the dreary corridor in the Property Room scrutinizing mummies and such.

"I dunno, Theo, sometimes I feel like an old relic looking at older relics. I miss the excitement, the new blood of youth." He paused momentarily before going on. "Which brings me back to the matter at hand. You ought to know that Dr. Greystone's got some pretty open ideas in his head. He's no extremist, mind you. He's no radical activist or anything wild like that, but I think you should be forewarned of the scope of his vision—anything's possible in his mind. He's been around the old mystic block a few times. He's quite accomplished, if you know what I mean."

The Boulder doctor snickered. "Seems I recall a time way back when. . .two young professors were the same way. Wasn't that what sparked life into our fledgling careers in the beginning? All that magic?"

"Yes, Theo, I remember. Memories are all we have left now though. We were some team to be reckoned with back then, weren't we."

Maybe the memories weren't so good to recall after all.

Remembering better, livelier, and more actively constructive times were not all that good for some folks to be doing. Boston picked up on the sudden change of Boulder's mood and immediately changed the subject.

"Theo, I also want you to realize that Michael's been away from the lecture halls for quite some time now. Teaching's not his forte anymore, you realize. He's used to working by himself in research."

"Dammit, right now I'd be happy with the janitor."

"Well yes, I can appreciate your position, I really can, but you've got to have patience with Dr. Greystone. Let him get used to the new situation and that altitude of yours; given time, I know he'll fit right in. In fact, although I hate to admit it, I'll probably have to beg him to come back here. A dungeon doesn't look so appealing to an energetic and bright young man after he's been exposed to the likes of Colorado country."

"You worried, Conrad old boy? Do I detect a shred of apprehension here?"

"More concerned than anything. Michael just may change his ideas about what he really wants to do with his profession and I sure an' hell ain't goin' to stand in his way. If he does decide not to come back, I'll sure as hell miss him though. He's the best damn assistant I ever had or probably will ever hope to have."

"Sounds to me like you're putting that cart before the horse. The man hasn't even gotten here yet."

"Just keeping an eye on the probabilities, old buddy, just keeping myself prepared for the worst scenario."

"You always did, Conrad. You always did."

After the two rang off, Dr. Weatherbee sat back in his leather chair. His peer's unexpected insinuation that the young Greystone may decide to stay on at the university was an interesting consideration. It certainly was an inviting thought to entertain, and it'd solve a multitude of future problems. Maybe things really weren't so bleak after all. And with a lighter heart, the elderly man muffled a groan as he rose from his chair, crossed the room and flicked out the light.

"Evenin', Dr. Weatherbee. You're here later than usual. You should be home havin' some hot supper."

The doctor smiled kindly at the cleaning lady pushing the heavy wet mop over the tiled floor.

"Doris," he chided, "I ate a late lunch and will probably just go home and have a nice steaming cup of tea." Then, inspecting the condition of the floor, he couldn't help but to comment on it. "This floor's so clean you could eat off it. Don't you think it's good enough?"

"Oh no, Dr. Weatherbee! Why, when Doris cleans you can bet it's almost as sterile as them fancy operatin' rooms in the hospital." She grinned as she looked down at her work. "Yep. One more good pass an' it'll be right."

"Don't know what we'd do without you, Doris," he said, patting her on the shoulder. "Don't stay too late and be sure to say hello to those beautiful kids of yours."

"Oh I won't be long now, an' you can bet I'll tell 'em that Dr. Weatherbee said a special hello to 'em."

He winked and turned down another corridor. His long footfalls echoed through the quiet building. He thought about how haunted an empty place could seem. Especially one that was full of bustling people and commotion during the day.

Passing the door of the Anthropology lecture hall, he paused and backtracked to peer in through the window. His hand involuntarily touched the door and pushed. Before he knew it he was inside and standing once again before the podium. He looked up at the raised rows of vacant seats. And within the eerie stillness, his mind echoed with the spectral voices of curious students. He relived his last lecture of the day, hearing every question and answer, every snicker, reprimand and long silence.

Oh, how he wished it could've gone on forever. To be young again and so full of energy was something he dreamed of—or was it? Perhaps, he considered now, perhaps what he was really searching for was the singular accomplishment to claim as his own—one little thing of great import. True personal accomplishment eluded him and that he regretted very much.

The room suddenly became painful and he quickly left for the parking lot.

The silver Lincoln Continental was new. He had somehow gotten into the habit of leasing one every year. His old friend was the general manager of a dealership and had convinced him that that was the only way to go. Of course he had to be talked into it at first, but after realizing all the advantages, he'd decided to give it a try twelve years ago. He'd been doing it every year since. After all, a man of his age and stature deserved some amenities in his autumn years. It was one of the rare occasions he treated himself to a thing of pure frivolous luxury.

Heading away from the campus grounds, the sleek vehicle turned up a secondary road that led into the mountains. He'd traveled some distance before turning off onto the unmarked road that led to his home of many years, one that'd been in the family for as long as he could remember.

Tires crunching on the granite gravel, he pulled around the

circular drive that fronted the remote house. A ski lodge, some of his students had called it once when a group of them had paid him a surprise visit. Well, he didn't know if he'd call it a ski lodge or not because he'd never been out to any of those fancy resort places, but he did know it was home—just plain home.

Snuggled within the secluded density of a thick evergreen forest of ponderosa pine, blue spruce, and fir, the three-story residence loomed like an overstated monstrosity. Constructed of eighteen-inch logs, the place looked more like a frontier fortress designed by a confused architect. Sections were reminiscent of the traditional Bavarian design while other portions were strictly more austere—more functional and plain. French windows contrasted starkly with the colored leaded panes. The wide-tiered balconies cross-sectioned a massive central A-frame. The blue metal roof was designed to withstand and quickly shed the heavy snowloads that were common for the high country. Yet with all its obvious exterior eccentricity, the place possessed a certain magnetic appeal that tended to draw the onlooker into a sense of security. The place not only looked formidably indestructible, it was. It had stood on the site for nearly a full century. It had endured the test of time by withstanding decades of snow blizzards—it'd most likely still be standing long after the last inheriting owner was long gone.

But the present owner was a long way from that final road. He cut the purring engine, climbed out of the car and surveyed his wooden castle in the pines. Breathing in the crisp mountain air, he scanned the details of the building and smiled. Yes, perhaps his ancestors had been a bit over zealous in its construction, but hadn't the place persevered without a single sign of deterioration? Although he'd admitted that there were times he cringed at seeing the mixed architecture, he also had to admit how much he loved it—monstrosity, ski lodge, or whatever—he dearly loved the old place.

The stone steps were as solid today as the moment they were first set into place. The porch flooring was as sturdy as ever too. And the heavy, carved oaken door swung silently inward on its ornate iron hinges. Just as quietly, it closed. A solid click broke the stillness as the latch caught.

The doctor stood and looked around into the shadowy duskiness that had befallen the interior. The old place was always so infernally dark, he thought. The dense forest made certain of that.

He flicked on the wall switch and immediately the shadows scuttled back into the corners and crevices. A soft orange glow flooded throughout the lower floor. Artificial light ignited the interior with flames of color.

Overhead, the massive crossbeams were draped with vivid Inca-inspired weavings. Navajo blankets decorated the walls. Brilliant Mexican serapes were used as furniture throws. Blazes of bright multicolors were everywhere.

Dr. Weatherbee crossed the thick Persian carpet of the great room, passed through the rarely-used formal dining area and entered the immense country kitchen. He heated water for tea and when the whistle shrilled, he poured it and sat at the long pine trestle table.

The house was as still as a mausoleum in winter. Not a creak was heard coming from anywhere. The solid logs were perfectly fitted together. The insulation had been doubled, sometimes tripled, to insure warmth and quiet. No outside woodland sounds penetrated through the standing walls of the sturdy fortress.

In deep silence the man sat alone and stared into his strong brew. He thought back to the recent conversation with his life-long colleague and wondered if the young Dr. Greystone really would want to remain in Boulder. He wasn't concerned that the mountainous terrain would capture the man's fancy, nor was he overly worried that the beauty of blazing aspens would prove compelling. What he was thinking on was the matter of his students' possible reaction to a new and younger professor who just might spark their interest or—more probable—gain their admiration. Would this Greystone lure them away from him? Could the young one be able to hold them enthralled like he could? Would students flock to his classes now?

"Damn!" he sputtered, getting up and taking the tea back through the silent house. He passed the oaken door and went into the east wing where the library and study were located. "Damn if I'm not beginning to sound like some insecure bastard," he grumbled.

The green glass shades of the three library lamps cast a warming glow throughout the large room. Packed bookcases encircled the room, except for the center of the outside wall where a massive walk-in fireplace had been set into the moss rock stones.

Leather crinkled loudly as the man slouched into one of the red wingback chairs. He gazed about at the floor-to-ceiling rows of books that decades of ancestors had amassed and added to the family's collection. Some were quite valuable by now and represented an impressive sum of money.

Still, the previous conversation plagued the man. Remnants of this and that replayed over and over through his mind. Tired now, he removed his spectacles and rubbed his eyes. Was this the end of all his years of intensive study? Was this solitude the grand finale of decades of extensive research?

He reviewed his accomplishments. They were few. Those that he could actually claim as being solely his own weren't that remarkable. Was old Neusome right about being over the hill and ending up in dingy offices in dank basements? Nothing better to do than to push pencils and shuffle papers? Were their days for breakthrough discoveries over for good? Were they indeed all gone? Finis?

The deeply depressing thoughts were bitter pills to take and the man thinking them was not about to voluntarily swallow more. Perhaps it was true that he was past his prime, but did that mean he was also deadwood now? Wasn't he still sharp of mind and relatively spry of body yet? By God! Was he going to allow himself to atrophy in some old dusty, forgotten office without having first gone out in a blaze of glory?

It was then that Dr. Theodore Weatherbee's adrenaline began pumping like an oil derrick. It was then that he decided to make the strong affirmation to discover something really new in his field—something so monumentally earth-shattering that his name would never be relegated to that of mediocrity. He vowed then and there to ensure his place in history as one of the finest and greatest anthropologists known to man.

He didn't know from whence this great discovery would come nor did he care. All he knew was that no man would ever be able to say that Dr. Theodore Weatherbee was a nobody. And, sparked by his new, rejuvenating sense of purpose, a nebulous something suddenly pricked at his sharpened consciousness. Vainly he tried to pull it forth but it remained elusively cloudy. Irritated now that he couldn't pinpoint the forgotten item, he got up and anxiously paced the floor.

Something. Something was desperately trying to come through. Something he'd read a while ago that was now far more important than it had initially seemed.

"Damn! What was it?" he demanded of himself. He paced and talked to the listening walls.

"It was some little tidbit of an article, some item half hidden in what. . .a research paper? No, that wasn't it. Let's see. Was it the scientific report?" But that didn't seem to ring a bell either. *"Anthropology Monthly?* No, no, that wasn't it." Then the light came on. "Yes! It was the damned newspaper! Yes, yes, that was it, the newspaper!"

The professor, now obsessed with the puzzling enigma, grabbed up his glasses and rushed into the study that adjoined the library. Like one possessed, he ransacked through the stacks of newsprint.

Although the precise subject of the article still eluded him, he knew it was of utmost importance. It was somehow relevant to his renewed purpose for ultimate recognition.

Papers were hysterically rummaged through, quickly scanned and, one after the other, were tossed in the mounding discard pile behind him. Anyone observing the maniacal scene would've sworn that the little man was finally certifiable—a crazed mind performing irrational acts of dementia.

The flutter of papers suddenly stopped.

Silence filled the room as the professor anxiously read.

"Yes. Yes. Yes! I knew it!" he exclaimed in triumph. "I knew it was here somewhere!"

Again he centered his concentration on the article. He ripped it from the page and scampered from the room with the agility of a mischievous elf.

Quietly giggling with heightened excitement, Dr. Weatherbee flicked two wall switches. The lower level pitched into darkness while the diffused light from the second level flooded down the central stairway throwing lances of yellow beams into the darkness below.

The ecstatic professor grabbed onto the varnished pine handrail and climbed the set of massive log stairs. To his breast he clutched the piece of newsprint like it was a priceless artifact.

Up, up he climbed. And upon reaching the landing, he veered off to the right where his private suite of rooms were waiting for him. The lights would be on. The entire floor could be illumined by switches on both the lower and upper levels. He'd found it most expedient to have the wiring redone so as to save the effort of walking everywhere needlessly just to turn individual lights on and off.

Once he got within his rooms he could control the rest of the floor from there, which is just what he did.

Inside his oversized bedroom, he flipped another switch and the second level was plunged into darkness—all except the room he now occupied. He grinned with the cleverness of the circuitry and closed the door.

The single light escaping from the colored glass of the bedside Tiffany lamp cast a warm and rosy glow over the room. The massive pine bed gave off a cozy feeling. The bright and cheery colors of the granny square afghan warmed the room. Thanks to the exquisite handiwork of his baby sister, he was not left in want of coverlets.

Hurriedly, Theodore undressed and scampered under the quilt. He reached down and turned the dial to LO. He may be old, but he wasn't so old-fashioned as to be adverse to such comforting luxuries as electric heating blankets.

Snuggling down into the plumped-up pillows, he sighed with the delicious warmth that slowly began thawing out his brittle bones. Finally he was content enough to pick up the precious article and take the time to reread it.

Adjusting the wire spectacles, the words on the newsprint brought new flutterings to his heart. He had a lot of questions about the article. He'd have to do some fancy footwork in order to dig up the required answers but, one way or another, he was confident he still had enough clout to get those answers. May have to call in a few favors owed him, he thought as he mentally went over the long list of potential debtors he could draw on.

Dropping the informative piece of paper to his side, he thought about what he'd read. Whatever drove the young researcher to suicide had to have something to do with the project he'd been working on at the time. The article didn't specify that aspect and that would have to be top priority on his list. He'd have to find out exactly where the man had been working in order to find out what he'd discovered, or was about to discover. This Clifton Westlake had been no amateur. He had to have been onto something big and Theo Weatherbee was going to find out what.

The professor removed his glasses and exhaled a deep sigh. What the devil gets into a young professional like that, he wondered. What in the hell makes him so mad that he blows his brains out? He shook his head confoundedly.

"The young'uns just can't cut it," he said aloud. "Guess it's up to the seasoned old folks to get things done properly."

And with that comforting thought, the man set his glasses and newspaper fragment on the nightstand before turning out the light.

Outside, a wind gathered its energy and hushed through the high pines.

The mountain nightfall was complete. Darkness extended its arms and stretched to encircle the secluded house within its being.

Blackness was absolute beneath the starless sky. Words whispered on the breath of the wind, and a peculiar chill reached icy tentacles through the ebony surround. It wrapped them tightly about the lonely lodge. Its grasp was firm, it was strong like. . .a deathgrip.

In his fitful sleep, the man under the mound of blankets turned and tossed. He twitched and moaned, then shot up to a sitting position.

Eyes wide with the suddenness of his start, he craned his neck to search through the blackness of the room. Reaching out, he pulled the lamp chain.

The bulb flashed like a bolt of lightning. . .then died.

The hairs on the man's neck pricked as he squinted through the congealed blackness.

"Who's there!" he called.

Silence. Darkness.

"Dammit! I said who's there?" Alert eyes darted about. The stillness was unnerving. He knew something had awakened him. Someone was in his room. . .right this minute.

"Look here," he spouted, "if it's money you're after, my wallet's on the bureau. It's all I have in the house. Take it and leave me be. I'm just an old man."

No sound of movement followed. No sound came at all.

"I know you're here," he whispered into the blackness. "I can feel you, you know. Yes I can. I can feel you. Now what do you want?"

Dr. Weatherbee sat like a frozen statue. Controlling his breathing, he strained to listen for any revealing sounds of footfalls crushing the thick carpet fibers.

None came.

He wiped at the cold moisture that beaded on his forehead. "What the hell," he shakily cursed, "now I'm getting spooked at nothing. I must be getting senile."

He switched off the heating blanket and, throwing off the

covers, flopped back down on his pillow in exasperation. "Damn mind's beginning to play tricks on an old man," he mumbled just before drifting off into oblivion.

The morning light cast a wavering filigree of shadows through the curtainless windows of the second floor bedroom. The large domain was awash with the cheery greeting of the autumn daybreak.

The sleepy man roused, grumbled a bit, and lazily turned toward the bank of multi-pane windows. It was going to be a clear Rocky Mountain day and his heart lunged with excitement as he called to mind all the important things he now had to accomplish.

And, filled with the rekindled sense of purpose, he nearly trembled with the heightened expectation of it. . .until his gaze rested on the nightstand.

The news article was now crumpled. It was crumpled into a small wad. It had been tightly crushed and, when he carefully reached out to open it up, he found it spattered with rust-colored droplets looking very much like old, dried blood. . .very old blood.

"Ahhhh!" he grimaced in horrified disgust as his fingers straightened and went rigid.

Frozen in stark terror, the old man could do nothing but helplessly watch the grotesquely stained fragment flutter to the floor.

Karen

The bright red convertible eased out of Vail and, once on the Interstate, sped west.

Auburn hair whipping in the wind, the driver blared the radio to keep her company until she reached the town of Eagle. It appeared this was the driver's day for gallivanting about the Colorado countryside visiting friends she hadn't seen in a while. She'd debated about the Eagle stop though, mainly because her friend, Terry, owned a small cafe there and whenever she stopped in for a quick chat, they hardly had any real time to talk.

The driver switched off the distracting music to give some serious thought to her friend's situation. She sighed with the heaviness of it. Maybe it wouldn't have been so bad if her friend had married again. Working twelve hours a day and being a single parent was a burdensome load to carry. But, she considered, Terry had admirably persevered. She'd been a caring parent for the little girl and, in turn, the tyke's eyes always sparkled with warm love for her mother.

The Eagle exit came up and the convertible signalled.

Parking directly in front of the crowded cafe, the redhead jumped out and bounced through the door.

"Karen!" the woman behind the lunch counter squealed in surprise. "What brings you out here on such a beautiful day?" Terry came out and gave her friend a warm hug. "Got time for coffee?"

Red grinned. "I got time and I'm buying this time."

They sat in one of the booths. "You look tired," Karen noticed.

"Oh, I'm all right. Had someone quit on me last night. It's not easy getting responsible help these days." Terry glanced over at her busy employees. "Most of my crew is great though. Guess I can't complain about a few bad apples."

Karen sighed in disgust. "Truthfully, I don't know how you do it. I mean, with the piles of paperwork you have to do and all that ordering and audits and hiring, not to mention having to handle the housework and caring for that sweet kid of yours. I dunno, seems you're one hell of a lady to be able to do all that an' not go nuts."

Terry half smiled. "I have my moments, but Annie pulls me through. All she has to do is give me one of her special hugs and I'm right back on track again."

Karen stirred her coffee. "Gosh you're lucky to have such a great kid." Then she scanned the cafe. "Any available guys around here?"

"You're very transparent, Karen," Terry quipped back with a chastising glare.

"Well? Why not? You're young and available."

"To answer your question, yes. There's plenty of men in this town, but I'm not after the first handsome face that smiles at me either."

Karen rolled her eyes. "Oh right," she playfully snipped, "you're not prepared to make the same mistake twice. Next time around your man has to be able to talk."

"I believe the word is communicate, Karen. Communicate."

"Whatever."

"Well that's not all I'm looking for either. Sure, he's got to be honest and open with his feelings, but he's also got to love Annie and want the same things I do in life. No more possessive or materialistic men for me. No way do I want to rush into something that's not absolutely right for me and Annie."

"I know, I know," Karen bobbed her head. "You and Annie and your mountain man will live up in the woods in some remote setting in a little cabin and feed the wild things all day."

Terry's grin was wide. "There's other considerations too."

"Well for heaven's sake, Terry, you could at least date now an' then."

"Who said I didn't?" she coyly hinted back.

Karen's eyes bulged. "Who? Tell me who you've been dating."

"Nothing serious so don't get your hopes up. One or two now and then, purely platonic. We date more out of the need for mutual companionship than anything else. When you're twenty-four and single, both parties need to be very cautious."

"Well I'm glad to hear you're not starving for male companionship anyway, even if it is only on a friendly basis. Maybe that's the best way for now." She glanced down at her watch. "Gotta run. Who knows what the canyon will be like today."

"I heard on the radio that they did some blasting last night. This morning they said there are twenty-minute waits."

"That's not too bad. I can handle that. It's the really long holdups that irritate me."

Terry suddenly remembered her friend's college plans. "Did you hear from Boulder yet?"

"Nah," she grinned, "but I'm a shoo-in. I've already started packing up some things. I can't wait. Just think of all those great-looking guys."

Terry shook her head. "Last time I checked, people went to college to learn a thing or two."

The redhead tossed her hair. "Well some people just don't have their priorities in order like I do."

They said their goodbyes and Terry went back to work thinking about her friend. The redhead may be a bit flighty and a touch too arrogant at times, but she was a good friend just the same.

Back out on the road, Karen Kendall left Eagle behind and allowed her lead foot to speed her farther west. The car was a blur of red streaking along I-70 until she reached Glenwood Canyon and had gone a little over three-quarters of a mile in.

"Damn," she whispered, applying the brakes as she suddenly became the tail end of the stopped convoy of travelers.

The montage caravan was dead still. Most of the engines had been cut and people had gotten out to mill around and enjoy the spectacular scenery of the high canyon gorge. There wasn't much else to do as cars, trucks, RVs and semi trailers were bumper to bumper as far as the eye could see.

A refrigerated semi pulled to within inches of the red convertible. Behind that, a cattle carrier screeched the air brakes. The line was quickly lengthening. The fiery convertible was no longer the little red caboose. It'd quickly become sandwiched like all the others.

Karen turned off the ignition and got out to stand at the guardrail. The intense roar of the rushing Colorado River was deafening as the sound of its power resonated against the narrow canyon's steep walls.

Across the surging waters an Amtrak musically clattered its wheels over the iron struts, then whistled. The shrill echo bounced off the craggy stone heights. People in the long passenger train peered out their windows for a look-see as the metal snake slithered precariously close to the whitewater river that coursed alongside the track.

Looking up to the top of the rugged walls, Karen suddenly felt a queer diminutive sense of being. Subliminally it gave one the mildly uncomfortable feeling of being no larger or of no more consequence than an ant. All of humanity was just one big colony of tiny ants. So overpowering were the canyon walls, they made all of the breathing life at their feet appear Lilliputian by comparison. It made one stop and think.

"Quite a sight, ain't it?"

The suddenness of the masculine voice startled the concentrating woman. She jumped at the unexpected sound at her shoulder. When she turned, a cowboy trucker was standing beside her at the railing.

"Didn't mean to scare you none, ma'am," he apologized before continuing. "It is somethin' though, ain't it?" he praised, gazing up the sheer cliffs.

"Yes," she smiled, turning again to the breathtaking scenery. "It's so massive. Sort of makes one stop and think. It's a real ego deflator."

The Colorado River surged and churned at their feet.

"Think they'll ever be done with this construction mess?" asked the trucker.

"Pardon me?" Karen said over the roar of the water.

The man grinned and pointed up the curving stretch of road. "I said, do you think they'll ever get this construction done? Seems like it's been going on forever. Sure plays hell with my schedules."

"I bet it does. They've come a long way since they started. I heard it'll still take another year to complete. Just think how you'll be able to sail through this canyon once it's done."

"Yeah, it'll be a lot faster than it was, that's for darned sure, but still I think they shoulda left it alone—natural—like it was."

Karen sighed. "A lot of folks share your thoughts on that one," she commented before looking back at the line of vehicles. "That refrigerator rig yours?"

"Yup," he proudly replied.

"Where're ya headed?"

"Utah. Provo, Utah."

A commotion began up the line. People were scampering back to their vehicles. Engines sputtered back to life.

"Looks like it's a go," the trucker announced.

"Take it easy, cowboy."

The man tipped his Stetson, "You too, ma'am. Nice talkin' with ya."

Back behind the wheel, Karen eased forward as the long line began moving out. As speed picked up, the vehicles traveled up over the newly constructed concrete lane that rose high and then dipped and curved through the twisting thoroughfare that followed the river. At Glenwood Springs, Karen exited the Interstate. She smiled and waved as the cowboy pulled on his horn for a last farewell.

Glenwood Springs was nestled in a warm, expansive sun-drenched valley on the Western Slope of the Continental Divide. The thriving community was the trading center for people within a fifty-mile radius. Aspen was located to the south and the region was a treasure trove for the locals as well as the many tourists who visited the region's famous mineral hot springs.

Driving through the central business district, Karen Kendall loved to pass the little shops that lined Grand Avenue. Book shops, florists, Bavarian restaurants, and craft shops rubbed shoulders with art galleries, coffee shops, and authentic Native American traders.

Down the tidy side streets, the full canopies of shade trees wavered lazily in the early autumn breeze. Trim houses, amass with colorful flowerboxes and blossoming walkways, lined the quiet boulevards.

Karen's immediate destination was not located within the city limits. Her parents had an executive home built in one of the more exclusive subdivisions that sprawled through the expansive Roaring Fork Valley.

The flaming convertible followed the highway that paralleled the surging Crystal River. It cut right and slowed to enter through the stone archway that elaborately announced that one was now on the prestigious ground of Crystal Valley Estates.

The auburn-haired driver waved to the uniformed man in the security hut as she passed through the iron gates. Then, picking up more speed, she drove the distance along twisting roads that curled up and into the sloping terrain dotted with homes of the area's wealthy residents. Privacy walls surrounded the individual acreage and, behind them, manicured gardens and the mandatory swimming pools stretched out into the mountains.

Approaching the last and highest house in the complex, the vehicle passed beneath the iron arch that marked their private estate. She gunned the engine up the curving road and screeched to a skidding stop before the large stone Tudor that teetered on the stony hillside.

The coolness of the interior was refreshing after being exposed to the hot sun all morning. The young woman sauntered across the foyer and shuffled absentmindedly through the stack of mail on the mahogany table. One piece in particular held her mild interest.

"Looks like it finally arrived," came the soft voice from the sitting room entryway.

Without looking up at her mother, Karen stared down at the formal envelope.

"Well?" Mrs. Kendall asked, while crossing the foyer, "Aren't you going to open it, dear?"

Karen tapped the envelope with a long lacquered talon. "Why should I? I already know what it says."

The elder woman raised a questioning brow. "How can you be so sure? Your entrance exam wasn't all that great, you know. Just maybe you were passed over. It could be possible that you weren't accepted after all."

The unopened missive fell back to the table.

"Oh god, mother, don't be such a pessimist. You know what it says as well as I do. Of course I'm in. You can bet ol' Beady Eyes made sure of that." She smirked sardonically, "Oh yes. You can bet your best antique on that one."

"Karen! I will not have you referring to your uncle in such a disrespectful manner!"

The young woman chuckled. "Well he does have beady eyes." She then mimicked the strained eyes of a peering mole. "They sort of always peer up at you like this."

"Ohhh, Karen! That's just terrible. My brother may be a good deal older than me, but he's one of the most respected and honored members of that institution. I will not have you making fun of him." Her back stiffened. "You should be grateful he put in a good word for you. God only knows what half-baked college would've accepted you if he hadn't."

Karen held up her hands with a flutter. "Okay, okay, you don't have to get your blood pressure up over it. I appreciate his pull, but just don't make it into some big esoteric mystery whether I got in or not." She hesitated a moment while deciding if she should broach the forbidden subject again. She decided to throw caution to the wind. "I'll have to apply for space in the dorm before they're all taken." Now she braced herself for the rampage she expected to fly forth.

Silence.

Karen shifted her gaze to the older woman who stood firmly frozen in place. Evidently she was admirably maintaining control.

"Karen," came the even tone. "We settled all that already."

"No we didn't. You and dad settled it. I didn't."

"It's decided where you're staying and it's not in some crowded dormitory with a bunch of juveniles."

The young woman rolled her eyes and exhaled a heavy sigh. "What's the matter, mother, you and dad afraid I'll catch some plebeian ideas or some low-brow philosophies or something? God, mother, I'm not Lady Di! And I am going to live in the dorm."

"No, you're not. It's all arranged."

Karen placed both palms on the foyer table and leaned far over it. "Then un-arrange it, dammit! I'm not going to live there! I am not going to live like some protected recluse in that godawful monstrosity in the middle of nowhere! How absolutely dreadful! What would the other students think?"

A gentle smile curled Mrs. Kendall's lips. "They'd probably envy you. That's what they'd think."

Karen smirked. "Oh, I'm sure. You think that because old Weatherbee is your brother. You think that way because you're coming from an entirely different direction. You can't even think like a student would. I know what they'd think. They'd think I was a spoiled brat who only got accepted because of who her uncle was. They'd think I thought I was really hot stuff living with the great Dr. Theodore Weatherbee in his mountain fortress. God, mother, can't you see how that in itself would alienate me from the other students?"

Mrs. Kendall was unconvinced. "No, not at all. As I said, they'd envy you. I'm serious, dear. You know how well the students love your dear uncle. Why, they'd give anything to be so near him all the time. The way they follow him around like puppies, crowd his lectures, fall over one another for his attention, is no secret. You'd be popular just by association with the man."

That last possibility didn't serve to placate a thing. It only made matters worse for the young woman.

"Oh great! That's just wonderful. Karen Kendall can't be well liked for who she is, but because of who she knows! That's rich, mother. That's real rich."

"Karen?" came the whispered response.

"What."

"He loves you. He loves you a great deal. Don't you think he's looking forward to having you stay with him?"

Karen sighed. "I'll only be in the way," she tried.

"He's lonely, Karen. Can't you see that? He's been all alone for so very long."

"He likes it like that," she flatly stated as if it were a well known fact of life.

"Does he?"

"Sure he does, otherwise he'd have moved into town ages ago. If you think you can change my mind by playing on my sympathies, you're wrong. He only agreed to put me up because you asked him to. You're his only sister, his baby sister. What'd you expect him to say? No?"

"Karen, he didn't agree to do it because I'm his sister. He did it because he really wanted to. You couldn't hear the excitement in his voice when I first approached him on it. He didn't even hesitate—not a second. Don't you think he's anxious to be able to help you with your studies? Especially when they're right in his own field? Think what valuable insights you'll gain from someone so knowledgeable. Think of the great advantage it will give you. Think of it, Karen."

"I have thought of it," came the sour-grapes tone. "No friends, no fun, no guys or nightlife. Just trees and more trees. Just darkness an' owls hooting at me. Thanks, but no thanks, mother. I'll work it out on my own, thank you."

"I've already worked it out, Karen."

"Well, like I said, I'll work it out."

"It's finalized, Karen."

"No it isn't, mother dear, not by a longshot." The arrogant

daughter spun with a flourish and skipped up the stairs to her room where she used her private phone to call the University Student Services Department. If it was the last thing she ever did, she wasn't going to lose this battle.

The older woman was left standing alone in the empty foyer. Out of a subliminal curiosity she slit open the embossed envelope. A wry smile bordering on defeat lifted one corner of her mouth and she almost wish it hadn't been verified. Ms. Karen Victoria Kendall had indeed been accepted.

The letter was carefully placed back into the envelope while the woman thoughtfully gazed up the staircase. She sighed heavily. Was it really fair to expect a twenty-four-year-old woman to still obey just because she was still living at home? Was it right to expect a bright young woman to be sequestered in a remote house with her aged uncle the entire time? Regardless of the morality of the dilemma she knew in her heart that she'd been defeated again. As usual, the young determined daughter would ultimately see to it that she got her own way. This the mother knew all too well. She supposed that's what became of an only child who'd been spoiled since birth. And, in the end, she realized that she'd had only herself to blame for the disappointing outcome she now had no control over.

Upstairs, new living arrangements were being finalized.

One week later, the flashy convertible was again making its way through the snaking byway of Glenwood Canyon. Soft leather luggage and an assortment of cardboard boxes littered the backseat. In the trunk, more of the same were packed tight with little room to spare.

The driver slowed the vehicle and eased over onto the newly-widened shoulder that edged along the Colorado River. This time that stop was not mandated by the construction crews and their creeping earth movers. The stop had been voluntary.

The redhead got out to stand by the guard rail. There was a powerful force that lived within the canyon. She could feel it in her bones. Looking up the jagged walls, she again felt diminutive in its ancient presence.

Ravens, wings spread wide, glided effortlessly on the air currents that swirled above the cascading waters. Their blackness glistened like oil in the bright autumn sunlight.

It'd be a while before she'd be back this way again and, even though she was quivering with the anxiety to begin her new venture, she knew she needed to take the time to say farewell to the things and people she loved most—the magnificent canyon and, a little further up the road, Terry.

For the moment, Karen needed a few golden moments alone with the canyon. She gazed up its height. Towering and powerful. A shiver speared through her. A chill swept coldly over her skin. Some nebulous unknown thing made her frown. The sensation came as a darkening force that shattered her bright mood. It felt like some kind of omen that hangs as a shadow that one never really sees. The redhead shuddered again.

She wondered what had caused the eerie sensation that felt like a warning. There was nothing in her immediate future to be warned about. Everything was going exactly according to plan. Everything was unfolding just as she wanted it to. She had gotten her way and the future was bright and full of excitement.

She smiled then. Yes, she'd gotten her way, just as she always managed to do. And with that satisfying thought, she shook off the dark feelings. She turned her back on the towering canyon walls and climbed into the overloaded vehicle.

Muttering to herself about it being too beautiful a morning for thinking about omens and dark thoughts, she engaged the gears and pulled out and away from the shadowed Standing Stones to head toward her last stop.

The town of Eagle was sleepy-eyed this sunny morning. Business in the little neighborhood cafe was slow and the owner had been in the back stocking up the cooler. Through the glass she saw the redhead enter. Terry peered around. "So. This is it," she chirped while coming out from the back room.

Karen grinned wide. "Yeah, this is it all right. Guess I won't be stopping in for a while." There was a look of resignation about her.

"Well don't look so glum. It's not like you're going abroad or anything. We'll write back and forth, make calls, and maybe if I ever get any decent time off, I'll bring Annie up and we'll have a real visit. You can show her what a university looks like."

Terry's friend's eyes sparkled with the thought of that idea.

Terry winked. "C'mon, I'll buy you a farewell coffee." And, after settling down in the corner booth, Terry raised a questioning brow. "So. Where are you staying?"

Karen's green eyes slid up to meet those of her friend's.

"If I tell you, you're not going to lecture me, are you?"

"Why should I? Obviously things are all set. So where is it?"

"The dorm." Karen paused to gauge the negative reaction she expected was forthcoming.

There wasn't any.

"I see," Terry said. "Are you in with anyone else?"

"Nope. All alone. I pulled a few strings myself and arranged for a private room." She grinned. "All I had to do was inform them that I was Dr. Weatherbee's niece! Isn't it great?"

Terry frowned. "I thought you didn't want anyone knowing he was your uncle."

"Well. One must do what one must do. Especially if it's imperative to getting what one wants."

Terry ignored the arrogant statement. "So why'd you opt for private accommodations? I was under the impression you didn't want to stay out at your uncle's place because you wanted to be in the thick of things. If you're in a private room by yourself, aren't you going to be alienating yourself by such a separation? Won't you be defeating your purpose for being in the dorm?"

"No way!" Karen beamed. "My magnanimous personality and busy social life will more than make up for such trivialities." It was an intended exaggeration, but true all the same. Few people could resist the young woman's beauty and outgoing personality.

Terry just shook her head and grinned. "I'm sure you'll make plenty of friends no matter where you're bunked."

"Well! I seriously doubt my social life would've been agreeable if I'd taken my uncle's offer." She rolled her eyes. "Just think how awful it would've been being cooped up in that musty old family heirloom of his. Bears and coyotes aren't exactly my first choice for companions, you know."

"I'm sure you would've been free to come and go as you please. I hardly think your uncle was prepared to play cell keeper with you. You're a tad old for a babysitter."

The redhead shook her hair back from her face. "I sure as hell wasn't about to take that chance. Besides, I didn't like the idea of living with the campus guru either. People wouldn't have treated me normally, if you know what I mean."

Terry did. Still, she would've jumped at the opportunity to live in such a wonderful house and to have the golden chance to learn from the knowledgeable man who owned it. What an incredible once-in-a-lifetime experience her frivolous friend was passing up, or more accurately, throwing away. Yes, if it were her, she'd have jumped at the chance to live with Dr. Weatherbee.

Karen flopped her hand back and forth in front of her friend's face. "Hey! Yoo-hoo! Come back to earth."

Terry's eyes focused on her friend. "Sorry."

"You still don't agree with me, do you," Karen muttered as she leaned forward over the table. "You still think I should've accepted my uncle's offer."

Terry shrugged. "Everyone's different, Karen. Everyone's got to use their free will to make their own choices. If this is really what you want, then fine, go for it. What I think one way or the other, or what I would've done if it were me isn't germane in the end. I don't live your life. You do."

Karen's mouth dropped open. She pointed a long manicured nail at her friend.

"That's exactly what I've been trying to tell mother these past months. I guess she thinks that just because I still live at home she's got some rights-of-final-say in my affairs."

Terry gave her friend a chastising look.

"I think you're wrong. She's only trying to help you out, smooth over the sharp edges of the transition. I know your mother, I'm sure she isn't into controlling anyone. You're going to be living in Boulder and your uncle's house is right up there in the mountains. It's nearby. . .convenient, not to leave out the matter of it being safe."

"What's that supposed to mean?"

"Has your brain been out to lunch or what? You've heard about the trouble that's been happening on some of the college campuses. I'm talking about crime here, Karen. I'm referring to some colleges that have been experiencing violence against the students."

"Oh that. I never thought that mother was worried about that sort of thing. But Terry, we're talking Boulder here. We're talking Colorado!"

"Wake up, Karen. There are nuts everywhere. You think just because you're going to be at a mountain college there couldn't ever be any trouble? Crime?"

"Well no, but I know I'll be just fine in the dorm. I'm a big girl now. What possible trouble could I get into anyway?"

The friend didn't respond, but let Karen continue.

"Well, no matter. In a few hours' time I'll be busy fixing up my own little room and making it all cozy and homey-like."

"Can you change rooms if you want later on?"

Karen's eyes widened. "Why ever would I want to do such a thing? I've always had my own room. I'm certainly not about to fight for extra inches of closet space with some little twit who probably doesn't know a Gucci from a K-Mart! You just never know what sort of weirdo or lowlife you'd end up with for a roommate. No thanks. There's just no way I'd share a room. What made you ask that anyway?"

Terry shrugged. "Ohhh, silly me, I just thought that maybe you'd have more fun being in with someone after a while. You know, gossiping and sharing shop talk, somebody to study with, company and all that. I should've known better, huh."

"Absolutely! You most certainly should have. My goodness, you've known me long enough now to understand me."

The sudden frown on Terry's face couldn't be suppressed no matter how hard she tried.

Karen narrowed her emerald eyes in suspicion. "Come on. Out with it. Why the frown?"

Terry waved her hand. "Nothing. Really, it's nothing."

"No deal, my friend. I'm not leaving here until you confess." And with that, she squirmed squarely in her seat for the duration. "Well? I'm waiting."

"You really want to know what brought on the frown?"

"Absolutely. My dear, I am not budging until you come clean with it."

"All right, but I'm not so sure you're going to like it."

"Fess up."

"An odd feeling came over me when you said that I've known you long enough. I don't know, I just had a funny feeling, that's all."

"Like what kind of funny feeling?"

Terry looked off in the distance. Her thoughts raced. How could she tell her friend of the darkness she sensed drawing close to her? How could she tell what she felt without scaring her? She couldn't, so she looked her friend in the eye and gave her a warm smile. "I think I'm only concerned about you. You will take good care of yourself, won't you?"

Karen melted. "Oh Terry, you're such a good friend. Of course I'll take perfect care of myself. Don't you worry about a thing.

Don't you worry at all over Karen Victoria Kendall. She's going to be just fine."

Back on the road and heading east, Karen smiled at the thought of what her friend had said. It warmed her heart and served to alleviate the darkness that the canyon had begun her journey with.

From habit, she checked her makeup in the rear-view mirror. Satisfied with what she saw, the image smiled back at her. Then thoughts sped to what lay ahead.

It had been an ingenious move on her part to have thought to mention to Student Services that she was the good Dr. Weatherbee's niece. She seriously doubted she could've landed the private room without the coordinator having known that juicy little tidbit.

A satisfied smirk marred her dainty features. Old Beady Eyes had come in handy after all. Now he could enjoy his reclusive privacy and she could likewise enjoy her own chosen lifestyle away from the prying eyes and open ears of other students—students not nearly as sophisticated as she.

Yes, how perfect everything had worked out, right down to the last detail. Life was looking up.

The weather wasn't. Ahead, an angry line of grey clouds lowered and began to roil.

By the time the newcomer's car rolled onto the Boulder campus, heavily-ladened skies had unleashed their burdensome load. Rain fell in torrents of shifting wind-blown sheets across the expanse of grounds. The various buildings, reduced to ominous shadows, loomed as breakers on the plane of horizon. And finally, after several unsuccessful attempts at following the layout map that'd accompanied her indoctrination material, Karen Victoria Kendall pulled up in front of her new domicile.

Drenched, with arms straining from the weight of the cumbersome luggage, she located the door of her private sanctuary—208-B. Nearly exhausted, she set down the load in the hall. She was anxious to get out of her wet clothes and be alone for awhile. She released a heavy sigh and opened the door.

"Hi!" came a chipper greeting from within. "You must be Karen Kendall. I'm Emmy Winter. . .your roommate."

Frozen in place, the redhead presented a pitiful sight. The once-fluffy mass of flowing auburn tresses had now been plastered down her face like freshly poured paint. Mascara that had been professionally applied a few hours before was now awash and running down her cheeks. The woman looked more like she'd been on a crying jag. Soaked clothes stuck like second skin. And eyes, round and wild, matched the mouth that gaped in shock.

Finally the dishevelled figure stirred.

She crept silently into the tiny room and, in a mesmerized state, noticed the double set of furniture.

Two twin beds.

Two dressers. *Small* dressers.

Two desks.

And. . .one closet.

"Ahhh," the drenched woman uttered with feigned uncertainty while double checking the number on the door. "I believe there's been some terrible mistake made here. Ahhh, you see, Emmy dear, you've got the wrong room."

The dark-haired woman frowned as she watched the drowned rat with the auburn fur frantically dig through the depths of her soaked Gucci bag and extract a folded paper.

"See?" the rat squeaked, holding it high aloft. "This is 208-B! *My* room."

"Yes, you're right," admitted Emmy, also holding up an identical piece of paper. "We've both got Room 208-B."

"No-no-no, honey," came the sweet voice dripping with rancid honey. "This is supposed to be a *single*. A *private* single."

Now the other woman understood the situation, for not half an hour earlier, some students down the hall had had the same occurrence happen. And, inwardly, she hoped the outcome of this one wouldn't prove to be as ugly. The other two students had nearly come to blows over the mix-up.

Ms. Winter smiled wryly as she stepped forward and reached out her hands. "Here, let me help you with your things."

The wet woman immediately recoiled. "Perhaps you'll allow me to help you with *your* things. It shouldn't take but a few minutes to put them where they belong," she said, noticing the sparse possessions set about on one side of the room.

Emmy glanced back at her meager belongings. "Oh, no thank you, I'm quite settled in." Then she eyed the woman still in the doorway. "I don't know what you've been told or what sort of arrangements they've promised you over in Student Services but

I'm sorry to say that there are no singles. This room's been reserved for myself and one Karen Kendall. If you're Karen Kendall then I guess we're both here rightfully."

Still unconvinced, the newcomer strode authoritatively across the room and picked up the phone. A patronizing smile tried to sweeten the sour attitude that fumed within.

"Well dear, we'll just see about this little mix-up," she sang, punching up the numbers with a long nail.

"Student Services? Yes, this is Karen Kendall in 208-B. There seems to be. . .oh fine, my trip was just fine, thank you. As I was saying, there seems to be some confus. . .pardon me? Did I meet Ms. Winter? No-no-no. You see I personally arranged it with. . .no, but I'm Dr. Weatherb. . .but I was told! I was assured! You must have me confused with someone else, I'm Dr. Weath. . .yes. I see. Thank you so very much."

Slowly the headset was returned to its cradle.

Karen looked over at the deeply tanned woman and smiled sheepishly. "Seems we're roomies."

The remainder of the day didn't turn out as gloomy as the weather had. Emmy Winter braved the rain to help the disappointed woman cart in the rest of her belongings and they ended up laughing as they tried to rearrange the room to accommodate them both. And, as it turned out, the two became more and more comfortable with each other while they chatted about their differing backgrounds and got to know each other better.

The only things Karen omitted were her romantic escapades.

The only things Emmy left out were her sacred, mystical experiences.

Though the two were only a year apart in age, one based her entire existence on riding the surface waters of life while the other survived in a much deeper current of reality.

Little did either woman know how their destinies would entwine.

Part Two
TO TREAD A TRAIL DARKLY

With Wisdom should you pause along the Wayside to contemplate upon that which you wish to attain, for not all Byways are hospitable inroads.

With Prudence should you pause upon the Threshold of a New Path to meditate upon that which you wish to accomplish, for not all Courses are benevolent open roads.

Listen and Hear　　See and Feel　　Sense and Analyze

For I say to you. If you are not mindful of where your footfalls land, and if you heed not the many omens that rise up before you, then do you foolishly close your eyes to tread a Trail darkly.

The Papyrus

T he campus grounds bustled with activity. Friends sought out friends. Returning students gathered in groups to talk about their summer adventures. Freshmen milled together, their unfamiliarity being their common bond. Fraternity brothers eyed the new coeds with a practiced eye. Sorority sisters lingered to catch a glimpse of any new professors who happened by.

It was a glorious morning. The light breeze brought fresh scents of pine and spruce wafting lazily through the mountain air. The bright sun splashed down out of a deep turquoise sky. Signs of new beginnings were in bloom everywhere one rested one's gaze, for colorful autumn flowers were planted in budding clusters throughout the grounds.

The students were anxious to begin the new academic year. Great adventures were about to begin. New roads were being traveled and charted courses set. The entire campus possessed a touchable aura of adventure and discovery.

Two women strode up the pathway that cut through the recently mowed lawns. With new textbooks in hand, they had the telltale grins of newcomers—the kind of smiles that were impossible for their high excitement and wonder to contain. Yet a little observation would show these two to be very different from each other. One walked with exterior haughtiness, while the other went forward in reserved dignity.

Suddenly one halted the other in mid-step.

Karen Kendall's hand hooked around the crook of Emmy Winter's elbow and she nearly dropped her load of books as she was pulled up short.

"What's the matter with you?" she sputtered in irritation, grabbing for a notebook that threatened to topple off the pile. She turned to further chastise her friend and found her standing statue-still, mouth dropped open and in a dead stare.

Emmy peered through the stands of aspens trying to zero in on her friend's point of new interest. There were too many people milling about to make a reasonable selection. Emmy quickly looked back to her friend who had finally found her voice.

"Ohhh my god," came the whispered words. "Will you look at that gorgeous man!"

Again Emmy tried to find the source of Karen's infatuation. Then, one individual did appear to stand out from the rest.

A dark-haired man with a briefcase was quickly cutting across an adjacent walkway. He could've passed for a student if it weren't for the fact that he carried himself with assurance and the worn briefcase singled him out as a professor. The young man nodded to a group of passing students. His broad smile exposed the perfect rows of pearly teeth.

"That guy?" Emmy asked of her mesmerized companion.

"Ohhh, pinch me," she groaned. "Pinch me so I know I'm not dreaming or died and went to college heaven."

"Oh for heaven's sake, Karen. He's a professor."

"Who cares?" came the dreamy response.

"You are going to have to care. You can't fraternize with them." Emmy yanked on the woman's sleeve and pulled the lovestruck friend along. "C'mon, we've gotta get moving or we'll be late for our very first class. You don't want to keep the good Professor Greystone waiting, do you?"

"Forget Professor Greystone. I want that one. Maybe I'll just have to do some course switching."

Disgustedly, the dark-haired woman urged the redhead forward. "Well fine, you find out what he teaches and then you can do all the switching your little heart desires, but right now we've got to get going."

Once they located the proper building, the young women quickly found their classroom and discovered it to be a large lecture hall. Rows and rows of seats descended in levels down to a center desk and lectern. The desks were filling from the top rows and the two women had to go down the steps toward the front where a few empty ones awaited them.

Settling in, Karen sneered. "We would be forced down here right in front. I hate being right in this guy's face. He's probably older than Methuselah and got dog breath."

Emmy arranged her notebook on the tiny chair arm that served as her writing space. She eyed her disappointed friend. "Well, we could've been sitting way up there in the back if you hadn't stopped so long to gawk at that professor. It's all your own fault we're stuck down here in front. Now we'll probably be called on, no thanks to you."

Karen noticed the microphone and nudged her friend. "Dr. Greystone's probably so old he wheezes when he talks. Notice the mike?"

But Ms. Winter wasn't looking in that direction at all; she'd been watching Dr. Greystone enter the hall. "Oh," she whispered with amusement, "I don't think he'll be quite that old."

Karen turned and blushed. Now she really did wish they'd come in sooner. How ever could she hide her attraction for this man while she was sitting right in front of him? This was going to be a difficult class, how would she ever manage to concentrate on anything that was said?

The chatter hushed to a low murmur as the new instructor entered. It fell silent when he stood before the lectern. If anyone had dropped so much as a pin, everyone would've heard it.

"Good morning. I'm Dr. Greystone and I'll be filling in for a while." His voice was soft yet confident. "Officially, I'm the Assistant Curator of Antiquities at the Boston Museum. . .that's my prime occupation," the man said with a grin.

Karen melted.

"Since Professor Weatherbee required a replacement for the department, well, you might say I was sort of drafted."

Twittering snickers sporadically broke out along the rows of students.

The professor's brow raised. "Oh, so you think that's amusing do you? Maybe you think I've no experience with teaching? Is that it?"

The student body grinned and nodded in unison.

"You are all wrong," the instructor informed. "For your information I taught for six years. I used to stand before an arena filled with young people just like you. I'll admit that it's been awhile but I'm no stranger to this job."

The crowd silenced after they realized they didn't have an inexperienced substitute on their hands.

The man smiled wide. "I'm so pleased you appear to appreciate my years of experience." He continued on a more serious note. "Now, I'm sure there are more than a few of you here today who've heard about the reputation of Dr. Weatherbee and were expecting him to be giving the classes. To you I apologize because I know how much you were looking forward to that experience. I won't claim to be as knowledgeable as he nor will I expect the same love and respect I know you'd feel for him."

Karen's foot shot out to nudge Emmy's leg when the instructor mentioned the word love. She missed her mark and the leg went flying up in a knee-jerk action.

Dr. Greystone noticed the distracting movement.

Their eyes met.

"You there," he addressed her, "do you have a comment?"

"Me? I. . .no. No, I'm sorry," she stuttered beneath reddened cheeks.

Emmy had to concentrate on her hands to stifle the outburst that threatened to burst forth. Clearly this Dr. Greystone was a very perceptive individual. Nothing escaped his keen sense of observation.

"Well then," he continued. "I don't expect much, just complete attention while I'm speaking and plenty of questions when I'm finished." He raised the textbook for the class to see. "This is your Anthropology text. It is filled with valuable information. Five hundred pages of in-depth knowledge that will require many long hours of reading, studying, and memorizing."

The class groaned.

"It took years of research to compile this text. And, it will take at least as many years to absorb it. Therefore, we will not use it."

The group was struck silent with the unexpected announcement.

"Instead," said the professor, "you will open your ears and minds while I talk. You will take thorough notes and ask many questions. This will be a lecture course followed each day by a roundtable of class participation. How well you do will ultimately depend solely upon how complete your individual notes are and how well you've listened. Do we understand the ground rules?"

A roar of assent rose up amid the sea of happy smiles.

He grinned with satisfaction. "Good. I'm glad we see eye to eye already." The man began pacing in front of the desk. He passed within touching distance of the front row. Perhaps he could hear a certain heart throbbing madly close by.

"Now, we're going to be discussing some very peculiar subjects during this course. We'll be covering the traditional belief systems of various cultures around the world. Some of these beliefs will appear quite fantastic at first look, yet you must keep in mind that there are realities to life that are yet unimagined."

This statement perked Emmy's immediate interest. She listened more intently as the young professor continued.

"Many beliefs are clearly contrived stories handed down through the ages while, conversely, many are clearly mystical in origin. . .but real all the same.

"We'll be covering voodoo ceremonies, paranormal feats as demonstrated within the differing cultures, Egyptian mythology and that great culture's concept of the afterlife. We'll delve deeply into the nature of American Indian shamanism and the incredible powers those people display even today. We'll be touching on Hindu mental control and obscure sects of remote regions worldwide. And I caution you now with a strong word of warning—do not, I repeat, do not allow it to carry you across the demarcation line of reality." His next words were cryptically whispered. "Because if you do allow this to happen, you may never see reality as you know it ever again."

Heads turned to eye one another in curiosity over the mysterious warning. Somewhere up in the middle row a hand hesitantly rose.

"Yes?" Dr. Greystone acknowledged.

A young man stood. "What did you mean by that last statement?" he nervously chuckled. "Are you trying to scare us? Because if you are. . ."

"Sit down, young man," the instructor gently ordered while beginning to pace behind the lectern. When he stopped, he grasped both sides of the wood and scanned the anxiously waiting faces.

"There are unexplainable things out there that defy all logical and rational reason. There are ways of power that transcend far beyond the laws of physics as we now know and understand them. There are byways that are hostile to all but the most adept. Do I make myself clear?"

Nodding heads waved through the hall.

"I'm not here to scare the pants off you. I'm here to inform you.

I'm not here to give you a new toy to play with or a new thrill to experiment with. I'm here to be your guide through a maze of nebulous and obscure realities. And I'm here to see that you don't go over the edge with it.

"Now I want you to listen to me carefully. If any of you, during the duration of this course, have any problems developing with the material or even think you're mentally heading for dangerous ground, I want you to immediately come to me for help. I've had a great deal of experience, so nothing you could tell me would sound preposterous. Rest assured, I'm familiar with all aspects of the illogical and mystical facets of reality. On the same hand, I'm equally familiar with their exits back to safety and. . .sanity."

Perhaps the good professor hadn't intentionally started out to put fear in the hearts of his new students, but now the thundering organs were full of drumming emotion.

"Now, if you'll place what I've just said on the back burners of your minds, we can get on with other things.

"We won't actually begin in earnest until tomorrow, so for now, I want to hear feedback from you. Feel free to ask anything you wish about the subject and I'll try to make the answer as concise as possible."

He then waited for a volley of questions to erupt.

When none were forthcoming he urged them not to be so shy.

A young woman stood.

"Yes?" the professor acknowledged.

"How old are you?"

The class roared.

Dr. Greystone blushed. "Is that germane to the subject?"

"Oh yes, Dr. Greystone," she grinned. "You teach it."

The class expectantly looked back to the embarrassed man.

Dr. Greystone shook his head and smiled. "I've got dark brown eyes, am five-eleven and the black hair is not dyed. I like to go hiking in my spare time, am thirty-five years old and yes, I'm single."

The hall broke out in an uproar. Clapping hands, hoots, and whistles brought the house down. The consensus was unanimous—this guy was all right! This class was going to see packed standing room from now on. Dr. Greystone had just made himself very popular, maybe just as popular as old Weatherbee himself. A new guru had arrived.

The man behind the lectern held up his hands for quiet. When he received it he chastised them. "You want them to fire me after just one class?"

The raucous group resounded with boisterous negatives. Boos and groans grew in volume.

Again the instructor held up his hands. "All right. All right," he laughed. "We've established some good mutual respect here, let's respect it. Many more outbreaks like that and you're going to get the Board breathing down my neck."

The students respectfully settled down and calm reigned once again.

"Thank you," the man said with heartfelt relief before beginning to pace the floor. He then looked up into the enrapt faces of his students. "I want to hear more questions," he said to them. "Real questions."

A skinny arm shot up.

"Yes?"

The young man stood and stabbed a finger to push on the bridge of thick, bottle-bottom glasses. "Dr. Greystone, I heard some of the upperclassmen debating a matter and I wondered what your opinion was on it."

"Shoot," the instructor urged.

"Do you believe that all the American Indian tribes migrated to what is the present-day North American territory?" After stating the question, the lanky fellow promptly sat down.

The response was quick. "Popular belief is that some U.S. tribes came up from the ancient civilizations of the Aztecs, Incas and the Mayans. Also from the Toltecs and Zapotecs from Teotihuacan in central Mexico's highlands. It is also believed that, from the uppermost Northeastern region of the U.S.S.R. Indian peoples ventured over to our continent from the land bridge that once spanned the Bering Straits. However, recently I have found reason to believe that all of the Native American People were just that— native to this land."

The questioner wasn't finished. "What proof do you have to substantiate your recently revised theory on this?"

"You may sit down, young man," he said, motioning with his hand. "It's not necessary to stand in my class when you speak."

Again he began pacing before the interested group. "Let me explain something. Over the duration of this particular course—

probably this one more than any other field of study—it's going to become clear that, with certain issues, the proof is not always the touchable finality we expect it to be.

"You're going to discover that when following accepted theories there will always be exceptions to the rule. Where do these then fit in? Do these exceptions nullify the theorem? So in answer to this young man's query I will say that I've come across some rather interesting exceptions to the Indian migration concept held today. There are certain fragments that just do not neatly fit into the mold and I tend to be wary of what has already supposedly been proven. One day I hope to personally substantiate my ideas and reverse the former supposition."

Another hand shot up.

"Yes?"

"Have you ever personally witnessed firewalking?"

"Yes. Three years ago I had the unexpected opportunity to accompany a group of researchers to Haiti. I'm very pleased to say that I ended up with extremely warm feet, however. . .they were not burned."

The class was impressed.

The same hand went up again. "Did you also witness any voodoo rites while you were there?"

"Yes. I did. And perhaps we'll be able to get into those more in depth later on in the course. That all depends on how well you do as a group." He pointed to another student who was wildly waving his hand.

"Dr. Greystone, have you ever performed any mystical rites or ceremonies yourself? And, if so, are you an adept at such things?"

The professor smiled wryly. "Are you asking if I'm a sorcerer, young man?"

Snickers rippled down the rows.

"No, sir. I'm asking if you've ever tried the various rites yourself and if you've had much success with them?"

Silence filled the room as the instructor hesitated. The stillness became heavy as the students anxiously waited for the answer that would make the young man their new mystic.

Finally a gentle voice pierced the stillness. "You must remember that mysticism is an integral facet of this course. Because of the subject matter, it cannot be otherwise. However, there are many other vital aspects that come into play here—important aspects. To center one's total attention on the supernatural portion is a very grave mistake."

Another student had an urgent question and, when acknowledged, she voiced it. "Dr. Greystone, I understand the importance of what you've just said, but you skirted the initial question. Have you personally performed any mystical rites or ceremonies and, if so, were you ever successful?"

The man facing the students conceded. "Yes and always."

Now it was official. Now it had been verified. Soon the entire campus would hear of the handsome anthropology professor who was indeed qualified to be their new wiseman. From now on, Dr. Greystone would be looked upon with complete awe.

Down in the front row, the instructor nodded his recognition to a young woman with long ebony hair that glistened in the room's rays of sunlight.

"Doctor Greystone, I'd like to know what right archeologists have to dig up Indian burial grounds?"

The question interested the group.

The instructor frowned. "I'm afraid that's one I can't answer unless we want to diverge into the realm of philosophy."

The new student wouldn't be put off so easily. "But I've asked a valid question and I fail to see why it matters what area of thought it encompasses."

"All right," he agreed. "What's your name, young lady."

"Emmy. Emmy Winter."

For most of the discussion time the young doctor had purposely attempted to avoid the distracting woman in front of him. She made him uneasy. Her smooth tanned complexion made the blue eyes stand out starkly like a pair of turquoise gems laid on a soft pelt of deerskin. They were full of intense awareness and he'd immediately sensed a depth to her that reached far beyond her young age.

Now, slightly unnerved by the unexpected one-on-one confrontation with her, he wasn't going to be able to circumvent the point in question. His dark eyes locked on her blues for a brief second and his heart thundered. He felt a force at work. . .one that magnetically drew him to this young woman.

He directed his attention to the class proper. "Emmy here has asked about the authority that archeologists have to enter ancient Indian burial grounds and dig them up. Does anyone have any specific thoughts on that?"

Several hands shot up and he indicated each one in succession.

"Their right is the right of discovery," one student confidently claimed. "How else could we possibly become enlightened about past civilizations if learned men didn't delve down and research their finds from the past?"

"In the name of historical research and documentation," another offered logically.

"People have a right to understand the history of their own land."

"Proof to verify theories," came the last.

Dr. Greystone looked again into the magnetic eyes of the woman. "What about your peer's answers?" he inquired of her.

The woman's back was ramrod straight. Her eyes pierced the man's. "Not one entered into the philosophical realm. Now I want *your* answer."

"That's fair," he said. "But first I'd like your own response to what you've heard here from the student body."

"The answers are nothing more than shallow excuses. They're flimsy screens for irresponsible actions. If I were to act on the basis of their reasoning then, this day, I could go to any city cemetery with a pick and shovel and begin digging without doing it illegally."

A gruff voice from the back broke in. "You can't trespass on private property!"

Another joined the growing raucous. "Grave robbery's against the law, lady!"

"You'd be *desecrating* consecrated ground that's *holy*!"

Emmy Winter stiffened. Eyes flared. She spun around to face her accusers. "Sacred ground?" she softly questioned.

The class fell silent while she stared them down. Then she quietly turned and sat.

Michael Greystone had to restrain the involuntary urge to clap his hands and applaud Ms. Winter's point. Instead he winked at her and proceeded to address the solemn group.

"And so we enter philosophy. Tell me," he addressed them all, "tell me what deems one race's holy ground more holy than another's? What makes one race's sacred ground more sacred than another's?" Patiently he waited for some response.

There was none.

"Well?" he urged with force building in his voice. "Is the law of the land upheld for one race and not for another?" His brow raised. "Is it *discriminatory* by chance? Does it really mean to say that all races must respect the holy burial grounds of every race *except* those of the American Indians? What does this mean here? What does this really say? Who was here first?"

The silence that filled the lecture hall was deafening. All were enrapt by the exposed paradox.

"*Well*?" Greystone shouted at their autistic faces. "Where's the justice? The precious equality we pride ourselves in? Huh? Where? Do we view the Indians as a people of no meaningful consequence? Of immaterial worth as human beings that we tramp over their sacred grounds and scatter their bones? Tell me, if these good people were of no valued consequence, then why bother trying to find out more about their ancient culture in the first place! And if we do actually view them so worthy of our extensive efforts at research, why are we so wantonly desecrating *their* sacred grounds? Huh? Why?"

Silence.

Greystone powerfully pounded the podium with his fist. "ANSWER me!"

After several prolonged minutes of squirming in the uncomfortable silence, one student braved a reply.

"I don't think we know how to answer this," she said.

The instructor shook his head. "That's a cop-out. It's a cop-out because it's easier to say you don't know rather than spending some deep thought over it. I see you don't want to admit that we are a two-faced, hypocritical civilization of asses with forked tongues and double standards that are utilized to suit our own self-serving needs."

His gentle gaze rested on the young woman in the front row. He was outwardly sympathetic and deeply moved by his own emotions.

"And now you have my viewpoint, Ms. Winter. Now you see why it is not an easy issue for an archeologist's mind to resolve. Personally I abhor the practice. It only serves to underscore how truly primitive some of us really are in this supposedly advanced society of ours."

Emmy Winter bowed her head in humble acceptance of the man's sincerity and compassionate perspective.

A student called out. "Dr. Greystone?"

The man's eyes were still locked on the woman's. He was irritated with the distraction. He looked up to acknowledge the student.

"What is it?"

"Doctor, all you said was very impressive and really thought provoking but science still needs to utilize research in order to discover our past. There appears to be no cut and dried formula for this issue of archeological digs and. . ."

"Really. Really?" the professor questioned. "Is that what happens then? We just say there is no solution?"

The student was visibly flustered. "Well. . .well from what you've been saying there doesn't appear to be anything that can be. . ."

"My dear boy," Greystone broke in, "tell me what is wrong with archeologists digging in ancient camp sites, in abandoned hunting grounds, in forgotten cliff dwellings? Huh?" Then his voice was little more than a whisper. "What is wrong with respecting the sacredness of burial grounds and. . .*leaving*. . .the bones. . .alone?"

The student had no answer.

The instructor glanced down at Ms. Winter.

She looked into the blackness of his eyes and softly asked, "Have you ever heard of Standing Stones that speak in whispers?"

For Michael, it was as if all the students had faded into the distant background except for the one who now stood out in such crystal clear relief before him. A warm current of pulsing energy passed between them.

He found his voice. "I've heard of such things, Emmy, but never have I experienced them first-hand nor have I ever met anyone who had." But suddenly he felt the last part of his statement was no longer true. He desperately wanted to ask the woman why she'd brought up the obscure subject, but was compelled to refrain from voicing it. There was something there that more than hinted at a deeply complex sensitivity. And without going further into the issue of the rare Standing Stones, Dr. Greystone concluded his first class.

"Tomorrow I expect you all to come prepared. A notebook and pen is all you'll need. If you wish to peruse the text, please feel free. If questions arise from your extra reading we'll have time for such discussions toward the end of class each day. So until then, take care."

The crowded hall of students whistled and hooted as their beloved new professor packed up his briefcase and left the noisy room.

Michael Greystone needed to see the head of the department. His appointment was scheduled right after his class, but before he kept it he had personal business to see to first.

Rounding a corridor he quickened his pace and when he came to the administration sector he pushed through the double glass doors.

"Ah, Dr. Greystone! How'd it go?" inquired the woman at the desk. Her rhinestone studded glasses sparkled with the reflected fluorescent lighting.

"Fine, Mrs. Dowd, just fine." He paused a little longer than was usual for his efficient pace.

"Can I help you with something?" she asked, peering up over the glittering rims.

"Yes, at least I hope so. Is it possible for me to see one of my student's files?"

"Of course, doctor. What's the name?"

"Winter. Emmy Winter."

"Oh, I think I recall her," Mrs. Dowd brightened with a smile that represented an orthodontist's dream. "Isn't she real dark complected and have hair down to her waist?"

"That's the one," he agreed. "I'd like to know a little about her background. Some curious things she said has got my wheels grinding."

"Sounds interesting," the woman commented while digging through the files. "Here you are."

Quickly he flipped over the few pages. "Mmm, she's from New Mexico, twenty-five years old and. . .mmm."

"What's the matter?" came the inquisitive voice, silently wondering if her records were somehow amiss.

"Well, isn't there a place to check nationality somewhere on these forms?"

"Why yes. Right here," she indicated with a brightly painted nail. "Oh my, she didn't check anything. Well, probably an oversight," she wagged through a smile. "These kids come in here and they're so excited it's a wonder they can ever remember their names half the time. She looks maybe Mexican, don't you think? With those big blue eyes of hers it's hard to tell though. Maybe she just has a great tan—it's warm and sunny down there, isn't it?"

The file was shut. "Thanks, Mrs. Dowd, you've been most helpful."

"Oh," she sighed, "any time, Dr. Greystone, just any time at all."

Clearly it wasn't only the impressionable students that were infatuated by the new professor's charming mannerisms and handsome smile.

Rushing now to his appointment, Michael burst through Dr. Weatherbee's inner sanctum. He expected a good tongue-lashing to be forthcoming as the old man had made it perfectly clear how vehemently he detested tardiness. Instead, Michael found the man standing at the bank of windows deep in thought.

"Dr. Weatherbee?"

Startled out of the contemplative state, the man jerked around. "Ah yes, come in. Come in, Michael."

The young man took the chair opposite the massive desk while the elder began to restlessly pace behind it. "How'd it go, Michael. . .the class, I mean?"

"Fine, Dr. Weatherbee. They're just as eager as you said they'd be. I think we've established a good foundation. I'm okay with it."

"Good. Good. That's good to hear." Then there was silence again as the elder doctor began pacing once again.

"Michael," he began solemnly. "Dr. Neusome thinks very highly of your expertise. He can't praise you enough, you know. Are you aware of his high regard for your. . .abilities?"

The statement and subsequent question took the younger man off guard. "We did get along very well together and he always wanted my opinion on things he was working on. Yes. Yes, I'd say our respect and admiration was always mutual and straightforward."

The department head mulled that over for several silent moments. Then he slowly opened his bottom desk drawer and extracted a messy piece of newsprint. "Read this."

Michael reached for the paper that'd been dropped on the cluttered desk before him. His spine tingled as he recognized the media coverage of his former colleague's suicide.

"This man was my friend," he sadly uttered.

"Mmmm, yes. Neusome told me how shaken up you were about

the unfortunate incident. I'm truly sorry to resurrect painful memories, Michael, but shortly you'll understand why I'm forced to do it."

Weatherbee took note that Michael was subconsciously rubbing a thumb over the dark stains. "That won't come off," he said in a deadpan tone.

And after the mystifying incident at Dr. Weatherbee's home had been recounted he eyed the younger man. "You sure your colleague never dropped any hints as to the location of his recent research?"

Michael simply shook his head.

"Think about it. Perhaps some slip of the tongue, some inadvertent word that could be a clue."

"I'm sorry, Dr. Weatherbee, he was always so open about his projects before this last one. He'd always been so full of exuberance and purpose that he'd blurt every detail out. He seemed to love sharing his discoveries with me before taking them public." He shook his head. "But that last time he was extremely secretive. All he'd said was that he'd be away in the Southwest for a while and that he couldn't be reached."

"And he returned from there."

"Yes, but only to end his life. I didn't even know he was back. Maybe he didn't find what he thought he would. I tend to think that's what happened. He just got himself so worked up about the prospects of his expected find that, when it didn't pan out, it was just too hard a defeat to accept. He'd come up empty-handed."

"I don't think so," came the unexpected reply.

Michael looked up into the frowning face. "What? You believe he actually did succeed somehow?"

"Ohh, in a manner of speaking, yes, I do."

Dr. Greystone was incredulous, but before he could speak again, the elder man halted it with his hand.

"Hold on a minute and hear me out. I've a couple more things for you to see."

He opened a folder and extracted another newspaper article. This one was unstained. "Look this over, will you, Michael?"

Dr. Greystone read about the young archeologist who'd shocked the scholarly community by claiming that he was setting out to prove the Indian Migration theory was false. The upstart had even suggested that he'd seen proof that not only verified the fact, but had also firmly substantiated ancient communications between Native Americans and other intelligences from. . .*out there.*

Michael tapped the paper. "I remember hearing about this guy," he recalled now. "I believe he was bent on also proving that ancient Egypt had some vague connection to the Indian people too." He chuckled. "I also recall how Neusome ranted on and on, railing this guy up one side and down the other."

Weatherbee didn't find the recollection the least bit humorous and gave no comment on it. "Now read this," he gravely ordered, passing a third newsprint clipping over to the seated man.

Michael read it in disbelief. "Was the guy ill?"

"No. He was in perfect health. Thirty-two years old and they found him dead of a heart attack, or so they say. They figured his body had been out in the desert for over two weeks before it'd been discovered. The way it'd been picked over by the carrion buzzards and coyotes it was pretty hard to tell exactly how he went."

Michael shivered with the horrifying intrusion of the unwanted vision of it. He listened to the additional information.

"Anyway," Weatherbee went on, "he wasn't actually on a dig. Near as anyone can figure, the man had been climbing around at the base of one of the larger mesas out there."

"Where was this again?" Michael inquired.

"Somewhere between Holbrook, Arizona and Zuni, New Mexico. . .the Southwest."

New Mexico. New Mexico. Emmy was from there.

"That's an expansive area," Michael said. "Anyone ever been able to pinpoint it better than that?"

"No, seems not. There are towering mesas all along that corridor stretch."

Michael thought deeply on what he'd just learned. "So what you're saying here is that my former colleague and this upstart, this Dr. Zavarro, died trying to get to the proof they needed to shatter the accepted concepts."

The elder man nodded. "It would appear they both were unnecessarily secretive about their precise locations. Now we know they were nosing around one of the high mesas."

Towering mesas. Standing Stones.

"Dr. Weatherbee, this morning a young woman in my class asked me if I'd ever heard of Standing Stones that whispered words."

The elder man's brow rose in high interest.

"And she's from New Mexico," the younger added.

"I see." The head of the department rubbed his hand over his face while contemplating his next move. "Now I'm going to show you something I doubt you've ever seen before, in fact, I'm sure of it. But first let me tell you how it came into my possession."

Michael's hands were clammy as he leaned forward to hear every word the respected man said.

"A few weeks after they found the picked-over bones of Dr. Zavarro, a Mexican man died in his sleep. This man just happened to be Zavarro's menial helper. His wife claimed a Night Spirit killed him. She believes he died of a terrifying nightmare."

Nightmare. Nightmares.

Michael swallowed hard. "That's a common belief, Dr. Weatherbee. The coming of the Night Spirit is very much like the traditional Celtic belief in banshees."

The good doctor sighed. "I'm not a novice, Dr. Greystone. Besides, I wasn't finished."

The seated man apologized.

"Now," the elder continued. "It would appear that this José had taken a little souvenir from Dr. Zavarro's explorations and the wife is adamantly convinced that that object is what the Night Spirit came for. She wants no part of the thing and, consequently, sent it to me."

"Why you?"

"I was doing research down in that region a time ago. José was hired on to run errands. We became friends and she remembered me. She knew of no one else to pass it off to."

"Why didn't she just bury it with the usual offerings?"

"Oh she tried that. She did indeed. When her husband began having the nightmares that's exactly what she did. However, it was no good. She claims *It* wanted it back. . .not buried."

"Had she urged her husband to return this object to wherever he'd stolen it from?"

"She did. The man refused to go anywhere near the mesa ever again—said he'd rather die than to hear the whispering stones again."

Dr. Greystone surmised the rest. "And, since burying it didn't solve the problem, and since her husband wouldn't take it back to where it belonged, she got rid of the thing by sending it off to you."

He gave a wry smile. "Not a very nice gift if you ask me. What is it anyway?"

The department head heaved a weighted breath. "Michael, I don't know about showing you this. I just don't know if I should involve you further. I can't seem to make a firm decision on this."

"I can appreciate that. I understand your concern. Everyone who has had anything to do with it ends up dead. Even my colleague who must have been awfully close to its discovery was driven beyond sanity."

"Michael, I believe it was not the actual discovery of this item that drove your friend mad, but was rather the discovery of the cache where it came from. Both your former colleague and Dr. Zavarro were in the Southwest. José's wife admits to the general area but her husband was too secretive about its precise location.

"What I have here in my possession represents a fragment of what is sequestered away somewhere within one of the mesas. It represents a milestone discovery, not only for history, but for science and religion and all lifeforms with intelligence."

This last wording was a peculiar choice.

"Dr. Weatherbee, I want to. . ."

"It represents an incredible Force that lives to protect its discovery—a Force that will stop at nothing to keep its secret hidden from human eyes. It represents death, insanity or both to those who know about it—especially to the owner of it."

Michael was eager. "You've made your point well, Dr. Weatherbee. I want you to know how much I appreciate your deep concern over this. You've been completely forthright and held nothing back. But in light of my expertise and professional curiosity, I must admit that I won't leave this office until I've at least seen this mysterious object. Please allow me to help you in any way that I can."

Weatherbee looked down over his spectacles. "And you completely understand the risks involved? You completely understand that your decision may ultimately prove fatal for you?"

"I do understand."

"Very well." The elder walked over to his wall safe and extracted a large manila envelope encased in protective plastic. He crossed the room, set it on his desk and locked eyes with Michael. "You're sure, young man?"

Dr. Greystone couldn't take his eyes away from the ominous packet. He merely nodded his head.

Carefully, painfully, Dr. Weatherbee slowly slid out the envelope, slipped out an inner folder and opened it.

Michael rose to his feet and bent low over the desk. His scalp crawled as eyes traced over the foreign symbols he'd seen so many times before. The mixed characters screamed out at him. He barely whispered. "Shit. I don't believe this. I don't believe I'm seeing it again."

"AGAIN!" Weatherbee roared. "Where in God's name have you ever seen this?"

Michael ignored the outburst. His concentration was complete as he mumbled to himself. "I thought it was only an aberration. A dreamscape fabrication. Jesus," he uttered, "I must've actually been there."

"WHERE?"

Dr. Greystone's eyes were glassy as they slowly lifted to level with Weatherbee's. "I've been where this came from. This papyrus came from somewhere I've been!"

Dr. Weatherbee was shaking. "Make sense, man!"

Michael lowered his eyes to the paper. His nose was but inches from its delicate surface. "This looks a lot like an ancient papyrus, but it's not."

"Sons of Hades, man! You say you've been inside this hellish mesa and here you are being picky over what the cursed thing's made of! I've already poured over it for endless hours! It's *not* parchment! It's *not* papyrus and it can't be carbon dated because the properties of its substance are of unknown origin! Now in the name of all that's sacred! Tell me what you know!"

Unknown origin. Unknown origin.

The younger man reached behind him to feel for the chair. He eased himself down into it. "We'll have to refer to it as a papyrus for now, of course."

"Yes, yes. Now tell me! What's all this you've been blathering about!"

"Sit down, Dr. Weatherbee. This is going to be some story."

After Michael recalled the sequential nightmares and confessed that moving to Colorado had actually appeared to intensify them instead of alleviating them, the older man was dumbfounded.

"There's something big afoot here, Michael. There's something bigger breathing around us—far bigger than anything we could've ever in all our lives imagined. I think from here on in you'd better drop the Dr. Weatherbee formality. Something tells me we're going to need a closeness like no other in order to survive."

Silence.

"What are you thinking so deeply about?"

Michael's eyes slowly left the perfectly formed glyphs to lock on the elder man's. "Theo? We've got a grave problem already."

"Oh?"

"Yes. And her name is Emmy Winter."

"How so, Michael?"

"She's heard the Standing Stones whisper. Emmy's heard the mesa's speak."

"Good God, man! Do you know what this means?"

"It means that Emmy Winter has heard the mesa's words. And, for some mysterious reason, she's the only one on earth who's been allowed to live to tell about it."

A Plan of Madness

The lectures of Dr. Greystone became famous.

Students and instructors alike, including some university employees, crowded into the hall to hear him speak. By the end of the first full month of classes he was as well-known and respected as Dr. Weatherbee himself.

Now the campus grounds were ablaze with the reds and golds of autumn. The aspens had reached their peak and their heart-shaped leaves continually quivered like a gypsy's tambourine.

A multitude of chrysanthemums colorfully graced the edges of walkways and the lawns were kept trim and watered. The smell of fresh-cut grass mingled pleasantly with the pines and spruces that shaded pathways from the heat of the blazing Indian Summer sun.

During the four weeks that Emmy and Karen had been together, a metamorphosis had smoothly taken place. The two had reached a critical stage of understanding before their relationship naturally matured.

Karen had initially been infatuated with Dr. Greystone, but realizing the wide chasm that delineated their individual personalities, she soon abandoned the pursuit in favor of the star receiver on the football team. Karen didn't bat an eyelash when her roommate began spending her free time with the academically-minded professor from Boston who always seemed to only want to talk shop.

Emmy had worried about her new friend's feelings when Dr. Greystone began asking her out for coffee, to a cafe for lunch or to dinner. And when Emmy realized the brainy man was actually turning her roommate off, she relaxed with the situation—especially after Karen swore she was in love with another.

For Emmy Winter though, life hadn't revolved around parties and sorority teas. She had little interest in such frivolities. Her relationship with the young professor had quickly progressed from the formality of calling him Dr. Greystone to just Michael. Word got around and everyone knew they were an item not to be tampered with, nor taken lightly.

Though they were a full ten years apart in age, to the discriminating observer, they looked as if they were made for one another. In class it was strictly business—their student/teacher relationship was like everyone else's—but outside the lecture arena, the two relaxed to walk hand in hand or sit on one of the stone benches beneath the wavering aspens to speak in lowered tones.

To some, the cozy relationship had developed all too quickly. For those who knew better, they believed that no other outcome would've been possible. The two just had too many things in common. Their interests and philosophies were so well matched it would appear they originated from a single mind instead of two. They hadn't reached the all important stage of commitment yet, but few would doubt it was far off, for it would seem that one was rarely seen without the other.

Emmy hadn't planned on attending college to snare a husband or steady male companion. Love was a complexity that was farthest from her mind. She simply wanted to learn more about the ancient civilizations and their mystical cultural beliefs and practices. She wanted to gain a deeper understanding of her own supernatural experiences. She wanted to comprehend the natural facets of other realities she knew were there.

Little did she dream that she'd meet up with one as knowledgeable and experienced as her own instructor but, from that first day, a nebulous energy passed between them. A silent recognition took place on both sides and neither one could ignore the powerful magnetic draw to one another. Fate had taken hold of their lives.

Deep in her heart, Emmy Winter felt an array of emotional conflicts. She felt excitement and strong attraction, security and fear. An unknown thing lurked like a moving shadow around them and she knew there was a special reason behind the relationship. As always, there was a reason.

Michael was as taken off guard by the romantic development as everyone else had been. He hadn't voluntarily chosen to be in Boulder, he'd been drafted into the unexpected position. Reluctantly he'd acquiesced in deference to his deep respect for Dr.

Neusome. And, right from the first moment his eyes locked on the brilliant blues of that young woman in the front row, he knew their destinies were entwined.

In Michael's eyes she'd been reserved, yet spunky. Innocent, yet a certain refined wisdom pulsed within her being. She'd been shy, yet straightforward. And there was that obscure something else that he'd perceived right from that first day—something in her unusual eyes—something that hinted at great intensity of sensitivity.

Michael sensed an ancient wisdom dwelling within Emmy Winter. He felt an incredible specialness—a mysteriousness—that he had to know better. The attraction was too strong to ignore, it was almost as if the gods had deemed it to be so.

They had not yet come together as lovers and, although it hadn't been planned, this night would prove to be most intimate in more ways than one.

The Volkswagen Bug puttered its way up the dorm drive and stopped before the woman waiting on the walkway.

"Hey lady!" the driver called, leaning over to the passenger window, "can I drop you off somewhere?"

Hands on hips, the waiting woman tilted her head. "Thank you so much, kind sir, but I'm waiting for my Prince Charming. He'll be along shortly on his trusty steed."

"Methinks my Lady Fair doth need glasses. Don't you see this fine steed?"

The woman bent to examine the scratched and dented chassis. "Why, I believe you're right." She peered through the opened window. "And you, sir, must be my shining knight."

"Climb in, Cornball, dinner awaits."

Quickly Emmy cut the playacting and scrambled into the little vehicle. "So where are we going tonight? Chinese? Italian? Mexican or what?"

"How about a new place?"

"Oh?"

"Yeah," he eyed her seriously. "It's called Greystone's. Interested?"

She grinned. "Very much so, but what sort of menu does this Greystone's place have?"

"Just about everything," he boasted.

"Everything?"

"Yep. If it can be home delivered, Greystone's can serve it up."

During the short ride to Michael's rented house they'd decided to order pizza and soon he was on the phone placing the order while his guest looked over the surroundings.

"Not exactly my style of furnishings," he admitted after hanging up the receiver. "But then again, the place came completely equipped so I couldn't very well turn down the price." He smiled. "It didn't take me long to find out how rare rentals were in this town, then again, I guess they're at a premium in all small college towns."

"I suppose so," she commented, still engrossed in her survey of the place. "This isn't so bad, though. It's a lot bigger than the place where I grew up." She ran her fingers lovingly over the smoothness of the pine mantle. "This fireplace is real nice, it adds a warm touch."

"Too bad it's Indian Summer or we'd have a cozy fire going in there."

Michael headed into the kitchen.

She followed. "Can I help with anything?"

"Nah, just need some plates and things."

Emmy spied the table. It had been covered with a red and white checked tablecloth. An antique oil lamp was lit in the center. Two wine glasses were already out.

"This is nice," she complimented.

He'd brought over the wine bottle and set it on the table. "Actually, you may not believe this, but I usually eat by the light of this old lantern. I dunno," he shrugged, "just seems to make the atmosphere so much more inviting and restful when one is eating—helps me to think."

She knew how he felt. "It's like the firelight of a camp. It's almost like having company when you're alone."

Michael turned off the light switch and then adjusted the flame. He held Emmy at arm's length. "You and I think very much alike, you know that, don't you?"

She nodded while noticing how the lamp flame reflected in his midnight eyes.

The doorbell rang then. After sending the delivery boy on his way, the two sat at the table in the darkness with only one flickering flame to reflect their images. Their conversation was light.

"What's it like in Taos?" he asked while they each dug hungrily into the steaming pizza.

"I never told you what town I was from. I never mentioned it."

He avoided her eyes. "It's in the files."

"And when did you spy into those?"

"The first day. . .after class."

"Did you peek into all your student's personal information?"

"No. Just one that interested me."

"You don't waste any time, do you." She held out her glass for him to refill.

"Emmy, you know the energy was there that first day. I felt it and I know you did too. I just wanted to know a little more about the woman who was pulling at my heart."

She smiled. "All right, professor, you're excused this time but don't let it happen again."

He winked. "It won't."

A few minutes of silence passed between them as they ate their first pieces of the stringy cheese pizza smothered with the works. Then Michael mumbled through a mouthful. "So tell me about home. I've never been to New Mexico."

The blue eyes deepened in color. They glistened with excitement. "There are many festivities where I come from. All seasons have special ceremonies that are joyous occasions. Most of the people participate in some way, even if it is a little.

"In the mornings the sun shines colors onto the sandstone and adobe buildings and, at sunset, the alpenglow is brilliant with orange and deep reds. The skies are nearly always a deep blue— clear and cloudless except for passing birds. We have many birds in Taos, the people like to feed them."

"Sounds nice. What about your family?"

"The five of us live in a small adobe house. My father, he works on a ranch outside of town. All his life he's worked ranches. My mother has been a good wife to him. She cooks wonderful dinners and great big breakfasts for us all." She smiled warmly. "They love each other very much and are very close. They talk without words."

"If they do that then they've developed some impressive paranormal communications. People have to be very close to do that."

"Yes, but also they know the Way. With that, no words are ever necessary."

Michael tried to be slick. "Do you know the Way?"

"I have two sisters. They're thirteen and six. They're good kids and help Mother a lot around the house." She paused before going on. "I was so happy when I finally received the news that my grant came through." She went on to explain how it came to be and the big surprise party her parents gave that evening. She told how all the neighbors came over to celebrate the joyous occasion.

Michael listened attentively but couldn't shake how easily she'd avoided his question. He'd wanted to find out just how much she knew about the sacred Native Way. He wanted to hear of her mystical experiences and to discover if she was some kind of sacred person. His peaked curiosity about her strange blue eyes was a constant nagging in his mind. But because of his growing affection for her he couldn't bring himself to push for answers just yet.

The two talked casually for the remainder of the meal. It felt good for each of them to have a gentle relationship based on deep feelings and common interests. Michael had told her much of his own background and about his work in Boston—he left out the bad parts though. There was no reason to complicate things and cause her to worry.

After dinner they remained at the table and talked long into the night.

The oil lamp burned softly between them until its light shifted to reflect new meanings in their eyes. Recognition was mutual. The time had come for them to do another kind of talking—the kind without words. And the communication was complete and good. They rested in the after-comfort of each other's arms.

Moonlight glowed through the bedroom windows and cast silvery shadows here and there as the aspens outside swayed in the night breeze. Voices, content and soft, whispered in the stillness.

"I didn't come here tonight with this in mind," she softly expressed.

He kissed her cheek. "I didn't have this in mind when I invited you here. I'm glad it turned out this way though."

"Mmm, so am I," she whispered, smoothing her hand over his arm that rested across her waist.

A warm silence settled between them for several long moments before she spoke again. "Do you think I ought to go back tonight?"

Silence.

"Michael?" she whispered.

He was already asleep.

Emmy gently lifted his arm off her and carefully eased her hair out from under his head. She pulled the covers up over them both. Turning toward the windows she watched the shadows move about in the night. She smiled. It had been good. And deeply content in the embrace of her new relationship, she closed her eyes.

"*NO!* Oh *SHIT!* GOD! NO-O-O!"

The blankets ripped away from the slumbering woman. Her eyes shot open in terror. The suddenness of the wild confusion left her befuddled until she remembered where she was.

Swinging her long legs off the bed she reached frantically for the light.

Michael was crouched in the corner of the room, blankets wrapped tightly about his trembling form. He was shivering uncontrollably with a wide-eyed stare. He was still asleep.

Looking quickly around the room, Emmy spied his shirt draped over the chair. She grabbed it to cover herself then hurried to kneel beside the quivering man. "Michael? Honey? Wake up."

"Get *away* from me! Oh God. No! Please. Please get *away!* Ohhhh no-o-o." The man's hands came up to shield his clenched eyes from some unseen threat.

"MICHAEL!" she shouted, shaking him awake.

The trembling subsided.

Eyes focused.

They slowly moved with sickening realizations.

His tense shoulders slumped. "Oh my god. Why now."

Emmy held him in her arms. She held tight and rocked the man she loved. "It's all right now, Michael. It's all over. I'm here."

He looked up at her with pitiful eyes. "I'm so sorry you had to see this, Em. I just never thought it'd come with someone else here." Shakily he rose and went for his robe.

"I'll make some coffee," she offered. "You going to be okay?"

He waved her away. "Yeah, I'll be right in. Just give me a minute to wash my face and clear my head."

She hesitantly gave him a weak smile and warily eyed him. "You're sure?"

"Yeah. Go start the coffee—we're going to need it."

In the kitchen, Michael was glad to see that Emmy had the lamp burning. He didn't think he could face telling her what he had to reveal in the harshness of the bright electric lights. The soft glow was more in keeping with the complex mystery she was about to hear.

After downing several sips of the fresh brew he sighed as he looked across the table at the only woman he'd ever felt so strongly about. "I'm real sorry about what happened in there," he said.

"Everyone has bad dreams once in a while," she comforted, reaching out to place her hand over his. "You shouldn't be embarrassed or feel you need to apologize."

"That's not it," he said, shaking his head. "It goes much deeper than that. You don't understand. . .yet."

At his words her delicate brows knitted together in a frown.

A light smile came over him then. "Not to change the subject but you look real good in my shirt."

The unexpected comment made her self-conscious of her attire. She glanced down at the opened top. Blushing, she buttoned it up. "Not my usual style but good enough in a pinch." Her grin faded then. "Want to tell me about it now?"

He looked down into his cup without replying.

"You don't have to if you'd rather not," she said. "I understand. Michael, if you'd be more comfortable, we can just forget it ever happened."

His eyes met hers. "That's the problem, Em, I can't forget it. How does one forget something like this, especially when it happens all the time."

A cold shiver crept up her spine.

"Emmy, half of me wants to tell you everything and half of me is afraid to."

"I'm here for you, Michael. I'll always be here for you. I'm not demanding. I wouldn't force you to tell me anything you didn't want to. You have to make the decision yourself. But I want you to know one thing. Whatever it is, I'm here to help you with it."

He wrestled with the dilemma now playing tug-of-war games within his head. Then his back straightened. "Would you pour me another cup?"

When both cups were refilled he began to tell the story of when the nightmares first started and what they consisted of. He revealed his conversation with Dr. Weatherbee and described what the elder professor now had in his possession. He told her everything. He told her about his deceased colleague who'd been onto something in the Southwest and how it'd frightened him—how it'd driven him to take his own life. The slate was wiped clean. Nothing was left out as he told the listening woman about how his friend's discovery appeared to be tied in with the dead Dr. Zavarro and his helper, José. He even spoke about his great interest in her question in class regarding the Standing Stones and how he and Weatherbee had realized that she'd been allowed to live after hearing them. Why? Why was that? What did it mean? And was her whispering mesa the mesa in question? And when he finished he concluded by assuring her of his deep feelings.

"Emmy, I don't want you to feel my interest in you was purely because of all this mystery. I'm very attracted to you. Since that first day, before I knew anything about you, even your name, I felt intensely drawn to you. My feelings of the heart have absolutely nothing whatever to do with all of this. I felt you needed to know what was going on—it was only fair." He sat back in the chair. "I'll understand if this changes things between us. I won't like it but I'll understand."

"You didn't think I'd understand or maybe that I'd be frightened off. Is that it? Is that why you've held all this mess inside?"

"No." His voice was weighted. "No, Emmy, I was the one who was frightened. I didn't tell you about it because it's too dangerous. . .everyone dies."

"Oh Michael, I know you just wanted to protect me and I do love you for that."

"Honey, I'm worried now. I'm worried sick about you. Don't you see? This *thing* Weatherbee's got has strings attached, tentacles fixed to some powerful force that wants it back, wants it returned. And the Force kills for what It wants. Oh god, why did I ever have you stay over. Now you're in danger too." In his dark mood he moaned, "What have I done?"

A deep silence fell over the room.

"Michael."

Her voice was strangely calm. When he looked up past the orange light of the lamp her countenance was restful. The eyes were fixed with the wisdom he'd seen that first day.

"What is it, Em? What's wrong?"

"Nothing is wrong. . .not any more. You asked what it is you've done."

"I know what I've done."

"Perhaps. But you don't know the why of it."

Curious now, he sharpened his attention. Something was different about his companion. An intense serenity had settled over her.

"Em, there is something wrong."

"No there isn't. That's just it." A warm smile broke the woman's solemn intensity. She appeared to be her old self once again. "It just came to me, that's all."

"What did?"

"The realization we needed to come to."

He shook his head. "You're losing me. What realization?"

"Why I didn't go to the University of New Mexico like I'd planned. Why I'm here instead of down there. Why *you're* here instead of back in Boston. Why José's wife sent the papyrus to Weatherbee and not to someone else. Why the nightmares have come and why I heard the Standing Stones."

The man eyed her in utter disbelief as her meaning became clear. "Oh, no. No, no. That's too incredible. That's way out there."

"Is it, Michael? Is it way out there?"

"You're saying that we've all been brought together so that we three know about the papyrus?"

"No, Michael. . .so we can return the papyrus."

"Oh," he sarcastically chuckled, "oh, really. That's royal, Em. That's royal insanity, that's what it is."

"Is it? How so?"

"Because of my damned dreams, that's why!"

Her voice was soft. "Has this Force ever actually attacked you in these dreams?"

"Well no, Emmy, but it. . ."

"It what, Michael?"

"It. . .it. . ."

"Scares you," she finished.

"Oh, now I see. You think the terror is coming from my own self-imposed fright—from within myself! Oh, this is great, Em. This is just great."

"Michael," came the calm voice, "you're being defensive. You need to look at this. Please calm down and think about it. If you were a threat to this Force your dreams would've symbolized that fact but they don't. From what you've told me, you're always terrified of it but never really attacked. You naturally try to escape but never stand firm to see what it wants of you."

The man was incredulous. "Stand firm? Stand firm? Are you telling me to communicate with that thing in my dreams?"

She smiled and nodded.

Michael considered the idea. His extensive experience in confronting and dealing with forces in other realities did justify her theory. The more he thought on it the more sense it actually made. His grin came naturally.

She grinned back. "You know I'm right, don't you."

"It is a strong possibility I never considered. In the dream I'd always let the natural reactions to fear direct my responses. If I could override those I'd get further along in the dream and, if I could do that, maybe. . .just maybe some type of communication could be established."

"Do you think you could do it?"

The thought of holding his ground to face the wide-eyed Force in those dark catacombs terrified him. "I could try," he bravely offered. "Only this time, if I can stay lucid, I won't forget to put new batteries in the flashlight."

Emmy shook her head. "That part of it isn't alterable, only your reactions will be when you get to that point in the dream."

"How do you know that?"

"Trust me."

"So when do you think I should try this friendly confrontation?"

She glanced up at the kitchen clock that was bathed in shadows. "It's already almost five. . .too late now. I want to be with you when you attempt this."

"Oh no, Em, not a chance."

"Let's see," she pondered, "how about tonight?"

"Em, you're not hearing me. I said you're not going to be with me on this."

"Michael," she whispered.

His eyes locked onto hers. Hers with the undefined power swirling within them. His scalp crawled with the intensity he saw. "Okay, Em. The sooner the better."

"Michael?"

"What?"

"It's going to be all right. It's not going to harm you. We were selected for this. It chose us—It brought us together—to help It."

"Theo?" Michael called while peeking his head around the man's office door.

Dr. Weatherbee looked over his spectacles. "Michael! Come in, come in."

Dr. Greystone entered with a small shadow tailing him.

The seated gentleman's heavy brows arched. "I see you've brought a friend. Good morning, Ms. Winter."

"Good morning, Dr. Weatherbee," she greeted, sitting down in the chair he'd indicated for her.

"This is a pleasant surprise. What brings you two in here so early?"

Michael doubted their visit would prove to be anything remotely resembling pleasant. Instead, he was certain it was going to be more like a bomb dropping. He cleared his throat. "Emmy spent the night at my place last night," he began.

"That's marvelous. However, I seriously doubt you two traipsed in here to discuss your romantic escapades with an old man. Get to the point, Michael, I've got a hectic schedule today."

Emmy blushed and lowered her gaze.

Greystone inhaled a deep breath of confidence. He surreptitiously snuck a furtive glance over at his companion before again returning his full attention to the man behind the desk.

"She witnessed one of my nightmares."

Weatherbee didn't immediately respond. Instead, he eyed the young woman who met his stare head on. "I see."

"I couldn't very well keep her in the dark after that. I told her everything."

The old man pushed away from the desk and stood. He stared long and hard at the silent pair before turning to face the windows.

Activity on the campus grounds was just now becoming evident. As the elder professor watched the sparse groups of students walk here and there between buildings he considered the security of their uncomplicated lives—so carefree, simple. Keeping his back to his visitors, he finally spoke.

"You've jeopardized the one you love, Michael. You've acted irresponsibly. I fail to see how you could do such a thing. The occurrences of nightmares are not that uncommon, even for adults. It wouldn't have necessitated your ultimate revelation."

Dr. Greystone disagreed. "But it would've constituted an untruth—the withholding of the truth—and that would've bothered me."

Ms. Winter felt like the proverbial odd-man-out the way the two men were talking.

"Dr. Weatherbee," she interjected, "Michael did what he had to do."

"Really," he said, turning to face her. "Is that what you think, young lady?"

"Yes," she defended. "He couldn't have done otherwise considering the overall situation. And, as it turned out, things are looking up toward a satisfactory resolution of the problem."

The man's eyes peered over his glasses to rest on Michael's. "Resolution? I believe you've got some explaining to do here, young man. Just what is this young woman blathering about?"

The younger man stood. Shoving his hands deep into his pockets, he began to pace the room. "Theo, last night, after my incident and the explanation that followed, Emmy suddenly had a brilliant idea come to her. This idea was, in effect, the resolution to our problem with the papyrus." He paused then, unsure of the elder's reaction.

"Go on. I'm listening, although I don't know why."

"Well it's all very logical really. She realized that she and I were brought here to Boulder under strange circumstances. See, she was all set to attend the University of New Mexico but, without knowing why, her grant came through for Boulder instead. And, of course, you already know the circumstances that brought me here—a terrible accident that left a good man in a coma. Theo, how much thought have you given that 'accident'? Wasn't it a bit too convenient? An innocent bystander is presently in a coma simply because he had to be out of the way. . .to make way for me."

Dr. Weatherbee chuckled and shook his head. "Young man, you need to go into a different field of work, this one's finally made you irrational. These were nothing more than coincidences. What sort of ridiculous half-baked idea are you building up to?"

Michael sighed. "It may very well be ridiculous sounding, but it's hardly half-baked," he defended. "In fact, it appears to be a very clever scheme." He ran his hands through his hair.

"Look, Theo, all roads lead to here, right here!" he emphasized, stabbing his finger toward the floor. "Ms. Winter and I are here under questionable circumstances and now that mysterious papyrus shows up. I might remind you that the esoteric arrangement of characters on the papyrus *identically* matched those on the wall in my dreams! And another thing, why have those same dreams become so much more intense since I arrived here?"

They remained silent.

The younger two waited for the enigma to sink in while they observed the man's reaction.

Finally he spoke. "It would appear there is more than casual coincidence here," he admitted. "But what does Ms. Winter have to do with all this? Where could she possibly fit in?"

"We don't know for sure yet. All we do know is that she's heard the Standing Stones speak. She understood each word just as if they were coming from someone standing right beside her."

As eager as the old man was to know what the stones had said to the young woman he didn't want to diverge from the issue at hand. "So what is this brilliant resolution you've come up with?"

Now came the hard part. Michael jumped right in before he lost his nerve. "There are certain solid facts here, Theo, that cannot be disputed. Three people ventured into the forbidden ground. My former colleague, Dr. Zavarro and his assistant, José. The two researchers had been onto something so big, so monumental, that they became careless in their greed to be first to discover it. Am I right so far?"

"That last may be speculation, but go on. I'm still listening," he said, eyes shifting back and forth between the two young people.

"So, in their excitement they trespass on sacred ground. I mean. . . .*really* sacred ground. Agree?"

"I'm still with you."

"Okay. So one of these guys gets too close. My colleague discovers the hidden opening and he enters the mesa. He finds what he's looking for and. . .bingo!. . .before he can return to examine it further he's driven mad by horrifying recurring nightmares.

"The other guy actually goes in the opening far enough to remove a piece of the treasure. He ends up dead and so does his assistant. A mysterious papyrus shows up that's like nothing mankind has ever seen."

"Michael," Weatherbee impatiently advised, "we already have those facts. They've already been established. Why the need to rehash them?"

"Because they *are* facts, Theo. Because they're facts that support our resolution."

The elder audibly exhaled. "Proceed then."

"If it's fact that all owners of the sacred papyrus die, then why are you still alive? If it's fact that everyone who even knows about the cache in that mesa is killed off, why are Emmy and I still sitting here?"

Silence.

"The three of us know about this incredibly sacred place and one of us even has the papyrus! Yet here we are. Two of us brought here under less than normal circumstances are drawn in with the owner of the fragment. One of us has been shown the sacred place through dreamscapes while the other has heard the mesa's words—all three *together*. . .in one *place*. . .very much alive!"

The elder conceded the point. "So it's not mere chance. But tell me, Michael, if your colleague was frightened to death because of the nightmares why do you also have them? Wouldn't that suggest you're being warned too?"

Emmy spoke softly. "No, Dr. Weatherbee, it does not mean that. Michael is not being warned. . .he's being called."

"Well," the elder said, "I suppose the two of you have determined what it all means?"

"Yes!" Michael explained trying hard to contain his excitement. His building emotions were ready to explode. "The others had to die because they were going to go in and open the seals. They were going to cart off the treasure that's buried beneath the sacred ground of the mesa. They threatened to desecrate a holy place. They invaded the temple before it was ready to reveal its ancient secrets. But, Theo, we three are different. Oh yes, we're very different. We were brought together because we were called. We were called for a reason and, that reason is to *return* the sacred papyrus!"

Dr. Weatherbee's face flushed red. "That's INSANITY! Pure *insanity!*" the man flared, standing and tipping his chair over. "Why, I never heard such balderdash in all my life!" He glared from one to the other. "You both are mad! Do you hear me? MAD!"

The door flew open and Weatherbee's secretary charged in. "Is everything all right in here, Dr. Wea. . .."

"Get OUT!" he bellowed at the bewildered woman.

"Theo, calm down, your blood pressure's going sky. . ."

"Damn my blood pressure! You two have got to be absolutely *demented* to think any of us would be allowed near that hellish place! Why, we'd never get within twenty miles of it! Just the *thought* of what you propose is grounds enough for this Force to kill us! Jesus! I can't believe this!"

"It was so obvious last night, Theo. And we're still here, aren't we?" Michael underscored.

The elder man was at a loss for words. "Oh God, Michael, I dunno. I just don't know anymore."

Dr. Greystone righted the man's chair. "Sit down, Theo."

He not only sat back down, he spent a long while considering the preposterous idea. The man thought hard on many things. One in particular was his own history of accomplishments he'd contributed to his profession—they were few. To be the one to reveal the papyrus to the world would insure his notoriety and bring fame. Yet the idea didn't set well. In his heart he knew it was because this sacred object and its dwelling place could never be revealed. No, his discovery would never be made public. But perhaps if they could manage to return the thing he'd at least have the personal satisfaction of knowing he'd been instrumental in *preserving* something incredibly sacred. That in itself would serve as his one great accomplishment in life. That would make all his years of service more than worthwhile. Yes, he considered, that personal accomplishment would indeed allow him to die a happy man. Then, with these thoughts, he suddenly realized the entire idea, as utterly absurd as it sounded, had indeed carried a certain appeal to it. His eyes slid up to fix on Michael's. "I dunno. I just dunno. It's a plan born of madness, that's what it is. . .complete madness."

"It's madness that makes sense though, isn't it?" Michael asked.

Weatherbee admitted the truth to that. "More than anything else we've been able to come up with so far, sorry to say."

"Surely we won't be harmed if our intentions are set on *returning* it," Michael reasoned.

"I'd like to take some comfort in that. So far it's all we have to go on. I'd like to think our safety has been preserved because of our purpose. Let's hope our good intentions continue to spare us grief."

"We're still here, aren't we?" Greystone said.

"Yes, for the time being." The elder paused to think. "One aspect of your nightmares still doesn't wash, though. If you're meant to return the object, then why the terrifying nights? Wouldn't it be more sensible if the dreams were peaceful ones? With some sort of indicative message that would reveal the master plan?"

"Emmy figures they're frightening me because, in the actual dreamscape, I'm afraid of the unknown and try to escape. That's a natural reaction. She seems to feel confident that I'll get my message once I stop to face the Force and confront it—stand my ground so to speak. What I need to do is to allow the dream to progress past the point my fear always stopped it at."

The look on Weatherbee's face made it clear he didn't like the idea. He didn't like it at all. "Could be dangerous, Michael. Could very well be a fatal mistake on your part. Maybe even be the last dream you ever have."

"I have to try it. It's the only avenue we've got open to us right now. We need more information and I've got to attempt a way to obtain it. We can't proceed without knowing where this mesa is located. How are we going to return it if we don't know where we're going?"

The elder man looked over to the woman. "You going to be there when he does this?"

"I wouldn't let him do it alone."

Theodore nodded in assent then became momentarily contemplative. "All right, I suppose we'll have to go with it." He then hesitated again. "One last thing still bothers me, though. Why us?"

Michael shrugged. "I wondered about that too. Then I thought that maybe it had something to do with our ideals and individual backgrounds."

"How so?" the elder inquired.

"Well, on that fragment are Egyptian hieroglyphs. Your mother was Egyptian. The papyrus has also got Native American symbols and I've got Cherokee blood. I think this Force, or whatever it is, wants a representative of all the symbols to join together in returning the papyrus to its rightful place."

Weatherbee raised a questioning brow. "It's also got characters of an unknown origin."

Both men simultaneously looked suspiciously to the third party of their group.

Emmy's eyes widened. "Hey, you guys! Do I look like an Unknown?"

Michael winked. "Your nationality was left blank on your application."

"Must've been an oversight," she excused away. "I'll have to stop in at the office and fix that."

The elder questioned her. "You sure about this oversight?"

She pursed her lips. She sighed and gave a look of resignation. "My name's not really Emmy," came the confession. "Everyone calls me Emmy because, over the years, it's just always been easier. I've even gotten into the habit of legally using it on forms and such, but it's not a name at all."

Michael was visibly taken aback with this new information.

Weatherbee's head tilted forward in heightened interest while the woman explained herself.

"It's not Emmy as in short for Emily. It's not a nickname for Emiline either. It's M. E.—my initials!"

Michael gave her a surprised look. "Initials standing for what?"

"Standing for Mourning Elk. . .I'm a fullblood."

The old professor leaned over his desk to squint into the woman's unusual blue eyes. He raised a brow as he prepared to question the paradox.

Emmy didn't wait for the man to voice his puzzlement. She self-consciously chuckled. "You're wondering about these blue eyes. Well. . .my people believe an old ancestral story that's been passed down by word of mouth since as long as anyone can remember. My eyes have to do with that. I don't brag about being a fullblood because I don't like having to explain about the story. That's why using the name of Emmy is just easier."

Weatherbee wasn't about to let her get off without a full explanation. "My dear, why don't you just share that story with Michael and me. We'd love to hear it, wouldn't we, Michael?"

"I'm all ears," he said, sitting back in his chair.

Emmy looked from one to the other and then sighed. "Well, as I said, my people believe an old ancestral story. Its range is very narrow because it only has to do with our own family line—our family clan."

"Go on," Weatherbee urged. "We want to hear it all."

"Okay. Just remember, though, you asked for it. The story is that our family clan's beginnings were of the stars."

Weatherbee and Greystone looked at one another.

"Stars?" Greystone repeated.

"Yes. Our family lineage is believed to have originated from fullbloods of the Starborn Tribe. Anyway, the story says that one individual is chosen out of every third generation to represent our Starborn origin. Tradition teaches that this person may possess special knowledge and abilities. And that person is known by being born with blue eyes."

Again the men's eyes were drawn to each other's. Then they simultaneously turned to settle on the woman's.

"Hey! Stop looking at me as though I was E.T.! It's only an old story. One out of every third generation has had blue eyes for as long as anyone can remember. It's just a story to explain the genetic fluke."

Suddenly the silence in the room was a breathing thing.

No one really believed it was coincidence. No one really believed it was a fluke.

Everyone at once realized that Emmy's so-called fluke was the one missing piece that pulled it all together. And, as a unit, they understood where the Unknown glyphs on the papyrus had come from. It was the language of the Starborn Tribe.

The stunned group sat in silence for a long time.

The rest of that day sped by.

Although Dr. Greystone had expected the time to drag on interminably he found that his students had served to fill the long hours and speed him through his classes.

As usual his lectures had been filled to over-capacity and the high curiosity of the young minds had actually made for such an interesting day he'd been able to get his mind off Emmy's revelation and his upcoming dream confrontation.

Waiting outside the lecture hall, Emmy watched through the open door as a dozen students excitedly plied the young professor with further questions. They looked like bees around a honey pot.

"You've become quite the campus heartthrob," she chided as he exited the hall.

The doctor blushed at her words. Young women from his last class lingered in the corridor and coyly looked his way.

He noticed. "C'mon, let's get outta here," he said, quickly taking Emmy's arm. "We've got some planning and preparing to do before tonight."

But the amused woman wasn't so easily put off. She talked as they made their way to the exit. "The word's already out that I spent the night with you. Campus is buzzing with speculation. I'm afraid you, dear doctor, have broken more than a few hopeful hearts around here."

"Get in," he barked, opening the car door for her.

She smiled and crawled in.

The door slammed behind her and she grinned to herself at the humorous thought of Michael's embarrassment with the unwanted situation. It was evident the handsome man never had to deal with a campus full of infatuated students. Most men would've been highly flattered, but not this one—this one was totally disturbed by the entire thing—he was having a difficult time dealing with his unexpected popularity.

Emmy continued to ignore him while he climbed into the tiny vehicle, slammed his door and shoved the shift in gear with more force than was necessary.

"I didn't ask for this, Em. I didn't plan on becoming the campus main attraction."

"I know," she agreed.

"Well it's absurd. The entire thing is just ridiculous, that's what it is."

"Is it?" she asked, bracing herself as the car swung out onto the boulevard.

"I don't know what that's supposed to mean, but yes! Hell yes! I can understand student admiration for a certain instructor. I can understand that natural attraction to a professor who makes his classes interesting and fun, but for so many young women to actually be fawning over me is quite different."

"And you don't like it."

"No, I don't."

"Not even a teeny bit."

He made no comment.

She grinned. "Michael?"

He softened. The corner of his mouth upturned a little. "Well, it does make a certain qualitative statement, doesn't it. It says that Dr. Michael Greystone is a very well-liked individual. It says that Dr. Greystone's class is the one to take because he makes learning enjoyable."

"Oh really." She gave him an incredulous look. "My dear Dr. Greystone, it says a hell of a lot more than that."

"Well maybe, but that's how I look at it. It's the only way I can look at it without getting upset. Let's change the subject, okay? What do you feel like for supper?"

"Oh, I don't know. Surprise me."

"To tell you the truth, I'm a bit on edge about tonight. I think just a salad will be all I'll be able to handle." His brows raised in question to the passenger.

"Salad sounds great here too."

During the meal neither of them again mentioned the infatuation phenomenon that had gripped the campus. Nor did they broach the issue of the upcoming nocturnal experiment. Instead, they talked of the interesting questions that had been popping up in the anthropology classes and Michael's concern over the student body's fascination with the supernatural side of it.

"You'd think they were in a metaphysical class," he muttered disgustedly.

Emmy shrugged. "Hasn't it ever occurred to you that at least three-quarters of your students are taking the metaphysical course?"

He frowned.

She smiled. "Naturally," she explained, "they're just trying to connect the two. They're naturally relating one complementary aspect to the other."

"I never considered that before. I see your point." He hesitated for a moment before going further with it. "Are you taking the metaphysical course too?"

She gave him a strange look. "Only if I could teach it."

He raised a brow. "You that good?"

"No, and that's not what I meant. What I meant was, after being raised in the culture that I have and after experiencing the things I have, I seriously doubt a class on the subject could come up with anything fresh for me. I've had metaphysical class every day of my childhood. I was brought up on it."

"I see your point," Michael said.

A weighted silence fell over the two before Michael's eyes raised to meet Emmy's. They hinted at more waiting to be done before he could ask the questions that were plaguing him about her.

"What's the matter?" she asked.

"Nothing," he hedged.

"No. Come on, you wanted to say something more. What was it?"

He put down his fork. "What exactly have you experienced, Em?"

Eyes lowered to her bowl of greens. She picked through it as if to stall the reply.

"Emmy," came the soft voice, "you know all about my recent experiences and about the mysterious circumstances behind that papyrus, but I don't really know anything of what realities you've gone through."

"I know," she sighed.

"Well?"

"Not now, Michael. Maybe at a later time, but not just now."

"All right. I respect that." He smiled wide and patted her hand. "Ready to go?"

Once safely within the privacy of Michael's house the two settled down on floor cushions with cups of fresh-brewed coffee. They exchanged separate incidents of their day and commented about general school events that were coming up. Then Emmy began talking of her roommate.

"Remember I told you about Karen Kendall? The one who shared my room?"

He grinned. "Yeah, I remember. She's the one who went catatonic when she first saw me. Sure am glad that one latched onto someone else."

"You really did luck out there because she's very possessive. She's quite demanding."

"So. What about her?"

"Did you know she was Weatherbee's niece?"

Michael's eyes widened. "You're kidding. No, I didn't know that. The old guy never mentioned her at all. I'd no idea he had any family here."

The young woman smiled. "Well I'm not surprised about that, but we just might have a snag in our plans. Seems Karen's noticed how often the three of us have been meeting in her uncle's office. She insists she smells a rat."

"That's bad news."

"That's what I thought. Anyway, she keeps pushing for information. Says we've got some big, dark secret and, since she's his niece and my roommate, she deserves to be let in on it. I keep telling her that I don't know what she's talking about, but Michael, underneath all that exterior flightiness of hers she's very astute. I don't know how much longer I can put her off. . .I never was very good at lying."

"Has she approached Weatherbee about this?"

"I didn't come right out and ask, if that's what you mean, but I overheard one of her telephone conversations to her friend in Eagle. She was all worked up. She insisted that some great mysterious thing was going on and, if it was the last thing she did, she was going to get to the bottom of it."

Michael whistled low. "Bad timing, Em."

"You took the words right out of my mouth."

"What's ol' Weatherbee said about this new development?"

She shrugged. "I haven't spoken to him about it. I'm trying to avoid being seen in his office as much as possible. I think she's got spies around."

He ran his hand through his hair. "Dammit, Emmy, that woman could really jam things up for us."

"I know. What do we do about it?"

"Listen, she can't find out anything. She's got to be kept in the dark. Tell her anything. Tell her you've been telling us about some of your traditional ceremonies or something like that. Yeah, that'd be good, she'd buy that. Tell her Weatherbee and I have been interested in hearing about some of your people's tribal ceremonies and things like that. She'd go for that."

"I don't know," she hesitated. "That'd still be lying."

"Not if you told *me* about those things. Then it'd at least be half truth."

She was pensive.

"Well?" he pushed.

"Are you coercing me?"

"No, not at all. I'd never force you to speak of private matters—the sacred things. They can't be spoken about until the time is right."

The woman seriously pondered his words. She gave deep consideration to their personal relationship and thought about their joint involvement in the new plan. And with the realization of the warm current that began flowing through her being, she looked deep into his eyes.

"The time is right," she softly announced.

The man smiled tenderly and nodded for her to go ahead whenever she was ready.

And the woman known as Emmy became Mourning Elk. Her voice was soft and reverent as she told the man of her childhood that'd been steeped in traditional ceremonies and the deep mysticism that accompanied the sacred rites.

She revealed that her uncle was a man of power who could

make things happen. One of her aunts had the powerful gift of healing hands. She recalled witnessing unexplainable occurrences as a small child and grew up accepting their realities as simple facts. And after she'd become a woman she began taking her private walks out of town to pray beside the buttes that pierced the moonlit desert sky.

Mourning Elk tenderly told of her private ceremonies performed at the foot of the towering Standing Stones. She reverently spoke of the gradual awareness that grew within her, how her senses suspensefully sharpened and the oneness she eventually felt with the buttes. Finally she spoke in lowered tones. Finally she revealed when the Stones spoke to her and how she felt their living heartbeat throb through her being and, finally. . .she revealed their words. When she was finished, a warm stillness filled the room.

A gentle aura of sacredness softly pulsed around the two.

Michael touched Emmy's cheek. His voice was little more than a whisper. "I know how sacred your words were, Em. I know what it cost you to tell me those things, but know this, your sharing has brought you more fully into my heart and I in yours. I'm glad you trusted me enough to open your heart the way you did."

"So am I, Michael, so am I."

After several moments of precious silence, Michael wondered aloud. "Why do you think the Standing Stones spoke to you?"

"I've no idea." Then she reconsidered her answer. "Let me change that to—I had no idea. But with everything that's recently transpired with this papyrus business and your dreams, with all the coincidences summed up, I think you and I both know why they spoke to me. Michael, we're players. We're the main characters in a design grander than anything we've ever imagined. We were hand-picked by a casting director like no other. And now all that's left is for us to play out our parts as best we can, because I've the distinct feeling we'll only have one take to get it right."

Michael sighed with the heaviness of it. "Yeah, one take is all we're gonna get, just one shot."

And the two sat in solemn silence for a long while as they thought about the most bizarre script ever written.

Long shadows stretched over the quietness.

All was quickly being plunged into a thick and spreading greyness. A weighted darkness grew and expanded until its mass filled the room.

Light fled.

A new surround of eeriness pricked at the spines of the two sitting on the floor.

"It's time, Michael," came the whispered words from Emmy.

"Not yet. I'm too tense. I'd never get to sleep. God, Em, I don't know about this."

"Yes, you do. It's just stage fright. I've brought a little something for that." She got up and turned the lamp on.

"What do you mean?" he asked, curiously watching her rummage through her purse.

"Just what I said. I've got something to help with your jitters. See? This," she smiled, holding it up for him to see. "It's an old herbal sedative. Take a little and you're relaxed, take a lot and you're out for hours." She handed the vial of grey powder down to the man on the floor.

He turned it back and forth from end to end. "If this had come from anyone else I wouldn't have touched it with a ten foot pole." His eyes twinkled with the appreciation of her thoughtfulness. "I'll take a pinch more than a little," he said, getting up. "C'mon, let's get this thing over with."

With that finality voiced they turned out the light and headed for the bedroom.

Michael entered the bathroom for a glass of water. "How do I figure the right amount of this stuff?" he called.

"I'll do it for you."

When he reentered the bedroom he stopped in mid-step. "What're you doing?"

She'd thrown a quilt over the upholstered chair and was busily lighting something that looked like twigs.

"You're the famous anthropologist. Don't you know?"

He crossed the room to the table where she'd been working. "Yeah, I know. You're burning cedar to clear the spirits."

"Only in this case, it's to appease them—make them more comfortable with what we're doing here."

"You bring sweetgrass too?"

She patted her bag. "Yes, for later, though. I won't bring that out until I see how things are progressing." She paused out of uncertainty. "Michael?"

"Mmmm?"

"I know you've heard of Nightwalkers, haven't you?"

"Sure. Nightwalkers are those who are believed to be able to send their spirits into another's dreamscapes. Never could figure why those people weren't called Dreamwalkers, though."

"Silly," she chided. "A Dreamwalker is someone entirely different and you know it. They are very wise individuals who are in possession of many ancient secrets and have strong powers. A Dreamwalker is also a Nightwalker, but a Nightwalker is not always a Dreamwalker too."

"That's because some Nightwalkers have not reached the level of being an adept like the Dreamwalker has. But hey," Michael said, "I know all that and so do you. How did we get into playing What I Know, What You Know?"

Emmy laughed. "Because the game lets me know if you're clear on the terms."

"And was I?"

"Of course you were. Now the next question is a little more touchy." She stopped her preparations and turned to face him. "Michael, have you ever seen a Nightwalker walk?"

"No. That'd be incredibly interesting, but I've never had the opportun. . ."

Dead silence hung thick between them.

". . .ity. Jesus. You're a Nightwalker, aren't you?"

"Does that really surprise you?"

"Well yes! Well. . .no, I guess not," he admitted haltingly, watching her complete the preparations.

"Here," she said, letting the powder fall from her fingers into his glass. "Drink this now and get into bed. It won't take but a few minutes to work."

He eyed her and brought the glass to his lips.

"Go ahead," she encouraged. "Down the hatch with it."

The man did as urged and prepared for bed.

The woman sat on the edge of the mattress. "Now just relax. Don't think of anything in particular," she whispered, smoothing his hair back in soothing strokes. "Just be calm. All your muscles are going to sleep now. Rest. Rest. I'll be there. I'll be with you, Michael. Sleep in absolute confidence. All will be well. You will not be frightened. You will be a strong warrior and hold your ground. You will hear what the Force has to say to you. Sleep now, Michael, just sleep."

The man's breathing leveled off. He was gone now and the

woman knew she wouldn't have much time to finish her work before she too needed to be gone from this room.

Quickly she went to her bag and extracted several deerskin bags of different colored sand. She ground her thumb into some of the cedar ash and hurried over to the slumbering man. Praying the sacred words, she smudged the ashes upon the man's forehead, cheeks, and chin. She repeated the same process on herself.

Then, taking the four bags, she began emptying them in a circle on the carpet. She made the circle wide enough to enclose the bed, her chair, and the ceremony table within it.

After the colors of the four cardinal points were complete to her satisfaction she turned out the lights, added more cedar to the smoldering mixture and rested in the chair with her legs pulled up and crossed.

Held loosely between her fingers was an owl wing.

Her breathing was paced to a metered rhythm while a low chanting began to emit from her throat. Behind closed lids her mind's eye watched the grey cedar smoke lift and curl. Fingers tingled with the feather's desire for flight—for freedom. And her consciousness took flight upon the spreading wings of the rising owl.

His hands touched the smooth cold stone.

Fingertips rediscovered the engraved characters he'd remembered. But this time it wasn't so dark. This time there was some faint light. And it came from somewhere in the maze of catacombs behind him.

The light was intensifying, casting shifting shadows as it wound its advancing way forward through the twisted corridors of rock.

The man froze in fear. He was lucid enough to remember that he had to control that, but what was coming? Was the Preserver nearing? Would he suddenly be faced with those unblinking eyes any second now?

His sense told him that the unknown light source had only one more turn to round before he'd be face to face with it. He inhaled a deep breath of courage and lifted his chin. This was it, he thought, this was going to be his moment of truth.

The light cleared the corner and shone upon him.

His eyes widened at the unexpected sight. He stood transfixed at the sight of Emmy—her shimmering spirit form—standing before him in a presentation of full tribal dress. Her traditional native attire was a breathtaking sight to behold and the man was full of deep admiration of the beautiful vision.

Her long hair hung loose and fell in a shimmering flow to below her waist. White rabbit pieces and eagle feathers hung in the ebony tresses. A turquoise choker encircled the delicate neck. White deerskin with hundreds of fringes softly outlined her youthful form. Intricate designs covered the beaded moccasins that peeked out below quilled leggings. And, in her hand, was an owl wing.

"Emmy," he softly breathed, holding out his arms for her.

She went to him. "In this place I am Mourning Elk. How I present myself will help our cause."

Wordlessly he led her over to show her the mysterious wall. The light from her exquisite aura shed a glowing illumination onto the curious glyphs. They examined them together.

"Michael, I know some of the Unknown ones."

"How? How can you know them?"

"I don't know what they mean but some of our elders have handed them down through many, many generations. Our old ones sometimes have drawn these same symbols."

His excitement grew by leaps and bounds. "Are you certain?"

"Yes. I am sure. The old ones say these characters were made by the Bird People."

"Bird People?"

"Yes," she sweetly smiled, "only nowadays we don't call them Bird People because we know better and don't want to reference an ignorant term. Now we have another word for them. . .Star People."

Silence filled the cavern.

Michael mulled her words over. "Mourning Elk, your people had contact with the Star People?"

She raised one delicate brow in response.

He stared at her and, between the incoming rush of thoughts he marvelled at how radiant she looked. A decorative hair feather wavered when she turned her head to the wall and touched one of the Unknown symbols.

He was nearly at a loss for words. He whispered, "Then these really are symbols of a whole, separate civilization, aren't they? These represent space language."

"Yes," she whispered back, tracing small fingertips over the marble wall. "These represent the words of my Starborn ancestors." Then her eyes shifted back to lock on the man's. "He's approaching, Michael."

Air flowed through the deep chambers.

The metered drumming sound of a heartbeat throbbed louder and louder.

Michael recalled how the sound in his dreams nearly caused his ears to bleed from the strong vibration of it.

The two turned and psychically braced themselves.

"Do not show fear," she quietly reminded. "Do not show any fear."

And, together, they waited for what was to come.

Labored but steady breathing grew louder. The wind was whistling and howling through the hidden caverns. It whipped and swirled before their faces, yet the two stood transfixed as the great blue eyes appeared to float around the passageway.

Glowing. Glaring. Unblinking, they came forward to lock on the two pair that stared back.

Michael's calm spirit communed with his terrified consciousness the entire time. Calm. Do not show fear. Stand your ground. Watch.

The floating eyes drifted up to Michael's, then over to the woman's. They were assessing the hearts of each.

A tension-filled moment passed before the great piercing eyes suddenly blinked.

The two startled at the unexpected movement. They stood firm to watch in fascination as the eyes softened into a brilliant jade color. The orbs then slowly drifted backward and stopped while a form began to materialize. The eyes turned from the green to a mesmerizing shade of blue, and an aura of undulating violet light backlighted the new form's silhouette. It was that of a man. The man had voice. . .a gentle voice.

"You return."

"Yes," Michael shakily managed to say.

"As well you both reentered."

The violet aura around the figure undulated with silver spears of light.

"Who are you?" Michael dared to inquire.

"I am the Guardian of the Seals. The Preserver of the Sacred Wisdom. I am the Appointed Keeper for the Ancient ones."

"Are you spirit?" Michael asked.

"My Ba has long fled this wondrous place where my old bones lie in final repose. I am the Ka of myself. I remain to protect the Wisdom Treasures that were placed in this Sacred Sepulcher."

Michael's trembling began to subside. "We'll return the papyrus to you. We're sorry this place has been desecrated. We'll bring it back."

"This I know," came the soft voice, "for I have chosen the Deliverers. When you have completed your task I will allow you to pass beyond the last Seal."

Greystone's mind was spinning with urgent questions. The only one that untangled itself was simplistic.

"Why us?"

"I have chosen you for that which courses within your blood and that which dwells within your hearts."

"When should we come?"

"Do not allow one more week's time to pass."

"Can you tell us about these writings here? This *Star* language?"

The shimmering man smiled. "That is of your own Brother's tongue," came the cryptic statement. "You have much to learn," he added while beginning to fade into the ether. "But one word of warning I give to you—two are safe, three are dangerous, four are fatal."

"What does that mean?" Michael shouted to the vanishing entity.

Fading.

Fading.

"Ka, wait! Ka!"

Silence.

"KA!"

When Michael awoke his eyes fixed on those of the woman kneeling beside the bed. "Guess we did it, huh," he sleepily whispered.

She nodded and a sweet smile tipped the corners of her full mouth. Light from the moon slivered into the dark room.

He grinned. "Your face is dirty."

Smiling back, she traced his own unseen markings. "You mean here, here, here, and here?" She held up her smudged finger.

"Of course, you marked me too."

"It was the only way I could be assured you'd be fully protected."

He wriggled his nose. "You've burned the sweetgrass already."

"Yes. All went well and in Thanksgiving I burned the Prayer Smoke."

He rested his head back on the receiving pillows. "We did it, didn't we, Mourning Elk."

"Yes, Michael. We did."

And after washing up, the two snuggled back beneath the covers to talk about all that had transpired in the dreamscape. Together they were content and, safe in each others' arms, fell into a deep sleep. . .a dreamless sleep.

The nightmares had come to an end.

The Journey

T heodore Weatherbee slouched in the worn leather chair behind the old desk. He peered up over the wire rims of his spectacles and eyed his two visitors. Then his full attention was directed at the woman.

"So you're a Nightwalker. Well I'll be. If I'd have known that beforehand, young lady, I would've been there last night." He turned to the young professor. "You ever witness a Nightwalker in action before?"

Michael smiled in amusement. "Not to observe one. Guess I'd have to say I've got personal experience with one, though."

"Yes, yes, I'd certainly say so too. Good grief, when will our surprises stop coming?" This last was more of a statement than a question.

The senior professor had been wildly ecstatic that the dream experiment had gone well. Of course, he'd had no idea that the woman had been an adept. And after listening carefully to both of them recount the sequence of events he became silent as he mulled over a few questions of his own that were forming.

"So this Ka vanished before you could find out what he meant by his last statement."

Two heads nodded in unison.

"Damned cryptic." He repeated the ominous message. "Two are safe, three are dangerous, four are fatal." What the hell did he mean by that, I wonder? Any ideas?"

Michael cleared his throat. "I've been doing a lot of thinking on that. I believe the numbers refer to a body count."

Dr. Weatherbee's brows furrowed. "What does that mean? There's already three people dead over this confounded thing."

Michael shook his head. "No, that's not what I meant. That's not the sort of body count I'm referring to, Theo. I believe the Ka was referring to the number of people who go back when the papyrus is returned."

The full intent of the insinuation struck the old man hard. He sorted it out. "'Two are safe.' That'd be you two, of course, since the Ka already acknowledged that fact. He accepted you both already and your passage would be assured. 'Three are dangerous.' I suppose that'd mean *we* three when you include myself. But why would that be dangerous? Have you given that any thought, Michael? Ms. Winter?"

Dr. Greystone spoke first. "I have. And I think it may allude to your health. It's very hot and dry out in that region, especially now during this time of year. Add the heat of this extended Indian Summer we're having and. . ."

Weatherbee guffawed. "Balderdash! I'm in top shape for someone my age. There's not a single thing wrong with this ol' carriage of mine."

"Still," the younger man pushed, "the desert can debilitate the youngest and fittest of people. The Ka probably meant for you to just take extra precautions. You know, take care and watch yourself while we're out there."

Ms. Winter felt the need to add to that. "Dr. Weatherbee, Michael never meant to insinuate that you shouldn't come along. The way we see it, the papyrus should rightly be returned by representatives of the three language glyphs. We wouldn't feel complete without you there."

That definitely sounded more acceptable to the elder's tender ego. Then he addressed the third part of the mysterious warning. "And then there's this 'four are fatal' aspect. Who could he have possibly meant with that? Nobody even knows about this except we three. . .well, and Rosa, of course."

"Rosa?" Emmy inquired.

"Yes, José's wife. The woman who sent the papyrus." He thought hard. "Who else could the Ka be referring. . ."

Everyone in the room suddenly had the same sinking notion.

KAREN!

The thin skin on Weatherbee's face tingled. And with wide unbelieving eyes, he dared to whisper, "Karen."

Michael and Emmy looked at each other before staring back at the shocked man behind the desk. No words of agreement were necessary. All knew they were right.

"But how, for god's sake?" the elder questioned. "I've assured her over and over again that there's nothing secret transpiring between the three of us. I'm sure she was placated. Yes, I'm damned well sure of it."

"I'm not," Michael said coldly.

"Nor am I, Dr. Weatherbee. She thinks we're all in cahoots and that we're hiding something monumental from her. I overheard her tell someone that she's determined to get to the bottom of this mystery even if it kills her."

"'Four are fatal,'" the old man mumbled under his breath.

"Yes, Theo," Greystone said. "You've got to come up with some valid way to keep her out of our hair. You've got to devise a diversion for her. Obviously the Ka is very perceptive. He's foreseen a strong probability that Karen will attempt to interfere with our plans."

"You really think he's foreseen her coming with us?"

"Why else did he give the warning against four? There's no one else who has wind of any of this but her."

"Mmm, yes, a diversion." The elder man tapped his pencil while his cunning mind spun. Suddenly the eyes danced. "I've got it! Yes, yes, it's perfect, so perfect!"

Emmy smiled wide. "What?"

"Well. . .since we have this little excursion to sidetrack us away from the university for a time I'll need to get a substitute to fill in for Michael. And I know just the young man." He eyed Dr. Greystone. "He was my second choice after you, of course. I've never met him, but from what I've heard, he's quite a lady's man." The senior professor's eyes danced. "Do you think Karen would turn down an opportunity to be appointed his official host to show him around?"

The other two grinned at one another. A lady's man would certainly be the perfect diversion for Karen. Their satisfied expressions said it all.

Weatherbee thought aloud. "Yes, yes. I'll have her so busy showing Dr. Gordon around she'll never even notice we've slipped away." He chuckled with his own cleverness. "The girl will be ecstatic. She'll be in Seventh Heaven."

"Theo," Michael beamed, "that is brilliant. I do believe our little problem has been solved." He turned to the woman sitting beside him. The smile faded. "Now what's the matter? Don't you like the idea?"

"Oh yes, I like it fine, but. . .well, I'm not so sure she won't still smell something fishy going on."

"Why would she do that? She'd be so full of plans that she couldn't think of anything else. You're just worried. It'll work out, you'll see."

The woman's doubts remained. She addressed Michael. "But isn't it rather obvious that if a substitute professor is being brought in, *you* must be going somewhere? And she's going to be wondering where that 'somewhere' is."

Dr. Weatherbee groaned. "She's right, Michael. We've got to come up with something plausible to explain your absence."

Michael swore beneath his breath. "This is getting more convoluted with each passing minute. Why can't we just say I've got to return to Boston for some museum business?"

"Sounds good to me," Weatherbee said. "Think she'll buy that?" he addressed Emmy.

She managed a weak smile. "I think it's as good as anything we'd come up with. Maybe I am a little too worried. I suppose she'd jump at the chance to hang on the arm of a new professor-- especially if he's as handsome as you say. It's just that we can't afford any kind of delays at this late stage. We can't afford any hangups in the plan because we need to get right on this." She looked back to Weatherbee. "When do we go for it?"

"Tomorrow morning, my dear. I figured four in the morning." He cleared his throat. "Perhaps, young lady, you could manage to make arrangements to sleep somewhere other than in the dorm tonight. Karen would follow you right out the door if she saw you slipping out at that hour."

Emmy blushed. "Yes, that can be arranged. I can't very well have her see me sneaking out so early. I agree, she'd be right on my tail."

Theodore smiled. "Splendid! Now I'm leasing a motor home for us to use for this little jaunt of ours. The expense, of course, doesn't come out of my own pocket—or yours either. I've managed to get a loaner from my car dealer friend so there's no expense involved except for the gas. He's assured me that we've got the use of a fully-loaded vehicle. I pick it up this afternoon and I'll spend the evening stocking it." He then addressed Emmy. "Ms. Winter, can you find the time to pack a few changes of clothing when Karen's out of the building?"

She could.

"Good. When you're done, bring them around to my office and I'll see they're put in the RV. We can't have my nosey niece see you or Michael with anything that even vaguely resembles luggage. Michael, I'll swing by your place precisely at four. You two be ready."

"Sounds like a fool-proof plan to me."

Dr. Weatherbee was beaming with their cleverness.

Emmy tried, but knew no plan was fool-proof and that Karen was nobody's fool either.

"So," Theo perked with self-satisfaction to Michael, "just make sure. . .whatever you do. . .don't forget the map."

Michael and Emily looked at each other. They were mute.

"Okay?" he said with a smile.

Greystone was at a disadvantage. "Theo. . .what map?"

Weatherbee, exasperated, shook his head. "*Your* map, man! How will we ever locate the right mesa without it?"

The blood drained from Michael's face.

Weatherbee looked disbelievingly from one shocked face to the other. He stood. "Good GOD! Don't tell me you didn't ask the Ka where you were?"

The two vacant faces staring back told him all he needed to know. The enraged elder paced in total frustration. "We've got less than one week to return that papyrus and now, now you sit here and tell me that neither of you know where the mesa is! This is incredible, absolutely incredible! *Preposterous*! That's what it is." He sat back down and let his head rest in his hands. "God Almighty, I can't believe this is happening," he groaned.

The thick silence that hung over the room was so weighted that everyone's shoulders slumped. It remained that way for a long while until a soft voice shattered the stillness.

"We don't need a map," Emmy whispered.

Two heads simultaneously looked over at her.

"I can find it. In the morning I'll have located the precise spot. I'll mark a map if you wish."

The two men were amazed beyond words.

The corners of the young woman's mouth lifted ever so perceptively. "Sacred owl wings take Nightwalkers to many places— dreams are only one of them."

And so it was that the three schemed and were determined to carry out their plans to fruition.

Emmy had selected a few extra clothes that wouldn't be missed.

She packed up her important ceremonial items, leaving behind many that only looked important. And, without Karen seeing, she'd deposited the case in Dr. Weatherbee's office.

When Karen returned to the dorm later that afternoon, she found Emmy studying her anthropology text.

"Emmy! Guess what?" Then her hands fluttered in her friend's face. "Oh never mind, you'd just never guess in a million years. My uncle chose me for a very high level administration job!"

"No. You're kidding!"

"Oh, my dear, I am not jesting! You know when you were so down about Michael having to leave for Boston for awhile?"

Emmy nodded then listened to her excited roommate.

"Well! My uncle's got his replacement coming tomorrow and he's supposed to be a knockout." The woman puffed up her chest. "Guess who's going to be in charge of showing him around?"

"You?"

Karen paraded proudly about the room in her thrilling anticipation of the event. "Yes! See? It does pay to know someone."

"I guess so. Karen, that's wonderful!" Emmy couldn't help but grin over the other woman's exulted moment of glory as she watched her flit to and fro about the room. Karen scuttled from dresser to jewelry box to closet fretting over what would be the most impressive things to wear. After a short time the woman completely forgot about Emmy. She was far too busy talking to herself and visualizing how wonderful everything was going to be in the morning when the handsome new professor laid eyes on her.

Yes, Emmy thought, everything is going according to plan.

That evening as Michael and Emmy lay together he asked her if she was going to take a Nightwalker journey.

She said she was.

"Don't you have to make some preparations?"

She snuggled her head down into the warmth of his chest. "No, I only did all that last night because I had an outsider to protect and watch over."

He remained concerned. "What about your own protection?"

"That's all done spiritually," she softly informed. "I go through all that in my mind and visualize how I'll be dressed and where my destination is before I even begin my journey. When I finally do leave, my spirit eyes will see the path I took to get to where I envisioned I'd be. It's like sketching out a drawing before the complete painting is filled in."

"You're pretty special, you know that?"

"Yes. I'm special because I have you."

He kissed her tenderly on the head. He inhaled the sweet fragrance of her glossy hair.

She kissed his cheek. "Good night, Michael."

"Good night, Mourning Elk. Sweet dreams and happy walking."

Within minutes the man was sound asleep. It'd be some time yet before the woman would follow suit, because she wasn't going to technically Nightwalk this night. Instead, she was going to send her spirit out to talk with the Ka.

Calmly did she lie upon the bed. Deep within her being she envisioned the white core of her lifeforce as it pulsed with energy and power. And like an opalescent bubble she caused it to rise up to her chest, along her throat and to her head where it hovered near her crown. Then, when she envisioned a gate swing open. . .she was floating free.

Up she drifted. The heavens shimmered in the altered perspective of her spirit sight. They were filled with an electrifying essence of life that swelled her being with a deep sense of eternal love.

Below, mesas towered above the desert that glistened with the surrounding auras of plant and animal life. It was a veritable fantasyland of pulsing colors and spiking rays.

Everywhere, life undulated.

She lowered and traveled above a trailing depression in the land.

Buttes rose shoulder to shoulder. Mesas nearly touched one another as they watched out over the vast land that stretched out at their feet.

A nighthawk, effortlessly gliding on the cool air current, took notice of her passing spirit.

Then Emmy saw it.

One mesa in particular had a stronger wakan. Its spirit energy writhed with a power few have seen. And she hovered above it for a silent moment to absorb its beauty, its exquisiteness.

A warming peace settled over her—through her. She looked again up into the endless firmament. Something nebulous had passed between her and the sacred mesa. Something incredibly holy had transpired because the sense of her being expanded and suddenly she was the firmament—she was All That Is.

Emmy's eyes shot open.

The man beside her was tossing fitfully in his sleep. Had he disturbed her traveling? No. Remembering the sacredness of that magnificent touching made her realize that that had been the signal that her journey had concluded for this night.

She and the Ka had communicated.

Now she snuck from the bed and crept across the carpet to where the map had been spread out on the table. Quietly flicking on Michael's lighter, she silently picked up the pen. Glancing down, she studied the paper. Yes, there it was. There was the exact location. And before slipping silently back into bed, she marked a cross where she'd seen the mesa's powerful aura of light.

Until her mind began riding the gentle waves of sleep, she wondered why she hadn't actually entered the mesa. She'd planned on speaking with the Ka. Why hadn't she followed through? Then the light of realization came to her—it just hadn't been the right time to enter and her spirit had perceived that. Instead, she'd been given a majestic type of communication that stemmed from deep within the heart of the towering Standing Stone itself. Instead, they had each given recognition of each others' presence and she had been blessed with a minute fragment of what lay buried below—a love and wisdom more sacred than anything yet known to man.

She could think upon it no longer. And the woman the mesa came to know as Mourning Elk was gently swept along the swirling current of slumbering oblivion.

Precisely at the stroke of four, a large RV quietly rolled to a stop in the street in front of Dr. Greystone's house. The two occupants inside had been watching for it and Emmy flicked the porchlight once to signal the driver that they'd seen him.

When they saw what pulled up, Michael chuckled. "Weather-bee certainly goes first class all the way. No plebeian little camper for him."

The two left the house and, walking out to the massive shadowed hulk of metal, Emmy couldn't help but think it looked a little like a Christmas tree the way all the running lights glowed orange and red in the early morning darkness.

Before the two had advanced halfway down the walk, Weatherbee leaned out the opened passenger door. "Got the map?" he rasped his whispered question.

Michael smiled and patted his jacket pocket. "Right here."

"Is it marked?"

"It's marked, Theo."

The elder man released an audible sigh of relief as he held the door open. "Welcome to home, then," he chirped as his new traveling companions climbed in.

Emmy was wide-eyed at the sight before her. She'd seen hundreds of the big roving vehicles as tourists passed in and around Taos, but never had she had reason to be inside one. She looked over the arrangement of furniture, the kitchen area and walked to the back where the bedroom and bath were located. Her eyes danced. "This is really something."

Michael smiled with amusement.

Weatherbee grinned with pride. "My dealer friend claims this baby is the absolute creme de la creme."

A crease marred the woman's forehead. "Do we need something so extravagant?"

Michael shook his head and put his arm around her shoulder. "Come on, Em, Theo said his friend loaned it to him. Why not travel in style when it's free? Huh? Look how comfortable we'll be."

She again glanced about the interior. Her blue eyes came to rest on the area above the driving section. "What's that?" she asked, pointing to the big shelf. "What's that shelf for?"

Weatherbee rolled his eyes and left to study the marked map.

Michael chuckled. "This isn't exactly a shelf. See." he said, grabbing the strap and pulling down the overhead sleeping compartment.

"It's a big bed!" she exclaimed. Although the man thought of resisting it, his urge to kiss his unworldly lady was too great. "You're so cute," he laughed.

Emmy remembered they weren't alone. She blushed.

Weatherbee frowned. "Oh for heaven's sake!" he grumbled. "This isn't some honeymoon! Let's get going. We've got a lot of territory to cover. Michael, sit up front with me and be my navigator. Emmy, make yourself comfortable."

Dr. Greystone winked at the woman before climbing into the

plush passenger seat. And just as the motor home pulled out onto the street, he looked over to the driver. "You ever driven one of these crates before?"

"Nope. Never too old to learn though."

"Oh great," Michael mumbled.

"What's that you say?" Weatherbee asked, leaning his ear to the younger man.

"I said, gonna be great, just great!" he covered, as he heard the woman behind him snicker.

"Yes, yes, going to be something to remember, all right," the driver emphasized.

"Theo?"

"Yes?"

"You do have the papyrus, don't you?"

The old man flashed his passenger an outrageous frown. "I may be an *old* professor but I'm not an absent-minded one. . .yet! Of course I've got it. It's safe in one of the bedroom drawers back there."

Emmy quickly changed the subject. "Which way are we going?"

"Open the map back up, Michael," Weatherbee ordered. "We'll follow Interstate 25 all the way out of Colorado, that way we avoid the highest passes. In Albuquerque we'll pick up I-40 heading west and follow that to Sanders, Arizona."

"Sanders?" Emmy questioned. "Why Sanders? I thought we were going all the way into Holbrook."

"Look again at that map. Look where your mark is."

She saw that it rested midpoint centered between invisible crosslines down from Chambers and directly east of Holbrook. A state road led south out of Sanders that would place them in the general vicinity of the marked area.

"We're taking the state road out of Sanders?" she asked.

"That's right."

Michael silently pointed to it and raised a brow in dubious question.

The woman's concern grew. "But, Dr. Weatherbee, that road's marked six-six-six!"

"That's right, that's what it's marked all right. What's the matter, dear, you superstitious about numbers?"

"Well that is a rather ominous one. Why couldn't we just continue west on I-40 until we get to Holbrook, then double back?"

He took his eyes from the road just long enough to peer over his spectacles at her. Then he returned his attention to the road. "You tell her why we can't double back from Holbrook, Michael."

"Sorry, Em, no roads. Oh there's probably the usual desert tracks through there, but it'd be too slow going, too time-consuming. Theo's right, we'd be better off heading into the region from the state road. As it is we're still going to have to pinpoint the exact mesa and who knows how long that'll take us." His shoulders rose and fell. "Sorry honey, but it really is our best course."

She rested back in her seat. "I just hope we're not going to regret it, that's all. I can't imagine anyone putting a number like that on any highway."

Weatherbee grinned. "Maybe they had a good reason," he said cryptically. "Does it make you nervous, dear?"

She straightened her back. "Not really, it's just not very comforting, that's all. The Ka has already proven how powerful he is and I don't think we need to be dealing with any more spirits than we have to."

Michael's look was grave when he turned to her. "But, Em, the Ka is on our side. From what we've seen so far I doubt there're any spirits that want anything to do with hampering his plans. I'd say we were about as safe as any. . ."

Just then the vehicle swerved to avoid hitting a big black dog that'd been in the road.

"My god!" Weatherbee spat. "You see how that damned thing just sat there?"

Michael righted himself and gathered up the papers that spilled to the floor. "Maybe it was blind. It had to be blind or it would've scampered out of our way. We weren't going that fast."

"What kind of a dog was it?" Emmy inquired.

The driver and navigator eyed one another. Their thoughts were on the same wavelength.

"Well?" she asked again.

"It was hard to tell," Michael hedged. "It all happened so fast. I dunno, maybe a Doberman or something like that."

The woman had been placated.

The two men up front were far from being at ease with what they'd just witnessed.

In the RV's headlights the animal had appeared to look more like a jackal. . .a very large jackal. The yellow beams of light had caught its eyes just right and the men vividly saw the blue iridescence that glared back at them. No, it was no common dog that had tried to block their passage—it was no common dog at all. Michael had seen those eyes before. . .he'd seen them in his nightmares.

Dr. Weatherbee merged the cumbersome vehicle onto the Interstate. He was ominously quiet.

"We need to talk about it," Michael said.

The driver nodded.

"Talk about what?" Emmy asked.

"That *thing* back there," Michael replied.

"What thing? The Doberman?"

The driver nodded.

Michael explained. "That was no dog, Em. It was the Ka."

Her scalp crawled.

"He took the form of Anubis. I've seen him like that in dozens of dreams. It was him alright."

Her eyes were wide. "You sure?"

"I'm sure."

"But why sit in the middle of the road like that? He must've known we'd swerve. We could've been seriously hurt. Why would he do something so threatening like that?"

Weatherbee's voice was cold. "To warn us."

Both passengers stared at the driver.

"My young friends," he softly said, "something is amiss. I suggest that Ms. Winter go back and check on our precious cargo." Emmy immediately scrambled to the back room. She was relieved when she saw the sacred object; yet, staring down at it now it was almost as if an ancient memory had subliminally speared to the forefront of her consciousness and then fled. What was so familiar about it? Her searching eyes scanned the characters. What was this intimate feeling she had for this prehistoric fragment?

"Em?" Michael called, breaking her concentration.

"Yes, everything's fine," she called. "I'm coming."

Making her way to the front of the coach she wondered why the professor hadn't secured the valuable piece better. "Dr. Weatherbee, shouldn't the papyrus be protected from the air?"

The old man's spine tingled. "What on earth are you prattling about?"

"Well, in your office, you had it in plastic and in double

envelopes to protect it. Now it's just sitting out on the dresser. It could fall and be damaged or something."

A tremor rippled through the driver. "I don't know what's going on here," he grumbled, trying to maneuver through Denver's heavy morning traffic, "but I left it just as it was when I took it out of the safe. I placed it inside the drawer. Michael, go back there and secure the thing again. The handling gloves are in the second drawer."

Dr. Greystone hurried to the back with the woman quickly following on his heels. Just as she'd said, the fragile fragment was there on top of the dresser. Michael looked to his confused companion then began pulling on the latex gloves that would protect the delicate paper from skin oils.

"What's happening, Michael? First that dog thing and now this. What's the Ka trying to tell us?"

"I'm not sure but I've the sinking feeling that the omens are just beginning." Then he concentrated on the delicate handling of the old fragment. When it had been safely replaced in its seal and the drawer closed, he removed the gloves. "I wish I knew, Em. I wish I knew what this was all about."

"Maybe today isn't the day to start out," she suggested. "Maybe tomorrow would've been better."

He shook his head in doubt. "No, that's got nothing to do with it."

"But how can you be so sure?"

His shoulders slumped as he stared out the window. "Just feelings, I guess. We've only got a few more days to accomplish this task and we can't afford to waste a single one. No, something else is wrong and he's trying to warn us about it."

"But what could be wrong?"

His dark eyes came around to lock coldly on her bright ones. "I don't know. And that, my love, is what scares the hell out of me."

The rest of the morning passed without further incident. The trio was, for the most part, silent as the RV covered the ground between Denver and Pueblo. In another couple of hours they'd cross the state line and be in New Mexico. It was past lunch time.

"Anyone hungry?" Emmy inquired.

No one was, yet they agreed they probably should eat something.

The driver inclined his head as he spoke to her. "You'll find everything you need in the kitchen. I stocked it full."

Michael went back to help Emmy make up some sandwiches while Weatherbee informed them he'd keep his eyes peeled for a good spot to pull over.

Another ten miles were covered before a rest stop came into view.

After eating, they got out and stretched their legs. While walking about the sage-covered ground they discussed the early morning's eerie events.

"Think something could be wrong with the vehicle?" Michael offered as a suggestion.

The old man pursed his lips in serious doubt. "I was personally assured that it was in perfect condition. The dealer knew where I was headed with it and said he told his mechanics to give it an extra going-over. Nah, that little baby is in great shape."

Emmy listened to the two men toss ideas back and forth while they strolled about the sunny rest stop.

The sky was a brilliant robin's egg blue. Not one ominous cloud formation was in sight. If there were bad omens for them at least nature wasn't guilty of presenting any of them.

A gentle breeze lifted the ends of her ebony hair and she deeply inhaled the sweetness of the sage. Little brown prairie dogs scuttled here and there, often nervously venturing near the other seated travelers in hopes of obtaining a morsel or two.

Happiness and serenity were alive everywhere the woman looked, yet why were they being warned? What could possibly be wrong? Weren't they on a mission of good faith? Weren't they helping the Ka regain the precious treasure? It was a baffling enigma that defied comprehension.

The trio finally climbed back into the coach and settled in for another long stretch of road.

Emmy had been seated on the raised floor between the two men and, as the passing scenery of lowlands began to lull her into a semi-hypnotic state, her sights were drawn to a small pinpoint of blue up ahead. Recognition broke the spell.

"Look! There's an old man up there! Where could he be going out here in the middle of nowhere?"

The vehicle soon closed the distance between it and the lone figure. As it passed the man wearing the bright turquoise headband, the three kept their eyes on him.

"I'd offer the old guy a ride but he appears to be going the other way," Weatherbee said. "He's probably been hitching rides all morning."

"He was Zuni," Emmy informed her companions.

"You know him?" Michael asked.

"No, I've never seen him before." And she then became solemn as she thought about the elder who shuffled along the roadside. "He never even looked up when we passed," she commented.

Michael shrugged. "We weren't going his way."

"Maybe. Maybe that's why," she whispered.

The driver chuckled. "Something wrong, Ms. Winter?"

"I'm not sure."

"I think you're spooked. You're finding mystery in normal things now. Give it a rest."

Emmy made no reply. She remained silent as another hour passed.

The new scenery was uninteresting. Dry and flat. Colorless. It made one feel as though one was getting nowhere fast. It created a surreal surround. Then the sign loomed up ahead: WELCOME TO NEW MEXICO — LAND OF ENCHANTMENT.

And, an hour out of Raton, they again passed the old man with the distinctive headband. All three travelers quivered with a peculiar chilling shiver.

"Damn!" the driver spewed, cramming all his weight forward onto the brake. "We are going to talk to that old man. He can't possibly have gotten way down here before us. Dammit! He was headed the other way!"

The RV bumped off the highway onto the fields of rabbitbrush and the three scurried out. When they ran to the back of the vehicle to call out. . .there was no one there. . .anywhere.

Afternoon shadows crept across the flat prairie.

The three stared up the desolate stretch of highway.

"What the hell!" Michael flared in disbelief. "Where'd he go?"

"Come on. Get in." Weatherbee barked. "We're turning around to see just where he went."

The long RV swung out and arced wide. It sped back the way it'd come. Slowing now, all eyes searched the level landscape. If the man had fallen, his bright clothing would stand out in the brush. From the center compartment the driver pulled out two pairs of binoculars. He handed one to Michael as the vehicle edged onto the shoulder and stopped.

"Michael, climb up top. See if you can see anything."

The agile man took the glasses and scrambled out to climb the ladder that led to the luggage rack. He stood tall and slowly panned the eyeglasses over the desert.

"See anything?" the woman called.

"Nothing. Not a sign of him."

She looked over to the driver, who'd also been scanning the brush. "Anything, Dr. Weatherbee?"

He shook his head. "No, and I don't expect we're likely too, either." He avoided her eyes. He knew she'd sensed something mysterious about the pedestrian and he didn't want to admit that he'd teased her over it. "Let's go, Greystone. We're not going to find anything out here."

After the vehicle again headed south, the three remained silent while each was lost in their own private speculations over the phenomenon of the vanishing Zuni elder.

Emmy was about to voice her thoughts on it when the vehicle hit rough road.

All three were startled by a sudden racket coming from the large storage closet.

Someone sneezed.

Everyone knew who it was.

Michael cursed as he flew out of his seat. Face red with rage, he flung open the door.

Karen meekly looked up. "Hi! Sorry, but there's sawdust falling all over in here."

Michael grabbed her arm and roughly pulled her out. "What the hell do you think you're doing in there?"

Unruffled by his outrage, the woman cleared her throat while brushing off her designer jeans. Her chin jutted up defiantly. "I'm coming with you. That's what the hell I'm doing here!" A long lacquered fingernail snaked out to shake in his face. "I knew you three were up to something. I just knew it! And from what I've heard all day it's something not only big, it's damned spooky, too!"

"You can't come," Michael spouted.

Her brow rose. "Oh, really."

The driver sighed. "Michael, leave her be. It's too late to do anything about it now. We'll just have to make the most of it."

"No dice, Theo. We'll drop her off at the first motel we come to. She can rent a car and drive herself back to Boulder."

"Michael, come sit down."

"No, dammit! I won't sit down. She's got to go! Don't you see that she makes four? Four is fatal, Theo! The Ka knew she was a stowaway and that's why we've had all the omens—the warnings!"

"*Michael*! Leave it I said!"

The stowaway smiled.

Greystone glared hard at the arrogant face. He strode back to his seat.

Emmy rubbed his arm in an attempt to calm his flaring temper. "We'll just have to work it out. We'll be all right."

"Of course it'll all work out," Karen sang. "This is going to be so much fun!" Her stomach growled. "Oh my but I am famished." She then busied herself in the kitchen with the making of an over-stuffed ham sandwich. When she finished she took it to the dinette and proceeded to tongue-wag while eating.

"Honestly, I can't believe you guys actually thought you'd pulled one over on me. I mean, that was really dumb. I watched you all like a hawk and when Trish told me she'd seen Emmy drop off something that looked like a suitcase at Uncle Theo's office. . .well, my dears, how obvious can one get?

"So then I really made the connection when I thought of that trumped-up excuse you made to keep me there at the university. I passed the job off to someone else and then I had a friend of mine drive me up to uncle's place.

"Dear man, you really were careless to leave this wonderful expensive thing unlocked! So I just snuck in and here I am! When you stopped off at the rest area I was able to slip out unnoticed to use the john. Man, did I ever have to go! Anyway, you weren't gone long enough for me to grab something to eat. I'm absolutely famished. I would've stayed hidden longer if you hadn't gone off the road back there and that awful sawdust hadn't been shaken down in my face. So then, as hard as I tried, I couldn't. . ."

"CAN it, Karen!" Weatherbee angrily ordered.

"For heaven's sake, you don't have to get rude about it. After all, I am your niece and I'm entitled to come along."

The three up front exchanged defeated glances. There was nothing to be done about the unfortunate turn of events. Though they'd been warned that "four are fatal," they were helplessly stuck with the situation as it now stood.

Karen sighed. "Look everyone, I promise not to get in your way or underfoot. I promise I won't cause any kind of trouble. I'll even be helpful. While you three are doing whatever it is that you're going to do, I'll stay here in this lovely motor home and read magazines. I'll even fix the food and clean up too. How's that sound?"

No one responded.

Guilt was slipping into her tone. "I promise not to be a bother. I really do."

The trio looked to one another with doubt written all over their faces.

"All right, Karen," her uncle acquiesced. "We're going to hold you to your word. Just stay out of our way, keep the place in order and, for god's sake, don't talk so much!"

The woman seated at the dinette smiled to herself and buried her nose in a magazine. "Yes, Uncle Theo, I'll be a good little girl. I'll be as good as gold, you'll see."

At six o'clock, the four stopped for a hearty dinner at a roadside cafe. The newcomer was quietly told about the entire scenario and how dangerous it was. She was informed that the high danger factor was the main reason her uncle hadn't wanted her to come along. That wasn't quite true, but it sounded as good a reason as any.

Karen felt sheepishly regretful. Deep inside she was scared. What had she gotten herself into this time? "Maybe I'll just go back. Dr. Greystone had a good idea about me renting a car. I don't mind driving myself back to Boulder."

"Too late," her uncle flatly said. "You're here now and nobody else can know about what we're doing."

She pursed her lips and half smirked. "Oh, I get it. You think I'll go an' blab, don't you. You think I'll go back and babble about it to everyone."

"That's not what I said, Karen," Theo soothed. "You're not being fair to me. You're being unreasonable. Now that we're together here, we have to remain and stick it out. Like you said, perhaps you can be of some assistance to us after all."

"Well I *want* to go back! I don't like the sound of any of this crap! Dogs that aren't really dogs, Indian men appearing out of nowhere and then vanishing in thin air!" She glanced over at

Emmy, then over to the young instructor. "Nightwalkers and nightmares! Thanks but *no* thanks!"

The entire dinner was spent convincing the frightened young woman that she had to remain with them, that there was just no other alternative. They succeeded in calming her fears and reassuring her that she wouldn't come to harm if she'd remain inside the RV while they did their work.

This appeared to placate her somewhat and all four had finally reached an acceptable understanding of the situation.

Two hours out of Albuquerque when the stretching rays of the setting sun were long and orange across the land, a shadowy greyness began to herald the coming of twilight.

The driver suddenly pulled off the road and stopped.

All four occupants stared wide-eyed out the front windshield.

An old Indian man walked toward them. The turquoise headband was bright in the headlight beams. Slowly did he walk forward to stop ten feet from the vehicle. His obsidian eyes, piercing, speared to lock on those of the occupants.

The passengers, held spellbound, were frozen as helpless rabbits before powerful snake eyes. And, while their hearts pounded like the thunder of a hundred war drums. . .the man vanished.

Karen fainted.

The Seventh Mesa

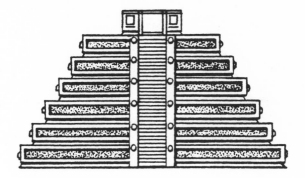

On the outskirts of Gallup the RV stopped for the night. The driver had pushed as far as he could before fatigue and the mental concentration of driving had taken its toll. It had been late when all four of the motor home's occupants fell exhausted onto the makeshift beds.

The elder man quickly drifted off to sleep.

The younger man tossed for a while before giving in to the peace of slumber. No nightmares came to disrupt his rest.

Emmy had a desire to walk through the quiet desert night to be alone with nature and to pray—but realizing she'd need strength and awareness for the day ahead, she too succumbed to the welcoming embrace of sleep.

Only one person remained awake for what seemed like hours. Only one person stared in fear up at the shadowed ceiling because, for the first time in her life, Karen Kendall regretted she'd gotten her way. With wide, darting eyes suspiciously shifting over her shadowy surroundings, she pulled the blankets tighter around her chin. Wrapped like a cocoon, she alternately cursed her stubbornness and then prayed for deliverance.

And the darkness passed over them without incident.

Hot breaths of air steadily wavered over the lone motor home that rolled to a stop just inside the Arizona line. It was as if the earth itself was breathing over the incapacitated vehicle.

Inhale. Exhale.

Inhale. Exhale.

Above, the burnished copper disc rose higher and higher through its wedgewood ocean of blue.

Below, the flatlands were beginning to simmer.

Heat waves rippled over the land.

In the distance, saguaros stood like watching totems.

The horizon wavered dreamily.

Lizards scampered about. The hiss of their cool bellies making contact with the hot rocks was nearly an audible sound as they settled down to bask in the baking sun.

Soon the heat would be torrid. Soon the orb in the sky would turn from yellow to a searing white hot.

From beneath the raised hood of the stranded vehicle, an arm waved out. "Try it again, Theo," shouted the irritated voice.

The engine coughed and sputtered.

"Again!"

This time it caught and purred like nothing had been amiss.

The man slammed down the hood and quickly scurried back inside.

The driver shoved the shift into gear. "What the hell did you do?"

Michael shrugged. "Beats me. If you ask me, it just decided it was time for us to be off again." The passenger shot a surreptitious look to his companion. "I don't think we'll find logical explanations for anything on this trip. I've the distinct impression this situation isn't entirely in our hands."

"Looks that way, doesn't it. You took the words right out of my mouth. Especially since this baby's been checked out from top to bottom. It's a case of everything from here on in being controlled by the power of the Ka."

As that sobering realization took hold, the four occupants were silent until the vehicle slowed and turned left at the road marker that indicated they were now on Route 666.

No one spoke.

A perceptible heaviness weighted the interior of the RV. Four hearts pounded with the expectation of the unknown while the solitary vehicle headed down toward their destination.

Emmy examined the map. "There's no road going in off this one," she whispered.

"Then we'll just have to make one," Weatherbee said. "Question is, where do we make one?" he hinted, peering over his wire rims at her. His intent couldn't have been more obvious. Clearly it was up to her to use her insights and recall the landmarks from her Nightwalking to guide them in.

Her awareness sharpened to a finely-honed edge as they

covered more ground. They passed a weed-choked road and the driver slowed. He looked at her for instruction.

Emmy shook her head. She held up her hand to indicate the need to go slower.

Weatherbee continued with caution while the vehicle crept forward.

"Here. Turn off here," she voiced when her spine began to tingle.

The group looked to the west where she had indicated. Sage and rabbitbrush blanketed the ground from the road to the distant horizon where ghostly mesas could be discerned through the hot, wavering haziness.

They stared out into the desolation.

The driver released an audible sigh and wheeled the cumbersome mass of metal and fiberglass off the paved road. The vehicle bumped and pitched. It inched its way over the uneven terrain of the desert.

"Going to be rough going," Weatherbee's voice rattled. "This crate ain't no four-wheel-drive Jeep, but it's all we got. Hang on, everyone."

As it tilted and rocked through the open land, supplies were heard toppling in the cupboards. Everyone ignored the sounds. It'd be fruitless to set things aright so soon. Faces were tense as all four watched the painful progress of the vehicle.

After an hour of constant jostling, the groundcover changed. They had reached a natural demarcation line where the heavy brush gave way to flat, cracked desert. The small wheels rolled quietly over the baked earth and, after forty-five minutes more, the mesas and buttes were no longer seen through a distant haze. They were towering realities. . .real as stone.

Emmy carefully scanned the monoliths then gently touched the driver's arm. "We're here."

"Which one is it? I'd like to get us closer," the driver said.

"This is close enough," Emmy whispered, not bothering to take her eyes from the massive Standing Stones.

"I'll be the judge of that, young lady. We'll need to move in closer so we can. . ."

The engine died.

Michael grinned at the timing of it. "Like the young lady said, Theo, this is close enough."

Dr. Weatherbee cleared his throat. "Yes. Yes, it would appear the gods have deemed it so," he agreed, gently engaging the gear in PARK. He sighed while scanning the austere geographic land features. "Damned miserable place. God-awful hot too."

Emmy peered out the windshield at the panoramic view of the desolation. "They call this the Screaming, Burning Place Above," she whispered cryptically.

Michael turned. "Who calls it that? Your People?"

She nodded. "Yes, them and others who know about it. To those who have always been close to the Earth Mother and have heard her whispered words, this place is very wakan."

"That means powerful," Karen informed.

"Powerful with sacredness," Michael added.

"I knew that," Karen snapped back. Then, trying a little too hard to stretch her knowledge, she said, "They come here to pray."

Emmy's eyes widened. "Oh no. Some places are too powerful. Their very force represents danger."

"Not to the elders," Karen quipped.

"Yes! Even to them. They do not tread this ground. . .ever."

"None of them do?" Weatherbee questioned.

"Only those entrusted with its guardianship. Only certain adepts are accepted here and do not come with fear in their hearts."

Karen had had enough. "Well, well, now, isn't this just a dandy day. Here we are in the middle of nowhere with the heat of hell itself blazing all around and now we find out that it's got some terrible force on it that scares the living bejesus out of the natives. Isn't this great?"

"Shut up, Karen." Weatherbee ordered. "*We* knew what we were getting into, it's *you* who jumped into the frying pan without looking first. And we'd all be eternally grateful if you'd just keep your mouth shut and stay out of it. We've got a monumental task ahead of us and we don't need someone flapping her jaws at us every step of the way!"

Indignant, Weatherbee's niece knew better than to utter another word of objection, so she flopped down on the couch and snapped open a magazine. She listened intently to the conversation that was taking place up front. The tone of her uncle's words were resigned, yet determined.

"I suppose we'd better get on with it. We're going to have to do some cursory explorations before we make the actual move on this thing."

It was agreed that it'd most likely take a while before they pinpointed the precise opening to the mesa and that they'd have to go in a ways to familiarize themselves with it. All three decided to leave the papyrus where it was until they were ready to make their final trip.

Emmy had worrisome concerns about the elder gentleman. She attempted to be nonchalant about it so as not to injure the man's sensibilities.

"It's awfully hot out there and I expect it's going to be pretty strenuous climbing about those foundation rocks." She glanced furtively at the man in the driver's seat. "Dr. Weatherbee, why don't you stay here and let Michael and me do the preliminary explorations. Then when we've found the passageway we'll come back and get. . ."

When the doctor turned his head, the look was frigid. "There is no way, young lady, that I am going to miss a minute of this. That papyrus was sent to me—not to you and not to Michael, but to me—and I am going to be damned sure that I'm there every step of the way."

"I didn't mean anything. . ."

"I know, I know what you meant. You're thinking that this godawful Burning Place is going to be too hard on an old codger like me. But I don't mind reminding you that, before you were a twinkle in your daddy's eye, I'd been poking around worse places than this. And as for my age. . .well, you'd be surprised what an old coot like me is still capable of. No, you let me worry about me. Now," he spouted, "shall we proceed?"

Michael tended to agree with Emmy about the heat and rough terrain taking its toll on the elderly man, though he also had the mind of an anthropologist and knew that his senior's adrenaline was pumping to discover the ultimate find—there'd be no way he'd stay behind on this one. At his ripe age this discovery was going to be the landmark experience of his entire career and, at this late date, he wouldn't care if it ended up killing him. Dr. Weatherbee would surely die a happy and fulfilled man.

Michael winked at Emmy in an effort to placate her. "Okay then, let's get on with it."

Karen looked up from the glossy pages of her magazine. "Guess I'll mind the store. Don't worry, though, I won't throw any wild parties while you're gone."

Dr. Weatherbee came around to stand in front of his niece. He leaned down and rested his wide palms on the table. Then he removed the magazine from the young woman's hands.

"Karen, you are my only niece and I want you to know that I love you." His warm mahogany eyes locked on her wide ones. "Now I need you to listen carefully, very carefully, to what I'm about to say." He pointed toward the bedroom area and slowly said, "Back there, secured in a drawer, is evidence of humankind's beginnings."

The woman's gaze hypnotically shifted from her uncle's eyes to look down the narrow passageway. They eased back to lock on the man before her.

"Karen, people have died because of the thing in that drawer back there." His voice was reverent, almost down to an inaudible whisper. "The Force of the Ka has killed to protect that sacred fragment. It's the secret proof—the ultimate proof—of this civilization's connection to intelligent star beings."

Karen was held entranced while her uncle spoke.

"Now my dear, do you know what your job is while we're gone?"

Her head slowly went from side to side.

"Your job is to protect it."

She tried to swallow but found her throat too dry. "M-Me?"

The man towering over her nodded. "Yes Karen, you. Can you do that for us, Karen?"

"Well. . .yes. . .I guess so," she said haltingly.

"Good. Very good. And Karen. . ."

"What?"

"Whatever you do. . .do not. . .touch it."

Her head again swayed from side to side. "Oh no, Uncle Theo, I won't even go anywhere near it."

While the doctor had been instructing his mesmerized niece, Michael and his companion had been gathering up their equipment. Now that they were supplied with the canteens of water, ropes and lanterns, they waited outside for the third member of their party to join them.

Emmy still held serious reservations about the elder man accompanying them. And, touching Michael's arm, she led him away from the vehicle.

"Are you sure it's wise for him to come along this first time?

We may be out there for hours." Her eyes drifted to the horizon of rugged mesas.

"No, I'm not sure. I'm not sure at all. Right now I'm not sure of anything. But, Em, we can't very well deny him the moment of the discovery. He's the senior member here and he's had years of experience. Let's just go along and see how it goes. I've the feeling that if the Ka doesn't want him in, he'll find a way to keep him out."

Emmy's blue eyes narrowed. "That's what worries me—the Ka's ways."

Her partner turned his head to the distant stones. "Shh, here he comes."

Emmy spun around to cheerily address the newcomer. "Well? Everything squared away back there?"

He eyed her curiously. "It would appear so, then again, it wouldn't hurt to keep our fingers crossed." Then he hesitated before asking, "Everyone use the. . .facilities?" It appeared that the question was directed more to Emmy than to Michael.

Both nodded that they had.

"That's it then," Weatherbee finalized before striding ahead in a pace a bit too vigorous for the desert heat.

And it wasn't too much longer before his energy waned considerably. The distance from the motor home to the towering pinnacles had been grossly misjudged. It was slow going across the smoldering, cracked ground.

Above, the searing sun torched down unmercifully upon the desolate land below.

The occasional appearance of circling buzzards cast ominous shadows over the dead earth. The three ignored the sight. They trudged on until they reached the first rocky foundation of red Standing Stones. They fell to rest in the cool shade of the massive boulders.

Though Dr. Weatherbee's breathing was somewhat labored, no one spoke of it.

They sipped from their canteens, each savoring the cold wetness that slithered down their parched throats.

The three sat in prolonged silence while tired bodies rejuvenated and active minds contemplated their next move. Three pairs of eyes scanned the massiveness of the structures that rose above their heads.

"They're like great tombstones," Emmy whispered in awestruck wonder at their size. "They're here and they've always been here. They're really ancient gravemarkers."

Weatherbee frowned. "Now's not the time to get morbid."

Michael disagreed with the elder's remark. "Oh, I don't know, Theo. Seems that that's just what they are. They're the American version of the pyramids—great Standing Stones marking the treasure graves that are hidden far below them. We know that beneath the seventh one are man-made chambers and mazes of tunnels. Maybe one leads to the greatest inner sanctum of all the ancient civilizations combined. Who knows, Theo, maybe there's even a sarcophagus somewhere down there."

"Oh come, come, Michael. Don't get carried away."

Dr. Greystone raised his brow in silent question.

Weatherbee frowned. "Well, whose would it be? If there was one, I mean."

Michael smiled. "I didn't say there actually was one, I was just speculating."

Theodore sighed. "Your imaginative speculation is rubbing off on me. After all that's happened recently, I wouldn't doubt you were right." Getting up and brushing off his wide trousers, he said, "Well we'll never find out unless we discover that opening. I've got my wind back, so let's get cracking."

After two hours of hard climbing over the precarious boulders, after exhaustive searching around the mesa's perimeter, Michael stopped to peer down into an unusual crevice. At the bottom there appeared to be a cave of some sort leading into the mesa proper. It would need further investigation.

He called out to the others. They scrambled up to see what he'd found and their hearts pounded at the sight.

Emmy stared down at the yawning opening. "How does it feel, Michael?" she asked in reference to his dreams. "Does it feel familiar?"

"It feels damned spooky," he admitted. "It's deja vu creeping up my spine. This has to be it."

Puffing, Weatherbee joined them. "This it, Michael?"

"I think it is, Theo. My dreams never began at the opening, they always started just before I reached the engraved wall. Still, my spine tells me that this opening will lead us to it."

The crevice hadn't been a straight drop. Nor had it been sheer.

The opening was a jagged cut that led down in a zig-zag fashion between outcroppings of boulders. At the bottom the blackness of a narrow opening was just visible from the proper angle of view. It didn't appear too hazardous if the climbers took their time and were careful.

Immediately the three set about the business of attaching the rope lines around their waists. No one wanted to take the chance of losing someone due to a misjudged step or loss of balance.

Michael began the descent first with Dr. Weatherbee bringing up the rear so he could keep an eye on the woman in the center. Behind the elder professor they'd secured the tether to an outcropping.

The descent was slow going and by the time all three were safely gathered in the shadow of the crevice, they needed to catch their breaths.

The opening yawned before them.

A chilling air breathed out from its mouth.

Emmy shivered. "I never thought to bring a jacket."

Theodore responded to that. "That's one of the reasons a preliminary investigation is made. By doing that we can determine what kind of equipment we'll need for the actual exploration."

"Well," Michael added, "hopefully we won't be in there all that long this first time. We only need to check it out far enough to be sure we're in the right place."

"Can you remember the way from your dream?" Emmy asked.

The man wiped a forearm across his forehead. "Sorry, this opening's all new to me," he said, glancing into the blackness. "But this time we have three flashlights with fresh batteries."

At the mention of the lanterns, each member automatically reached for their personal light. Beforehand, they'd attached them to their belts with small clips. They had meticulously planned out the gear and weren't going to be caught off guard like Michael had been in his dreamscape.

Now they simultaneously checked their lights and shined them into the blackness of the cave.

Excitement pulled them forward. And they stepped into the coolness.

Dr. Weatherbee closely examined the interior walls. He was visibly shaking with excitement. "Natural formations," he muttered as he shuffled in further. Then he gave his full attention to the overall structure of the cave. His light beam was added to the two already spearing through the ebony blackness. All the walls were naturally formed. The ceiling was nearly thirty feet above them. As the joined light beams moved downward to eye level again, they were lost in a tunnel opening. Its dimensions were small. It was only waist high.

Michael's voice echoed eerily within the embalmed stillness. "This entry cave is like an anteroom of some sort. It's all quite natural, geologically speaking, that is. But that," he said, indicating the tunnel with his light, "that is something else again. See how it's arched on top?"

The three now moved over to the opening. They crouched and scanned their beams along the interior of the tiny passageway. The lights were bright on the wall directly ahead, for the tunnel took an immediate turn ten feet in.

"I wonder how far it goes at that height?" Emmy questioned. She'd been thinking of the elder professor and how difficult it'd be for him to crawl for any length of time.

Michael had shared her unvoiced concern. "I don't know, I never crawled through anything like this in my dreams. Maybe I should go in a short way to see what's what." He looked over to Weatherbee for the go-ahead.

The elder man had been oblivious to the couple's conversation. He'd been deeply engrossed with the wall of the tunnel that'd been chiseled.

"Incredible, just incredible," he uttered to himself while glancing his fingertips over the glassy smoothness of the surface.

"Theo?"

"Yes, yes, my boy. Amazing, isn't it?"

"Theo, we need to get some idea as to the length of this low passageway. You can't grovel around on your hands and knees for any length of time so Emmy and I thought I could go in first to see how far this thing goes before. . ."

"Well go ahead, boy! We're right behind you," he prodded with a flick of his wrist.

Michael looked to the woman.

She rolled her eyes. "Go on, like he said, we're right behind you."

"Theo, I really don't. . .oh never mind," Michael said, seeing the old man's rising anticipation. And, on hands and knees, he began to move cautiously through the tunnel.

Like moles the trio inched forward along the twisted maze that sloped first downward then up a good distance before finally heading down and down for what seemed like an eternity. By now they'd lost all sense of direction, yet were relieved to still be breathing good air. After over an hour on their knees the passageway opened up and they could finally stand.

Weatherbee's bones creaked with the effort of uprighting himself.

Before them, a corridor stretched for the length of twenty yards or so before it veered off to the left. The walls appeared to be natural formations again.

Michael's sense of deja vu returned full strength when he stood and leaned on the wall to balance himself. With the perception of the eerie feeling, he slowly turned his head to Emmy. "I've touched this wall before. This is usually where the dreams begin. This corridor will angle off and make three left turns before it meets the smooth wall."

"The one with the glyphs?" Weatherbee gushed.

"Yes."

"Good god, man! Let's go!"

Emmy's hand shot out to rest on the man's. "No."

"*No?*" the man shouted. "What do you mean no? Why, we're so close!"

Her voice was expressionless. "We're too close this day. We can't go farther without the papyrus. He's waiting for it and we can't go in empty-handed."

The two men looked at one another.

Weatherbee was incredulous. "You don't believe that, do you, Michael? You can't think that the Ka would harm us now—not when he knows our intentions!"

"I'm sorry, Theo, but I got this feeling in my gut that says she's right about this. We came in here to make sure we were in the right place and we found out we are. There's just no reason to continue on without the papyrus. We came here to. . ."

". . .explore!" Weatherbee barked, charging ahead. "And explore is exactly what we're going to do!"

Just then a muted peal of rumbling thunder reverberated through the thick mesa walls.

The old man stumbled. He staggered. "Damn!"

The two rushed forward to support him.

"You all right?" Emmy worried.

Michael helped Weatherbee regain his balance. "What happened, Theo?"

"Well dammit, man! Can't you see I tripped over that cursed rock there?"

Emmy aimed her light to the ground, then into Weatherbee's confused face. "Dr. Weatherbee? What rock?"

The elder man impatiently grabbed at the flashlight that swung from his belt and frantically scanned its beam erratically over the dirt floor.

Shadows danced on the walls. No obstacle was to be found.

"Well dammit! I did stumble over a rock. Maybe it rolled somewhere."

Three yellow beams searched the dusty floor. No such obstacle could be found anywhere.

Theodore shuddered. "Oh let's get the hell out of here," he growled in defeated frustration. "We'll be back early in the morning and have all day down here. I suppose there's no reason to go further now."

Back outside, the long slant of the late afternoon sun cast an orange tint to the surrounding landscape. It looked like an old tintype photograph in sepia colors.

The three explorers had expected to exit into a raging desert storm, yet the sky was cloudless. No one spoke of the mysterious clap of thunder that vibrated through the seventh mesa. No one had any doubt in their minds as to its powerful source.

As before, the younger man took the lead with Emmy in the center. Dr. Weatherbee found the ascent up through the crevice more difficult than the descent had been.

When the trio had reached the top they stood in transfixed wonder at the landscape that spread out below them.

From horizon to horizon, the expansive burning land had been transformed into one that silently smoldered. Its dying embers glowed in coppery colors. The terra cotta citadels appeared ethereal.

In rapt fascination the three people stood upon the umber rocks of the seventh mesa—the Fountainhead—and felt the retrograde of time as they were surrealistically carried to the fringe of reality.

Enchantment took hold.

In the mystical light of the primordial surround a palpable presence could be felt.

A hushed tranquility fell over the land and penetrated their souls with a gentle pulsing that was thick with magic. And, upon the land between the towering totems of time, they could nearly discern the sound of the Ancient Ones' slow footfalls. From somewhere deep within their souls they perceived the embodiment of a Causal Eminence—a slumbering Knowledge.

Suddenly the longest flaming arrows of the lowering sun flashed out to spear the incoming clouds. And the roaring fire in the sky emblazoned the land below in preternatural reflections that instilled a clear vision of a slowly rotating Medicine Wheel. The mystical surround became a sacred place where all points converged and the three were subliminally drawn into the Center of All Things.

Flaming reds faded to brilliant oranges.

Light pinks muted to lavender, then to grey.

The spell was broken. The expansive robe of dusk spread across the land.

A new chill in the air lanced through the trio's consciousness and brought the observers into sharp awareness.

The three looked at one another.

"God, that was magnificent," Michael whispered.

"Spectacular. Can't say as I've ever been so moved before," Weatherbee expressed, full of emotion.

Emmy's eyes were closed. Long black lashes rested delicately together. She had no words for what she'd felt. All she could do was to remain silent and absorb the ageless Benevolence that touched her receiving spirit. Slowly her lids opened and, gazing out upon the spreading hem of darkness, she knew something wondrous was going to happen in this high place of great wakan, for only she had heard the Standing Stone's whispered words that came on the soft wings of this mystical twilight.

The earth cooled. It sighed with the entrance of evenfall and, as the trio trudged back across the variegated shadows of the painted desert, they were silent in their personal perceptions of it.

Here and there armed saguaros loomed like mummified giants, their thick limbs frozen in time.

At the halfway point of their return trek, the scene was drenched in a silvery light that transformed the landscape into a mystical vision. Everything appeared to be alive with the mercurial glow of the moon. All was silent except for the crunching of human footfalls upon the dry, crusty ground.

Then, in the distance, a movement caught Emmy's attention. "Look," she pointed, "Over there. Is that a person?"

Someone shouted out to them. "Hey, you guys! Is that you?"

"It's Karen! What the hell is she doing out here after dark?" Weatherbee exclaimed. "KAREN! Over here!"

The crunching sounds quickened. Soon her labored breathing could be heard. And as she came running up to them she babbled nonstop in their faces.

"Oh God. Oh God. Am I glad to see *you* guys!" she spat breathlessly. "Shit! I never been so damned scared in my life! That's the last time you go off an' leave me all alone!"

Michael grabbed her shoulders. "Is the papyrus all right?"

The woman's eyes widened in anger. The whites showed in the moonlight. "What! I tell you how friggin' scared I've been and all you can ask about is that damned. . .*thing*? I don't believe this shit!"

"I'm sorry, Karen," Michael apologized, "but you know how valuable it is. Is it all right?"

"YES! Your precious paper is just friggin' FINE!"

Michael breathed easier. "Okay, Karen, now tell us why you're so scared?"

Her voice cracked with nervousness. "Well. . .right after you guys left I got to thinking about all that stuff my uncle told me about. You know, about that thing in the bedroom drawer an' how people have died because of it."

"Go on, go on," Weatherbee prodded.

"Well. . .it made me kinda jumpy. And then. . .then when I was sitting at the table thumbing through a magazine I got this real scary feeling. I mean, really *creepy*! Oh God. These *goosebumps* popped out all over me an' my hair felt like it was moving! I was so scared! So I turned, expecting to see someone standing in the passageway behind me, but nobody was there. Then I went back to the bedroom and peeked in that drawer. Well. . .the thing was still there, but I still had those goosebumps. Then. . .when I went back to the front and. . .when I sat down. . .something *outside* caught my eye. When I turned. . .when I turned to look out the window. . .that Indian was there!" The woman was trembling uncontrollably.

Dr. Weatherbee hugged his niece. "There, there. It's all right, we're here now."

"But," she cried hysterically through tears, "he just stood there *staring* at me! Oh God. I didn't know what to *do*! I was so scared! I couldn't bear to keep looking at him, so. . .so. . .I pulled the sh-shade down and ran to the bedroom to peak out through the bl-blinds. God, oh God. He was *gone!* I raced to every window but he just wasn't *anywhere*! I can't deal with this sp-spooky shit!" Bravely she tried to mute her sobs.

"He can't hurt you, Karen," Emmy tried to sooth. "He's not real."

"Ohhh shit," she moaned.

"My dear," Weatherbee spoke with refined dignity. "There is much of reality you've yet to learn about. These things. . .these manifestations. . .are not at all uncommon in native cultures."

Karen stiffened. "I'm not native and I don't care if they're as common as mom an' apple pie! I got the living crap scared out of me today and you weren't anywhere around. Do you know how hard it was for me to stay in that stinking RV all day never knowing when or where that, that. . .that *ghost* might reappear next? Well, I can tell you one thing Mister, I am not letting you three out of my sight again! Maybe *you* don't mind playing footsies with spooks, but I don't want any part of it!"

Weatherbee grew irritated with the new situation. "Karen, dear," he humored, "we need you to hold down the fort. Tomorrow's going to be the big day and then we'll be finished here. Then we'll be on our way."

"Fine," she said haughtily, "four will be fun."

"Ahhh, dear. . .no. . .no. Four is quite impossible, you see."

She spun to flare at her uncle. "Then make it possible!"

No one spoke after the woman's final outburst. The group walked back to the RV in heavy silence—each one deep in their own private thoughts—each one full of personal determination for the ultimate outcome to end their way.

Someone was going to lose.

Once inside the lighted vehicle a minimum amount of conversation was voiced. A cold politeness and cursory replies passed between Karen and the others. They all knew there was much more to be said yet nobody dared approach the subject; it was still too raw. In the morning when some of the tenderness had healed it'd be broached again.

Emmy, unused to strained relationships, bid Karen a goodnight and announced to the others that she was going outside to take in the beautiful night.

The coolness of the silver-splashed desert night was immediately refreshing. Overhead a multitude of heavenly bodies winked down from the high firmament. A gentle breeze hushed over the land. Out in the expansive surround it was hard to imagine that there were crowded cities with millions of people in them. Out in the sweet serenity of nature it was hard to visualize any type of thriving civilization.

Emmy strolled over to a tall saguaro and stared thoughtfully up at it.

"What does it say?" came a soft whisper from behind her.

She turned to smile at Michael. In the gleaming moonlight she saw the flash of his teeth behind the wide grin.

"Saguaros don't speak, silly," she replied.

"Oh? I thought all of nature spoke. I thought Indians could hear all their different languages."

"You ought to know," she said in seriousness, "you're half Indian."

"Yeah, well," he hesitated, kicking at the dusty sand with his boot.

"What does that mean?"

"It means that I haven't had time to get in touch with my native half," he responded with embarrassment.

Silence.

"Em? You hear what I said?"

"I heard, Michael." She paused before speaking again. "The issue isn't one of race. That's not what counts. It's one's inner sensitivity that matters in such things. It's what's in their hearts and spirits that make them receptive to nature's tongue."

He raised his head to peer up at the giant cactus. "So why doesn't Mr. Saguaro here speak then?"

Her tone was reverent. "He does, but not like the Standing Stones that whisper words. Nature does not speak in words. It speaks to us through conveyed *feelings*."

"Em?"

"Yes?"

"She can't come with us tomorrow."

"I know that."

"What're we going to do?"

"Don't you know?"

Her cryptic reply puzzled him. A long silence fell between them before he offered his guess. "The Ka?"

"No, Michael, someone else. Tomorrow you and I must have a talk with our silent observer."

"That spook that keeps vanishing?"

"Listen to you. Now you're talking like Karen. Now you're talking like a fullblood Caucasian. Where's my knowledgeable anthropologist?"

"But Em, he's just a created figment of the Ka's mind."

She smiled sweetly. "Is he?"

He made no comment.

"Michael?"

"What, Em?"

"It's time to get in touch with your other half."

Part Three
REALM OF THE KA

The Fledgling Seeker grasps at Illusions and calls them Enlightenment, while the Seasoned Seeker possesses no desire for the empty Shells of illusions, but rather walks beyond them toward the Pure Reality of True Wisdom and Enlightenment.

The Shaman

Desert sunrise.
Tongues of flame.
Vermilion mesas.

The golden Eye of Ra looked down upon the singed land and watched the slow advancement of the two humans as they made their way across the expanse of cracked earth.

The high drama being played out upon the Burning Place Above was intense. Ra would watch the movements of the players. The final act was going to be something to remember—something auspicious. From his high royal vantage point he would watch and wait.

Upon the surface of the baked land Emmy and Michael were headed toward Zuni. Weatherbee had driven them back as far as the highway and he had been able to go a ways into the brush until the RV was halted at a deep wash. He and Karen were going to wait there for the couple's return.

The senior member hadn't liked the unexpected delay in getting back down into the Seventh Mesa, but after listening to the pair's reasoning he'd eventually seen the logic of the delay and finally acquiesced to the plan.

Clearly, the old Indian man was an elder of great wisdom and power. It hadn't made much sense that he was appearing and vanishing just to warn them. A confrontation had to be made before they could continue with their purpose. And so it was that the couple now trekked across the desert to seek the adept sage who kept sending his spirit out to meet them along the wayside of their long journey.

The couple's boots crunched on the stony, dry ground. They'd been walking in the early morning light for over an hour.

"This isn't as bad as I thought," Michael commented.

Emmy glanced up into the sky. "Sun's barely cleared the horizon. You'll change your mind in another hour or so."

He shielded his eyes with his hand and followed her gaze. "How much farther do you think?"

"A ways yet—maybe a little over an hour—maybe less. Depends."

"On what?"

"On how difficult our friend wants to make it."

"I thought we concluded that we were supposed to talk to him."

"We did." She turned to look at him. She eyed him with a hint of exasperation. "You don't know Indians very well, do you?"

Silence.

"You really should've taken some time to get in touch with your heritage—get to know your own people. For your information, professor, the native people don't allow their days to be run by clocks. Their entire systems are in tune with the Grand Timepiece of Grandmother Earth. Mechanical time is irrelevant. Their time is based on their personal readiness for the performance of certain actions. Inner *feelings* determine the precise time for certain actions."

Her companion thought long on that bit of information. "You didn't have to go into all that explanation but, when you think about it, that's really quite a beautiful way to live."

She smiled. "Few native people have ulcers. Those come from time and the pressures of it. Clocks don't run our lives—we do."

Michael became thoughtful. "When this is all over, Em, I'm going to do some serious thinking."

"Oh?"

"Yes. Just look around, Emmy, just look around." His arm extended and swept through the heating air. A quiet excitement was building in his voice. "I've seen deserts before, but before I've always just been there for research purposes. Now, suddenly I've got this deep urge to spend more time here." He shook his head. "I dunno, ever since we started crossing New Mexico that first day, this strange feeling's been growing inside me. It's like a strong pull—a powerful magnet—that wants me to stay for a while. Do you know what I mean? Am I making any sense at all?"

She grinned with understanding, but said nothing.

"Em?"

"What?"

"Do you think it's the Ka? The strangeness of it all? Do you think he's the source of this feeling I have?"

"Could be." Her tone wasn't the least bit convincing.

"But you don't believe that, do you."

"Does it matter what I believe?"

"Of course it does." He skipped around in front of her and walked backwards. "Tell me what you really think."

The delicate corners of her mouth tipped up. "It could be the anthropologist in you. This area reeks with native history—prehistory. Could be that's what you're sensing."

He gave her a smirk. "I asked you to tell me what you really think."

"It's what you think, Michael. It's what you feel in here," she said, pointing to her heart.

He stopped and gently held her arms. "Emmy, I do feel certain things there, but they're too confusing yet. I can't seem to sort them out into distinct ideas."

Her sapphire eyes sparkled with love for the man before her, yet they also held a sliver of compassion.

"Michael, each one must travel within to clearly see their own path ahead. It cannot be otherwise. One must walk the Within Trail before the Without Path can be approached."

He gazed past her to scan the horizon behind her, then his eyes locked on hers. "I don't want deep philosophy here, Em. I need answers."

"Yes. . .answers. They are found along the Within Trail, Michael."

His hands dropped to his side. He sighed. "You know, don't you."

"Perhaps."

His head tilted to peer questioningly at her. "Em?"

She was gravely solemn. "Yes, Michael, I do know. But. . ."

He finished her thought. ". . .but I have to travel within."

She nodded.

His palms came up in defeat. "Okay. All right. But answer me this—can you help me do this? Can you come with me on this trail?"

"I can lead you to its entry gate but you must walk through it alone."

"Oh boy, that's what I was afraid you'd say."

"Afraid? You?"

He chuckled. "Well, maybe afraid isn't exactly the word I want. Maybe I meant something like lonely. Maybe I just wanted some company on this journey inward."

"Lonely? Company? You surprise me. The Within Trail is never a lonely one. It's all those paths we choose to walk Without that are the solitary and desolate ones. Those are the ones we feel most alone upon."

And again, the woman had given him much to ponder over while they continued walking in silence over the desert floor.

Forty minutes had passed before they spotted the scattering of adobe dwellings in the distance.

"That can't be Zuni," Michael frowned.

"No, but it can be a settlement."

Soon they were close enough to hear the laughter and giggling of playing children. When they gained more ground, the child's game abruptly halted. All pairs of ebony eyes were on the two strangers.

Emmy spoke softly. "Hi. I'm Mourning Elk. This is Michael Greystone. We're looking for an elder who wears a blue headband."

Suspicious eyes widened and looked to one another.

No one spoke.

The little ones stared at the brilliant blue eyes of the fullblood. They'd heard stories of such a one. . .magical stories.

The woman realized they noticed. She didn't like their awestruck expressions. She tried to be extra friendly. "That looked like a fun game you were playing."

Silence.

"We need to find where the elder lives. He's expecting us. Do you know of him?"

Nobody moved a muscle. It was as if the group of little ones had turned to stone.

Emmy eyed Michael.

And that small movement broke the spell. The kids scattered like autumn leaves before the winter wind. In a flash, not one could be seen, they'd all disappeared into the adobes.

Michael shrugged. "Guess we start knocking on doors."

"You do that and you'll be knocking till your knuckles are raw—nobody will be home."

"What do you mean, nobody'll be home? Those kids just ran home."

The woman sighed. "Come on, just follow me. I'll show you how to get answers." After several minutes, she said. "For someone being half Indian you sure got a lot to learn about native ways and respectful protocol." She tossed her head back in a teasing manner. "You've been locked up too long in those eastern museums."

Her off-the-cuff remark struck a thundering blow. What she'd said was true, but now the realization of it held new meaning for the man. Now those words pulled at his heart and tugged forcefully. He had been sequestered in the cellar recesses of the ivy-covered buildings back east. He had all but ignored the culture of his ancestors in deference to delving into those of others. What had he missed all these years? From deep within the depths of himself he now had the gnawing feeling that he'd ignored his heritage far too long. Deep within, he knew some major changes were in the offing.

Side by side, the two travelers strolled into the center of the clustered buildings. They were simple structures, but good houses didn't necessarily have to be elaborately constructed in order to be beautiful homes. And these possessed their own unique beauty.

The square was empty. Silence pervaded the tiny village.

There was a touchable sense of suspended time—of waiting. Inside the dwellings, the occupants waited.

Outside, the two strangers waited.

Even the breeze had stilled itself in anxious expectation—it held its breath while the village waited.

Emmy spoke in lowered tones. "We'll sit here," she said, indicating a wooden sun-bleached bench. "It's best if we don't speak. We'll just sit here to show our respect for their own time."

And the two outsiders sat patiently in the growing heat of the climbing sun. Rivulets of sweat dripped from their brows and stung their eyes. Occasionally a tattered window curtain moved ever so slightly.

Thirty minutes passed. Ten more crawled by.

Emmy's blouse stuck like second skin.

Michael's shirt was soaked through.

Yet they remained tolerant of their discomfort for another twenty minutes before their perseverance paid off.

A door creaked open.

A woman in a colorful flowered skirt stood in her doorway and stared out at the strangers for a long moment. She stepped out from the cool shadows and slowly crossed the square.

The two stood.

"You lookin' for old man with blue band?" the woman asked, in awe of Emmy's unusual eyes.

"Yes," Emmy softly admitted.

"Why you lookin' for him?"

Emmy explained how he'd been calling to them.

The woman's expression remained unchanged as she stared deep into the younger woman's blue eyes, then into the man's dark ones. Her head slowly turned to the north. Her arm came up and a finger uncurled to point their way.

"Thank you very much," Emmy said, nudging her companion out of the drama.

"Yes, thank you," he said, nodding his head like a dancing fishing bobber.

The Indian woman made no comment. She stood and watched the pair amble off to the north.

"Don't look back," Emmy advised under her breath. "And don't look at the other houses either."

Michael dutifully kept his eyes straight ahead. "Why?" he whispered.

"It's not polite."

"Oh."

The turquoise canopy of sky was too bright to directly look up into. Wispy white clouds stretched here and there in their bed of blue, and the fiery orb paused lethargically at its midpoint before drowsily ambling down its dusty trail of sky. The desert slowly simmered as the landscape strained to breathe. Yet amid the burning intensity there was a stark beauty that couldn't be denied. A subtle brilliance pulsed through the torridness. There appeared to be a gentle peacefulness where Grandmother Earth rested in sweet repose.

Upon the scorched land, scarlet blossoms smiled out from their spiny homes of green and grey cactus. Here and there, fresh yellow flowers grinned up to greet the passersby. Lizards comically sunned in the caustic heat. A land untouched by the ravages of civilization sighed in its primitive purity.

Cobalt blue flowers. Saffron yellow petals. Silvery blue-green sage.

It was a forgotten place where time stood still. Bleached cattle bones stood out in stark relief from the bronze and cinnamon-colored backdrop. Redstone arches. Sandstone buttes. Flaming mesas. It was an artist's study in still life. The unmoving scene had been artfully painted upon an eternal canvas.

Nothing moved.

Chalky buffalo skulls stared.

Nothing moved.

Except for a lone nighthawk that suddenly sliced down through his deep sea of blue to disappear beyond a distant ridge. And when the desert walkers reached the deep-cut arroyo, they looked down across the wide ravine and saw a single dwelling perched upon the dusty ridge of the opposite side. The ground surrounding it appeared to shimmer like an oil slick.

Michael wiped his forehead. "Almost looks like a mirage, doesn't it."

"Yes. But then again, that is how some medicine people's place can look."

Her companion grinned. "It better be there when we climb up out of that ravine."

She returned the smile. "It will be there."

They wasted no time scrambling down the dry dirt of the jagged crevice. It'd been wider than it initially appeared from above. It took ten minutes to cross its littered wash. Remnants of flash floods scattered its floor. Dried branches of juniper, cattle bones, and piles of stones were haphazardly strewn about.

Picking their way through the debris they reached the far side and struggled to ascend the steepness of the rise. Once they had managed to gain the ridge crest they stood tall to see the tiny dwelling piercing the horizon plane.

"Told you it'd still be here."

"Yeah. Well, let's just hope our friend hasn't run down to the mall for a new headband or something."

She clicked her tongue. "Tsk-tsk. That was disrespectful."

And again they struck out across the cracked earth, only this time, their destination was clearly in their sights.

"We gonna have to sit it out again when we get there?" Michael groaned with the dreaded remembrance of the last time.

"Depends. If he's not immediately visible we will."

"Still don't see why we can't just go up an' knock on his door."

"I told you, it's not. . ."

"I know, I know. It's not polite. But why isn't it polite?"

Her voice was soft. "One's home is their sacred ground. It's where the occupants have established their own surround of personal energies and circle of protection."

"Kinda like setting up individualized vibrations," he said.

"Yes, kind of. It's much more complex than that, though. Listen. What if the occupant were praying—meditating? What if they were in the middle of performing a precise ceremony, like a Healing Way, for instance? It'd be the height of rudeness to interrupt such things. So the visitor patiently sits quietly outside until the occupant takes notice of him and is free."

Her companion mulled that one over. "And what if the occupant doesn't want to acknowledge the waiting visitor?"

"Then, after a reasonable amount of time that becomes apparent and the visitor goes away, maybe trying again another time or another day."

His brow rose. "Are we going to have to try again another day?"

A sudden movement caught Emmy's eye. She followed the exit of the nighthawk. Intently she watched it climb high in the sky until it was nothing larger than a dark pinpoint vanishing within the depths of the blue.

"Depends."

"Depends?" he repeated.

"Yes," she sighed, sitting on the ground before the dwelling. "Depends how long that hawk stays away."

Michael sat beside her and peered around into her face. "What's the bird got to do with the old man?"

Her eyes were cold. "Everything. Our man's not at home right now."

Michael stood again. He scanned the horizon.

"What're you looking for?" she asked.

"Movement. I'm trying to see if he's coming yet."

The woman slowly shook her head. "Sit down, Michael. He won't be coming from that direction."

He turned east and scanned the rugged terrain of that direction.

"Michael, he won't be coming from that way either. He won't be coming *across*. . .he'll be coming *down*."

His eyes locked on hers. He sat. "Then he is in there—his *physical* aspect."

She shrugged. "I can't say for sure. Some native adepts have ways of truly leaving. . .of. . .altering."

Silence fell between them as they each became lost in private thoughts while they waited for the adept to return home.

The young professor gazed out over the dry landscape and, seeing a new beauty to it, he no longer wondered what the remote desert held to attract and keep its human dwellers. His new perception had a definite connection to the growing awareness that welled within his spirit.

There was something primordial about this place.

His sights rested on a nearby saguaro. Its arms, crooked at the elbow joints, poised in frozen greeting, or was it warning to stay away? This primitive land was indeed a timeless place that minimized all the absurd trivialities of the world. And here, the plastic and chrome civilization felt like it was a figment of some child's wild imagining. Out here, in the gentle pause between nature's heartbeats, you could actually hear the earth's soft sighing as it breathed.

He looked up into the brilliance of the sky. Where was the bird? He'd heard of such feats performed by certain adept sages. The actual concept was far from new to him. Down through the ages, certain cultures had believed such transformations were possible and that their secrets were passed down from one adept to the other—the precise mechanics always remaining secret and sacred, always elusive to the outsider.

Had the old Indian really managed to alter his physical form? Was the dwelling now empty as suspected? Or was his *spirit* gone with the bird's consciousness? Was the man's *body* inside waiting for its consciousness to return?

The experienced anthropologist had never seen actual evidence of the performance of the feat. It had always been a grey area where the more obscure legends and folklore were relegated to because there were no verified eyewitnesses or solid evidence. No authoritative figure of science had ever been able to document the highly mystical feat of transmutation. And the more Dr. Greystone thought on it, the more it both bothered and excited him. Was the body of the old man in there or not?

The researcher in him came forward to dominate the moment.

Like a rampaging buffalo, the scientist charged to the forefront of his mind to override his finer sense of propriety.

From his sitting position in the sun, he silently leaned forward to rest his weight on his hands.

The woman beside him frowned at his curious action.

Slowly. Slowly, the hands and knees worked alternately as he crawled stealthily forward.

Realization struck like white lightning. Emmy's eyes flared. "Michael!" she whispered. "What're you doing?"

His head craned back as a finger came to his lips. "I've got to know," he whispered back.

"That's insane! You might ruin everything if he finds out."

His hand waved at her as if to say everything would be just fine and to calm down. . .not to worry.

The woman heaved a great sigh of peaked exasperation and fearfully scanned the blue expansiveness above them. A tight knot began to twist in her stomach. One minute her eyes were on the sky, the next they were on the man. Anxiously, back and forth they darted.

He'd reached the open window on the side of the dwelling. He crouched beneath it and slowly rose. His eyes cleared the ledge and scanned the one room interior.

A simple bed wedged up against the far wall, neat blankets pulled across it. Bundles of feathers, herbs and a medicine pouch hung from the wall. Handmade pottery and jars lined a makeshift wooden shelf. In the center, a rickety table stood with a lantern on it. Two chairs. The faint scent of cedar and sweetgrass wafted out.

But that was all.

No man sat within the tiny room.

The place was empty.

Michael quickly slunk back to the waiting woman. "Hope you're right about the hawk," he muttered. "Or we've come for nothing."

"He gone?"

Michael grinned. "Flew the coop."

Emmy rolled her eyes. "Oh, that was real cute."

"Yeah, I know. I couldn't resist it," he said, smiling sheepishly.

"Well? Do we wait?"

"We wait."

And they did.

They waited and waited.

Suddenly Michael perked up. "You hear something?"

Emmy had.

They scanned the sky.

The sound of flapping wings grew louder. The nighthawk came from behind and flew over them. It descended behind the lone dwelling.

The two stood and brushed off their clothing. When they again looked to the adobe house, their man was standing in the doorway.

Two hearts lunged.

Michael cleared his throat. Without taking his eyes from the elder with the blue headband, he whispered to his companion. "I see him but I'm not sure I believe it."

"Believe it," she managed to say back.

"What now?"

"We wait."

The old man then backed into the shadows of his dwelling.

"What's that mean?" Michael mumbled.

"It means we follow."

"How do you know that?"

"Protocol," she said, stepping forward.

The little room was surprisingly cool beneath the late afternoon sun. It felt good to be in some shade. Their eyes took several minutes to adjust to the darkness.

The old man sat cross-legged in a corner that faced the eastern doorway. He stared ahead.

The two sat in front of him and Emmy spoke first. "We came because you called us."

Silence.

Michael looked from one face to the other.

Emmy hadn't taken her eyes off the man who appeared to be staring through her. "You've followed us," she said.

Silence.

Michael was about to speak but the woman held up her hand in caution while she continued. "We've come to hear your wisdom," she said, pulling some tobacco out of her medicine bag that hung from her belt. She placed it on the floor between them.

A flicker of light flashed from his ebony eyes.

Emmy continued to speak to him. "You know why we're out there."

"I know," came the deep and slow voice.

Both visitors were intent on the wrinkled face that'd been leathered by years in the desert sun. The features were permanently etched into a striking character.

He spoke again. "You tread upon the Screaming, Burning Place Above. . .the sacred ground."

"Yes, because its spirit called us there."

Silence hung like thick smoke between them before the elder spoke again. "Spirit has much powerful medicine."

"We've seen his medicine," Emmy softly admitted.

The man's eyes flared. He studied the woman, then the young man before returning his attention back to her. "Yes," he whispered. "Nightwalkers see many things. . .dreamers see too."

Now it was clear that the aged one was a true visionary. Emmy recalled seeing a nighthawk that took notice of her spirit's presence when she took her spirit journey to the mesa. Now she knew the nighthawk and the man sitting before her were one and the same.

Her voice was reverent. "Along the wayside of our journey here, were you just observing us?"

His nod was barely perceptible.

"To warn us?"

Again the head moved up and down.

"Warn of what? The spirit of the mesa called us. He's expecting us."

This time the head went the other way. "Spirit expectin' two," he said, holding up two fingers. "Maybe three. There are four of you. Four are fatal." While he talked, the man's wizened eyes kept shifting over to Michael.

"Us two?" Emmy asked.

The native elder nodded.

"Us two and Dr. Weatherbee?"

Again a nod.

Michael spoke. "The other woman is a great problem. We know that. She wasn't supposed to be with us but she snuck on the vehicle without us knowing of it."

"Spirit of mesa, he knew. He tried to warn you."

"Yes, we know that now but we didn't know what he was trying to warn us about at the time. When we found out it was too late."

"It never be too late. I tried to warn too."

Emmy smiled at the thought of how he'd tried to warn Karen away.

"Your warning caused her to be so frightened now that she won't let us out of her sight. She's very scared," Emmy informed.

"I do not bring harm to living things," he said in return.

"Yes, we know that, but she doesn't."

"That is why she is dangerous. Her mind, it is not opened."

"So," Michael said, "how do we keep her from coming with us?"

"Been taken care of already."

The three remained silent for several minutes until Emmy broke the heavy stillness. "How? How has it been taken care of?"

"That is not important. The woman is safe. She will be out of your way. Four is fatal."

Michael didn't know what was going on. He wasn't sure he wanted to know how Karen had been taken care of, but if the man said she was safe, that would be the least of their worries now. The researcher in him took over. "You've known about the Seventh Mesa, haven't you."

The elder's eyes closed and he nodded.

"For how long have you known?"

"When the grandfathers gathered to tell what their grandfathers heard from their grandfathers, I listened. And I believed. We know about the Burning Place Above that Screams. We always knew."

Michael leaned forward. "And what about what rests beneath it?"

"That too," came the soft reply. "The People keep sacred things sacred. . .always." The old man slid his eyes over to the woman. "Ones with blood of star brothers also know. In here," he whispered, pointing to his heart, "in here the knowing is like a living thing."

Emmy's scalp prickled. Yes, she knew. "We won't tell anyone, Grandfather."

"Yes, we know that too. We all know that."

His statement was clear and the woman expanded on it. "The children, the ones in the village back there were afraid of us, weren't they."

He nodded.

"Because they knew who we were."

"Yes. Because they are fearful of those who are called by the

Spirit of the Seventh Mesa out there. The Spirit has great power. Them little ones see your eyes. They know what them eyes mean. That scare them too."

"Have you been beneath the Seventh Mesa?" she asked.

Silence.

The answer was written in his knowing eyes. He had.

"Can you tell us?"

"Mourning Elk, do not ask this. You will see for yourself if the Spirit allows it. But. . .you will see nothing that you do not already know here. . .in your heart. The old stories are alive. They are true."

"Old stories?" Michael remarked.

The wise elder looked suspiciously to the young male visitor. "Yes. . .old tales. . .the stories. You are of the People yet you are not. By your own choosing you have cut the mind off from the native heart that beats in your chest and from the native spirit that lives inside you."

Michael's cheeks flushed at the man's directness. He lowered his head in embarrassment, for he knew the man spoke truth.

"But," the elder continued, "that is not how it will end for you. Your ears will hear the whispers that ride the wings of the Wind Spirits. Your eyes will open to see the old wonders. Your fingers will touch things you thought not touchable. Your heart will feel new things and. . .one day your spirit will walk the path of the Way. It can not be any other way for you. Already you know this is true."

Michael was moved to silence.

Emmy picked up the thread of their former talk. "Why did the Spirit of the Mesa choose us?"

The old man looked away, then back. "Maybe he will tell you this thing. It is not for me to say the words that can only come from his own mouth."

"Then you know."

He nodded, then spoke of the mesa. "Beneath Grandmother's breast are many secrets that were buried long ago. Men believe they have it all figured out. They think they have all the answers. But they like to make all the ends nice and neat. They do not even believe in those others."

His eyes raised to the smoke-stained ceiling. "Long ago. . .our People called them the Bird People because they came out of the sky. . .but now. . ." he smiled, "we know better." His eyes squinted with twinkles while he moved his arms to animate his words. "Now we know who they really are. Now we know all about those other people who came here from places among the stars. They were the ones who taught our people long ago. They were the ones who taught our people to love Grandmother Earth and they gave us our sacred ceremonies and wakan ways.

"Today we still keep those same secrets safe here, in our hearts. Those others, those people in the world out there do not believe." He grinned wide. "That is okay. They are going to find out one day how wrong they have been thinking all this time."

An orange ray of light speared through the window opening. The sun was setting. The tiny room glowed with the brilliance of nature's colorful display.

The old man rose.

The visitors followed his lead.

Outside, the flaming disc had descended below the western horizon and a greyness began to wash over the land. In the distance, a faint sound of a roar could be heard. Two gold headlights bounced toward them.

The old man grinned when his visitors looked to him. "My grandson. He is going to take you back. You would never find your way in the dark. Besides," he smiled, "your camp moved." And with those final words he turned to disappear back into the darkness of the desert dwelling.

The Jeep screeched to a skidding stop. Dust billowed around the vehicle. "Hey, let's go!" said the driver. "I got a hot date waiting for me."

And the three took off in the dusty Jeep.

Five minutes away, Michael slapped his knee. "Dammit! I needed to ask him something." He looked hopefully to the young driver. "Can we go back. . .just for a minute? It's really important."

The teenager looked to the sky, then to his passenger. "Could. Then again, it wouldn't do any good."

"Why not?"

Emmy jabbed Michael's arm and pointed to the moonlit sky.

A winged creature sliced through the silver disc. "He's not home."

"Yeah man," said the boy, "he's always flyin' the coop."

The two passengers eyed each other. Evidently the young driver was used to his grandfather's mystical journeys and didn't think it was anything special.

"Hey!" the boy said, "I'm supposed to tell you two that your lady friend walked into a rattler's nest and they weren't none too thrilled about it."

"What!" Michael spat.

"Hey, it's cool. Lucky for her I came by when I did 'cause I was able to drive her over to my aunt's house. She's a medicine woman and real good with snake bites. Anyway, the lady's over there resting. Probably shouldn't move her for a couple days, though." The driver chuckled. "Man, your lady friend sure was hysterical. Can't do that crazy hysterical stuff with snake bites."

"You sure she's all right?" Emmy worried.

"Oh yeah. Not to worry. My aunt really knows her stuff."

Emmy was pensive for a moment. So that's how Karen was taken care of, she thought. It appeared that the gods had everything taken care of.

Michael interrupted her thoughts when he spoke to the driver. "Your grandfather mentioned something about our camp being moved. What'd he mean by that?"

The grandson concentrated on maneuvering in the rough terrain of the desert. "Seems the old guy you left behind took it in his head to move your RV in closer to the mesa."

Michael and Emmy glared at each other. Then Michael stared at the driver's silhouette that was outlined in a silvery aura of high moonlight. The feeling he got was more than unsettling. "How come you just happened to come along when they needed you out there?"

The driver shrugged. "Guess it was their lucky day. Some coincidence, huh man?"

"Yeah, some coincidence," Michael whispered suspiciously while eyeing Emmy.

Both knew there was something not quite right with the entire scenario that the driver had outlined. Both had heads full of unanswered questions. It had all happened a bit too smoothly.

Michael squeezed Emmy's knee, then looked to the man beside him. "So, how come you were out there in the first place?"

"Just passin' through."

"I thought that region was high wakan," Michael pushed.

"It is man, it is!"

"Then why were you there if the place is so sacred?"

"Hey, what is this third-degree stuff? Can't a guy go four-wheelin' through the desert?"

"Well yes, normally he could, but you were four-wheeling through sacred ground. Weren't you a little bit scared to go there?"

The driver turned to face the questioner. His teeth glistened in the ghostly light of the moon. His grin was wide. "Scared? Nah, only *people* get scared."

The two riders felt a cold chill ripple up their spines and didn't dare pursue the matter further.

When the Jeep bumped to a stop they realized how far Weatherbee had moved their site. They climbed out and thanked the driver for the ride.

"No problem, man. I'd move mountains for that old man of mine." He gave them the high sign, stepped hard on the accelerator and wheeled off into the night.

The pair stared after the distancing vehicle.

"There's not a fog out there, is there?" Michael asked, peering hard into the darkness.

Emmy knew what he'd been referring to. She strained her eyes to spy the taillights that should've been visible for miles around on the dark flatland. And she strained her ears to hear its engine.

But the vehicle's sound had been as abruptly cut as the red eyes of its taillights.

Her voice was mildly hypnotic. "Fog? In the middle of this arid desert?" She chuckled nervously. "A dust devil would be more plausible. Maybe a dust devil came up suddenly out there."

"Yeah," he whispered back, "probably one of those dust devils."

But somehow neither of them believed it.

The air was still.

The desert was as still as a photograph.

Michael, groping around in his mind for some semblance of rationality, reached for another excuse to explain the sudden disappearance of the vehicle.

"Think maybe he had engine trouble?"

Emmy's head slowly turned to look up into the man's hopeful eyes. "Do you?"

He sighed heavily then. "Em?"

"Yes?"

"I'm beat. Let's call it a day."

The Descent

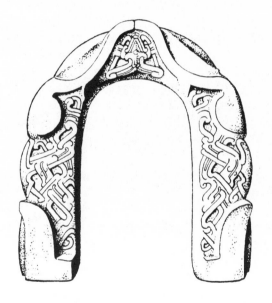

T here was a note from Dr. Weatherbee on the dinette table. The incident with Karen was explained. The elder professor had accompanied Karen and the young native man to the healer's house and afterward his niece appeared relieved to be away from the mesas. Theo had been driven back to their campsite where he moved the RV closer to their objective. The note expressed the doctor's amazement over how everything had worked out. The gods are with us, he'd written. He also conveyed his tiredness and apologized for going off to bed before they returned. Although he was anxious to hear how their meeting with the Indian went, he needed to get some solid rest before their explorations tomorrow. He'd talk to them then.

The pair turned and spotted Weatherbee sound asleep on the sofabed. It was clear that he'd left the double bed in the back room for his companions and, a few minutes later, the exhausted pair had gone to bed too.

The desert night wore on.

Above the spacious silent land the silvered circlet of moon arced high in the heavens. It arced like the wide swing of a great pendulum. The grand Universal Timepiece ticked through its designated constellations. And the gentle passing of time was marked by the mechanism's soundless movement through the sparkling firmament.

Far below, sitting incongruously out of place upon the quiet desert, the RV was dark. Within, the couple snuggled together. Window shades raised, the occupants found sleep hard to come by. They gazed up through the screening. Millions of twinkling eyes winked down at them.

"It's so beautiful," the woman reverently whispered, "So incredibly pristine and majestic."

198

The man tightened his arm about her shoulders. He'd been thinking like thoughts. "Looking up like this makes me feel as though we're the only two people in the world. It's like there's just us two floating in an endless sea of stars tumbling through the vastness of the eternal cosmos. It's so quiet. . .so peaceful."

"Mmm," she mumbled in agreement, nestling down further into the warm crook of his arm. "I'm used to seeing this whenever I walk out into the desert to pray beside the buttes. I'm used to seeing it, but I never have gotten used to the feel. Every time is just like the first. Every time is just as magnificent as the one before it. It never gets old."

Michael squeezed her. "And you won't ever get used to seeing it, will you?"

She smiled into the darkness. "No, not ever."

"Em?"

"What?"

"That elder was right about me, you know."

"Oh?"

"I have to come back here. I have to touch my roots, my heritage."

She silently listened to her companion's thoughts.

"I know the Cherokees weren't from around here, but this is where I feel I need to come."

Her tone was heavy with a hint of pain. "You sure you really want to do that?"

"You sound like I have reservations."

A shooting star burned across the heavens.

Emmy spied it. "You see that?"

"Yes. You make a wish?"

His question brought a heavy sigh. He really did have a lot of catching up to do. "No. My father used to tell me when I was only a little tyke that a shooting star was just Grandfather Sky letting a star fly from his mighty bow. It was Grandfather's way of letting his people know that, even though it was dark—nighttime—and we couldn't see him, he was still up there protecting us. It was Grandfather Sky's way of saying 'sleep tight, my children, for I'm still watching over you.' We always returned our thanks with a private silent prayer—never a wish."

The grave import of her words were not lost on the man. He felt somewhat embarrassed. "See, Em? That's just what I mean.

I've missed out on so much richness that I never had growing up. I've got to go back and learn all those beautiful things I've missed."

"They're not all beautiful, Michael. The Peoples' lives have been burdened with many hardships. There's much hatred alive in this country. Things are not all sweetness and beauty in our way of life."

They listened to the silence. They watched the Great Spirit's trail above.

Michael's voice was solemn. "That's what makes me feel so bad. That's what really hurts inside when I realize my own neglect. I've worked my way into the scientific community and I really believe I can begin to make some good changes."

She sighed. "Things don't change overnight. The country's opinion of the native People can't alter in one day—not when they've been set for centuries."

"It has to start with someone. At least I'll be able to shed some influence in my own field."

"In what way?"

"Remember that first class day when you spoke up about our Peoples' sacred grounds? The burial grounds?"

She grinned with the recall. "I remember."

"Well, that's just one area I may be able to help with. I may be able to initiate new guidelines for the archeologists who go around with their shovels digging up whatever they please. They've got to realize that Indian grave sites are just as holy as the consecrated grounds of their own churchyard cemeteries."

And on the tail of that idea, others quickly followed. His excitement grew rapidly. "And another thing, people need to see that the earth really is their mother. They've got to stop dumping all that hazardous waste into her. They've got to restrict the runaway mining. They've got to stop the nuclear insanity that's threatening the planet. Also, all that senseless. . ."

"Michael!" she soothed, leaning up on her elbow. "Settle down! What are you? Some red knight charging through the country like a great buffalo?"

He sheepishly grinned and pulled her back down to his chest. "Guess I did get a bit carried away. But now you see how intensely I feel about it. Things have got to change, Em. They've got to change."

"And you're going to do it?"

"I'm going to give it one hell of a try."

The weighted silence returned while Michael entertained visions of his new mission and, beside him, the woman's head was filled with the many worries that accompanied his images of valor. She refused to dwell on them further. "Michael?"

"Mmmm, hon?"

"Have you thought any more about the old man's grandson and what happened out there tonight with the Jeep?"

He stroked her silky hair while staring up into the starry sky. "Not really, I guess I felt it wasn't that important for us to understand everything we encounter."

"Well, I meant, have you wondered what he meant by what he said about only *people* being scared?"

"Looking back on it now I'd say he just meant other people. You have to consider the different childhood he probably had. Having an adept shaman for a grandfather would naturally alter your perspectives to some degree. He's been brought up with his mind steeped in mysticism and its realities. I hardly think the Burning Place Above would frighten him."

"That's the conclusion I'd come to too. The kid is most likely the elder's helper. He's probably seen it all. Did you notice how nonchalantly he commented about his grandfather not being home when you asked to go back?"

"Yeah," he smiled, "like it was no big deal that the old guy had spread wings."

"I would imagine someone growing up with that sort of reality wouldn't blink an eye at crossing the Burning Place Above or being near the Seventh Mesa." She sighed. "How wonderful to have been raised with all those beautiful beliefs and secret ways."

Michael pulled away to look down at her face. "You're not exactly a stranger to them either. You weren't raised in an isolation chamber. Far as I know, you're one of the few people still walking around who've heard the Standing Stones."

She wasn't flattered. "Yes, but we know why."

"Hey lady, don't dismiss it so lightly. There are people who'd give all they possess just to have one experience like you did."

She rolled her eyes. "Maybe so, but those kinds of experiences are highly sacred—they can't be bought."

"Good thing, too."

Silence drifted between them for several minutes.

"Em?"

Silence.

"Em?" He allowed the tired woman to fall asleep in his arms. The high firmament winked knowingly down at him. And he then realized how long the trail before him was. He had much learning to gain before his new path could be tread upon. He closed his eyes and, holding the woman he loved, drifted away on the warm waves of oblivion.

White heat.

Waiting.

Empty adobe.

Waiting.

A swift shadow swept across the simmering land. The man didn't have to look up into the blinding sky to know what had caused its passing. He'd heard the whoosh of air, the flutter of massive wings. And he waited, for soon his patience would be richly rewarded.

A subtle movement caught his eye. He looked up to lock eyes with another's. When the old man backed into his doorway, the younger one rose and followed.

Within the cool interior of the one-room dwelling, the atmosphere shimmered and wavered.

The shaman was seated on the dirt floor in the corner—facing east. Sparkles of light flickered here and there around him like a nebulous aura of dancing fireflies.

The young visitor sat before the elder and waited again. Michael stared intently into his eyes and they began to pull him in. He felt a dizzying sensation that swept him around and around in the strange weightlessness. He felt as though a great whirlpool was sucking him around and down, down deeper and deeper.

The old man blinked.

Suddenly Michael was jerked back into the present surround. He'd been released from the powerful force of the magnetic pull. Again he stared hard at the old one whose black orbs swirled with ancient wisdom.

The Indian spoke. "You have returned after all."

"Grandfather, am I dreaming?"

Silence. The shaman looked up to the square of golden sunlight that flooded the small open window. Then his gaze rested again on his visitor.

"Some call it that. . .others know better."

"Teach me Old One. Teach me what I need to know."

"Are you dreaming?"

The young man's eyes moved to rest on a ray of sunlight upon the dirt floor. It sliced between them. Dust motes floated aimlessly within it. Then he raised his eyes to fix on the elder's. "My spirit has done Nightwalking. This is no simple dream."

Weathered brown fingers unfolded to point to the golden ray spearing through the open window. "Where then is the night, Nightwalker?"

Michael frowned and stared at the wavering beam. He had no answer.

The Old One waited for one.

"You're powerful. You altered the surroundings," came the reply.

Grandfather merely stared intently. No comment issued forth.

The younger man reversed his assumption. "You didn't alter the time of day."

The elder remained unmoved.

"I'm *not* Nightwalking."

Ebony eyes closed slowly, then opened.

The student tried again. "*You're* Nightwalking into *my* dreamscape. You're the Nightwalker. I *am* dreaming."

A bushy grey brow raised.

Michael was frustrated. "Then tell me. Straighten me out."

"What is dreaming?"

Silence.

The gentle man smiled.

Michael reasoned again. "I'm dreaming."

And without clarifying the matter at hand, the shaman suddenly changed the subject. "Why are you here?"

"I don't know," came the honest answer.

"Where are you going?"

"I don't know that either. Can you tell me?"

"Could," came the short response.

"But you won't."

The bright turquoise headband went slowly from side to side. The man's eyes closed and opened.

Michael pleaded. "Why won't you?"

"Before you can know where you are *going*, you must first know why you are here."

Silence.

"Before you can know *why* you are here, you must first know where here is."

The thick atmosphere wafted about. It appeared to be a living entity of itself. It appeared to be breathing.

Michael let out an exasperated breath. "I can't know where I'm going or know why I'm here until I journey the Within Trail. Right?"

The Old one smiled.

"And you're going to help me do this thing, aren't you?"

But again, the head turned from side to side.

"Okay. I have to do this alone. I understand that. But can you tell me what I'll find along this Within Trail of mine?"

Grandfather's eyes deepened into great black holes. "That Trail is never the same for all. It is as different as those fingerprints that tell one person from another. No two are ever the same."

The student prodded further. "In generalities then, what can I expect to discover?"

Eyes flared, then melted into gentleness. "Always there are certain things the same. It is the little things that are separate and special to each person. Always a person finds his true self when he takes the Within Trail. He finds many things that are hidden from the world during waking hours. He finds the quiet waters and looks at their reflection. Always he must accept what he sees in those waters before he can go on."

"What else is on the Trail to discover?"

"A person's purpose in this life. His future burdens and hard times, his happy days, his sad. The reasons for things. . .the whys."

"And?"

"That depends."

"On what?"

"On how much he accepts what he sees. All other paths depend on this great acceptance and what he does with it."

"What blocks acceptance?"

The elder tilted his head. Hands upturned alternately. "Love of yourself. Love of stuff. Not believing. Being lazy. Self."

The small room darkened as a large nighthawk landed on the window ledge. Its massive bulk filled the opening as it cocked its glistening head this way and that to peer around inside the adobe. Lids blinked down over its round cold eyes. The thing was huge.

To the visitor, it appeared more than threatening.

"And Fear," came the quiet voice.

The young man looked to the shaman. "Fear?"

"Fear stops one from taking acceptance into his heart. Fear of the unknown. Fear of failure. Fear of others. Fear of self. Fear of what others say. Fear of the battle. Fear of the fight."

Michael shifted his eyes to the bird. Now it appeared as though it'd shrunk to a normal size. Now it wasn't nearly as menacing. And the shaman's words replayed in his mind. They echoed. Fear of ridicule or the fight. . .the fight. . .the fight.

"Fight. *Fight*! FIGHT!"

"Michael! Wake up!"

The thrashing man's fists flailed in the air before they were grabbed and restrained. Opening his eyes, he stared in confusion at the concerned woman beside him. He relaxed the tense muscles and raked his fingers through his tousled hair. "Jesus, Em, I'm sorry."

"What was it? What were you dreaming about? Was it the Ka again?"

He rested back on the pillow and stared up at the ceiling.

"Go on, tell me about it," she urged.

And he recounted all the details he could recall.

"Mmm, sounds to me like he's cautioning you to proceed with care."

Silence.

"Don't you agree?"

Again no answer came from the man.

"Are you afraid to pursue this new trail, Michael?"

He remained deeply pensive. Then, "Em, how could he know what I was planning to do? How could he know about what you said earlier about the Within Trail? It was just as if he'd picked up the conversation where you'd left off."

"I guess the matter needed expanding." She hesitated. "Michael, some things aren't to be questioned. Some things don't logically hold up under close scrutiny or intensive analysis, but that doesn't make them untrue."

"I know. I teach that."

"Yes, but maybe you need to really understand it as it applies to you now. It's fine to *say* that some things can't be explained and that there's no proof to verify them, but when these very things touch your own life, you need to have acceptance of them without searching for the hows and whys of them. You can't do that because you'll never find them. It's a hard thing to be able to just give yourself over to acceptance, but it's even harder to expect others to do that. And that last is what can make it the most difficult trail to tread. It can affect your life like no other situation you'll ever experience."

He thought on the rationale of her words. He thought long and hard while his mind conjured up the vivid images of his extensive research into the unexplainable feats he'd seen performed throughout the world. And just in the last few days, they'd been building with increasing speed. Today would be the culmination, the grand finale that nothing else could ever begin to surpass.

"What time is it?" he asked, peering out into the darkness of the black night.

Emmy squinted over at the illumined digital display. "Two forty-seven."

Her companion groaned and fell back on the pillows. He pulled her down to him. When she'd finished nestling into him, he spoke softly, yet with firm determination. "I've made some decisions, Em."

"Oh? So soon?"

"I'm not returning to Boston. There's too much for me here. I've got a lot to do." He smoothed his fingers down her loose hair. "And it's not too soon, either. If anything, it may already be too late."

"It's never too late, Michael."

"That's why I've got to get moving on this thing. Just formulating a step-by-step plan will be a big undertaking. There's so much to do. The preliminaries alone will eat up a lot of valuable time."

She understood his new sense of urgency and patted his chest. "We've got time for all that, Michael. It'll all work out, you'll see. Right now the most important thing is that you've discovered yourself and found direction. Things usually fall into place after that."

He closed his eyes and kissed her head. "Destiny's brought us together, that's all I know. Right now that's all I care about."

She smiled in the darkness. "We natives don't believe in accidents, you know. Everything that happens occurs because it was meant to."

The two remained silent for a long while. The darkness wrapped around the solitary RV and the soft desert sounds lulled them back to sleep. This time, neither of them were disturbed by visitations of night shadows. No spectral shades came to invade their slumber.

No Ka.

No old man.

No nighthawk.

And no omens.

An arm, knotted with muscle, held the mighty bow out before the Entity of Night. Fingertips curled around the taut string and slowly did they pull back. Back and back they pulled until the bow arm trembled with the powerful strain of it. The firetipped arrow flared and roared fiercely as it was drawn back. The arms, gathering added strength, held strong while the practiced eye of Apollo took masterful aim.

Time held its breath.

Then, within a blink of an eye, whitened fingers uncurled, the bowstring twanged. And Daybreak streaked across the desert sky.

The land below Apollo exploded to life with the flashpoint of combustion. Mesas blazed in the raging flames of the sudden fire dance. Grey buttes ignited to flare like orange licking tongues. Shadowed monoliths erupted in a burst of backfire, their redstone bodies turning vermillion—a rich red—the color of lifeblood.

Then the raging inferno waned. It settled into a soulful silence and smoldered steadily. All the land below smoldered. And Apollo smiled down at the three humans who had witnessed the spectacular release of his mighty Daybreak Arrow.

Her spirit overcome with the splendor of daybreak's magnificent beauty, the woman known as Mourning Elk halted her journey across the desert land and raised her arms to the sapphire sky. A low chanting came sweetly from her throat. Eyes closed, the slender body gently swayed. Tears coursed down the high cheekbones. And she offered her Sunrise Song to the Great Living Spirit.

When she was done, she turned to gaze at her companions.

Michael was seated cross-legged on the dry earth. His eyes were closed. The Ka's precious envelope rested in his lap. A quiet moaning came from deep within him. She knew he'd been deeply touched by the spirit of his heritage. She also suspected that the Ka had in some way influenced his openness.

Above, a hawk glided silently over them.

The low moaning stopped after a long, drawn-out tone and the man opened his eyes. The chant had concluded. He smiled up at his waiting friend, then took notice of the high flyer.

"Guess the old man doesn't want to be left out today. Looks like he's coming along for the ride."

Emmy smiled. "You didn't really expect him to stay away, did you?"

Michael stood and brushed off his jeans.

Dr. Weatherbee came up beside them. "That was the most spectacular sunrise I've ever witnessed." Then, as he looked up to watch the circling bird, he said, "I've the feeling that he's as anxious as the Ka is to have this thing returned." He watched Michael pat the envelope now safely sequestered within his jacket. "Sort of like the Touchable joining forces with the Untouchable for a common cause."

Michael reached out for Emmy's hand. And the three crossed the Screaming, Burning Place Above that already began to simmer in the torrid heat of the Indian Summer.

This time the climb down into the crevice had been easier and all hearts drummed wildly when they stood before the opening.

Michael unzipped his jacket to readjust the sacred package that snuggled protectively against his chest.

Emmy pulled on a heavy woven sweater.

Weatherbee buttoned up his jacket.

And when they looked at one another, eyes locked.

"It's going to be all right," Theo said, trying to soothe the nervous couple. "We're expected, remember?"

"I'm not scared, just nervous," Emmy said, patting her stomach. "There's a hoard of butterflies in here."

Michael pulled her to him. "I do love you, Em. When we're through here, I won't let this be the end." And he kissed her gently—meaningfully.

Dr. Weatherbee politely pretended to be rechecking their supplies. He'd come to understand the strong bond the two young people had formed. Though he'd never married, he knew what love was. He heard the woman's response to Michael's words.

"Done? End?" Her lips curled up in a smile. "I've the feeling that what we're talking about doesn't have anything to do with endings. My heart says we're just beginning."

Michael kissed the upturned tip of her nose. "We need to get this behind us first." Then, turning to the elder man, "Ready, Theo?"

"You bet, son. Let's go."

Emmy cautiously followed the men's lead. Triple beams of yellow light illumined the dirt floor of the stone anteroom. And, once entirely inside, they separated to examine it closer.

"C'mere," Michael called softly to the others. A hint of echo followed.

When his companions drew up beside him, he pointed to the wall. "Bring your lights up here. We need to have a better look at this."

The area he indicated brightened as they added their lights to his.

"Theo, you thought this cavern was formed naturally, but look here," he said curiously.

The doctor went over to Michael.

Emmy raised on tiptoe to squint at the stone. "What is it?" she asked, watching him bring a testing finger to his lips.

"Limestone."

She didn't understand and he didn't bother explaining.

"Anyway, see these indentations here? And here?"

"Uhuh," she said, while Weatherbee stood back in fascination.

"These aren't natural." He and Theodore stepped further back and in tandem aimed their lights along the separate crevices.

Emmy watched them with growing interest. "They *look* natural," she expressed. "I mean, they're irregular and run between the outcroppings of the rock."

"So it would appear," Weatherbee said.

"Appear?" she repeated.

By now his own lantern moved erratically up and down the wall. Back and forth it went as his excitement grew. Again he backed away, eyes wide with discovery.

"Dr. Weatherbee! What is it! You're scaring me!"

The elder's voice was barely perceptible in the cavernous vaulted room. "I don't understand why we didn't see it before, Michael."

"See what?" Her eyes went from the mesmerized men to the wall behind her. "Michael! Dr. Weatherbee! See what?"

Michael lunged forward, grabbed her arm and pulled her back

against the far wall. His light beam was directed into her startled face. She lifted her light to his face. Wild eyes glared back at her. "Emmy, you know those massive markings that are found around the world? The ones that can only be deciphered from the air?"

Her head bobbed up and down. "Yes, there's a couple of them in California's Sonoran Desert near Arizona."

He grinned with the secret he was about to reveal to her. "Well then, feast your eyes on this baby!" His light moved slowly across the floor and crawled up the far wall. Hers followed and joined with Michael's and Dr. Weatherbee's. Together, all three beams illumined the detailed outline.

Emmy gasped. "I've seen this symbol before."

"These are called intaglios, Em. This one in particular is an exact replica of the one on a Peruvian mountainside in the high Andes. No one has been able to determine what it means and how it was created," Michael explained.

The woman stood in silence as she looked over the design. "Is that right, Dr. Weatherbee? Is it really true that nobody knows what this symbol means?"

"Yes, dear. Michael's quite right," he said while touching the engraving.

Her voice was low and slow. "The outside forks represent humankind. The double circles on each symbolize the dual sexuality of the human reproduction system. The center spire is the longest because it represents the Supreme Being. Man. . .Woman. . .God.

"The center spire also extends far below the other two. That's because it incorporates the life on earth. So on the whole, this symbol represents Man. . .Woman. . .God. . .Earth—their bonded oneness with each other."

Dr. Weatherbee turned to stare at her.

Michael's expression froze on his face as she continued the explanation.

"And they were made by the Bird People—other planetary intelligences—who visited here long ago to help and guide our development. I've heard that scientists still believe that the intaglios of the Sonoran Desert—one man, one horse—were actually created by the native people who lived along the lower Colorado River. Of course, this is impossible for two reasons.

"One, they're far too massive for proportionate designing unless seen and directed from an aerial vantage point." She grinned. "And as far as I know, centuries ago when they were made, Indians had no airplanes. And the second reason being that, also centuries ago when they were made, the Indians had no horses, nor did they have knowledge of them until the Spanish brought them. When that happened, the Indians called the horses Elk Dogs. So, how could they possibly have made an intaglio of one when they'd never laid eyes on a horse?

"I've heard some people try to justify that fact by claiming that the animal intaglio is actually a representation of a cow buffalo. This too is wrong thinking because the symbol's neck and legs are far too long. One of the remarkable characteristics of the ancient intaglios is the fact that their proportions are so precise. If the animal at the Sonoran Desert site were a buffalo, it would've looked much different, more representational."

"Are you finished?" Weatherbee asked in stunned amazement. She grinned. "Pretty much."

In disbelief he shifted his weight from one foot to the other while running his fingers over his chin. He walked over to the young woman and peered down into her face. "Do you mind telling us where you learned all that from?"

"Not at all. When I was just a little girl, my family gathered with others around the desert campfire and we listened to the words of the Grandfathers. They talked of many wondrous things and. . ."

"Wait a minute," Theo cut off. "Are you telling me that your people know all about the intaglios that've been mystifying mankind for. . ."

She put up her hand. "The carvings *haven't* been mystifying mankind. Indians are mankind, Dr. Weatherbee. And some of us have known about them for centuries. Our family clan saw how they were made. They learned their symbology firsthand from the mouths of their creators. And ever since, we've preserved the stories through generations of Storytellers who keep the history pure and unadulterated."

The elder professor was stunned.

Michael's hands came up to rest gently on her arm. He squeezed it as if to applaud her burst of knowledge in front of two professionals.

Weatherbee whistled. "We've not made it past the anteroom and already it's proven well worth it. Young woman, do you realize what you've said indicates that your People really *have* communicated with the other intelligences of the cosmos? Do you realize that their story explaining your blue eyes may, in fact, be true?"

She simply nodded her head.

Weatherbee sighed and looked over to the younger man. No words passed between them.

And, together, they all turned once again to gaze up at the massive intaglio that covered the anteroom wall.

Emmy's light traced up and down the three-pronged fork. "It's meaning is quite beautiful, isn't it."

"Yes indeed, my dear, it surely is that. Too bad it's been lost to man. . .er. . .to so many."

She gave him a playfully chastising look and pointed her light toward the small passageway. "There's our next step," she smiled. "Who's going in first?"

The two men looked at one another. Dr. Weatherbee offered a solution. "Michael, you take the lead. Emmy will follow and I'll take up the rear."

Dr. Greystone thought that'd be best, but out of politeness, turned it around. "Theo, you're the senior member here. Why don't you take the lead and I'll bring up the rear."

"No, no, my boy. My seniority has no place here. I'm just glad to have lived long enough to see this. You go ahead and blaze the trail. We'll be directly behind."

Crouching down on hands and knees as before, they made their way through the twisting tunnel that varied its slant.

Michael advanced while talking to the woman following him. "Em?"

"Yeah, I'm right behind you. Weatherbee's okay, too."

"Good. You ever see any pictures of the Great Pyramid built for Khufu at Giza?"

"Yes, and I know what you're going to ask next. You're going to ask if I've also seen the interior layout."

"Sounds like you're way ahead of me."

"No, just on the same track. This corridor does remind me of the way those passages tilted up and down and angled off. What do you think, Dr. Weatherbee?"

The good doctor was puffing along on all fours. "Yes, it would appear to resemble the entryways to the pyramids. They were done much like this. Michael!" he shouted ahead. "I'd have to agree with your theory on this."

Michael spoke softly to the woman behind him. "You doin' okay?"

"So far, so good. Knees are complaining a bit, but they'll survive."

"How about Theo. He still doing all right?"

"He's still right behind me. He's fine so far."

After the changes in the passageway's slant, Michael's lightbeam flooded into a larger passageway. The three climbed out and straightened their backs. A groan or two escaped before they felt more like themselves again.

"This way," the younger man pointed, "this looks like the corridor I was in when I came to the engraved wall. We follow this until we get to it."

"Michael?" Emmy asked.

"What?"

"Have you ever gone beyond that wall. . .in your dreams, I mean?"

"No. I've no idea what's beyond it."

"Think we'll go farther this time?"

"I don't know. The Ka's always showed up at that point."

Dr. Weatherbee joined in. "Michael, didn't the Ka say he'd take you beyond the Seal?"

"That's right, I forgot about that. Well? Looks like we'll be going the entire way." And he turned to lead them through the rough tunnel that'd been the dark beginning of so many terrifying nightmares.

"Sure is good to be going along here with light!" Michael commented. "In my dreams I never could tell where I was going. I'd imagine drop-offs or water pools at every step of the way. Now I see it's just a tunnelled corridor."

The three walked on. . .and on. There was nothing remarkable about the corridor to note and they advanced in silence, following the passageway's three left turns.

Suddenly the lead man stopped and the two behind him nearly plowed into him.

Three light beams reflected off smooth black stone.

"Shit!" Michael exclaimed at his first sight of it.

The wall glinted to life. The stone surface was flawless. It reflected their images like a mirror as they advanced to the masterpiece and hesitantly touched the expertly carved glyphs.

Theodore pointed out smudges on the marbled surface. "Zavarro's sloppy handiwork," he sneered disgustedly, pulling out a handkerchief to wipe them clean. "I'm sorry the man's dead, but he sure must've been sloppy and careless to have marred this all up like he did. He should've known better."

The elder's companions didn't reply. They'd been examining the wall. Emmy in particular had been drawn to the more familiar symbols—some enclosed with the ovals of cartouches.

With interest, Michael noticed her high concentration. "Find any family names?"

She flashed him a teasing look. "This is really amazing. These are some of the same ones I've seen in the Anasazi region. And this one here? This one I've seen done by a Pueblo friend of mine. And there," she pointed. "That one's done by the Zuni."

Michael pointed to another character. "And this?"

She moved in closer to inspect it. Her small finger traced the outline. "That design was on my grandfather's medicine bundle."

Dr. Weatherbee, although intensely involved in his own inspection of the massive wall, couldn't help but hear his companions' conversation. He moved over to them. "You sure of that, Ms. Winter? Absolutely sure?"

"Oh yes. I especially recall this one because, when I was just little, I used to stare at it a lot. It fascinated me so much that I'd trace the design in the sand and draw pictures of it. One day my grandfather asked me why I liked the word so much and I. . ."

"Word?" Weatherbee barked.

The import of what she'd said hit home. Her eyes locked on the man's. "Dr. Weatherbee, I never realized. I was so little."

"Go on. What else did your grandfather say?"

"Well, he asked me why I liked the word so much and I said that I didn't know, but that whenever I drew it, I felt good inside."

"And?" he gently prodded.

"And then he'd just nod and smile at me."

Theodore thought that over. "He ever tell you what the word meant?"

She shook her head.

Michael entered the conversation. "Emmy, who was your grandfather? I mean, was he anyone special?"

"He was a shaman."

The two men stood silent.

She watched the men exchange meaningful looks. "What's the matter?" she asked.

"Em, that character you loved drawing so much when you were little. . .that word that made you feel so good is from another language."

"I know."

His brow rose. "Do you? I'm talking about an entirely different culture here. . .an entirely different race!"

"Yes, I know that."

"Honey," he humored gently. "I'm talking real different here."

She sighed. "I know, Michael. The Bird People wrote like that."

"You know?"

"I said I did."

He shook his head and looked to his peer.

Weatherbee scratched his head. "Seems the little lady is way ahead of you, Dr. Greystone. Maybe she should be in the lead on this expedition." Then he turned to concentrate on the wall. He set both palms gently on the cool surface and scanned its amazing size. "Michael, this is the Rosetta Stone all over again. . .only bigger. . .much bigger."

Emmy looked up at the enormity of it. "It is big, all right."

Michael chuckled. "No, Em, he means it's a much bigger *discovery* than the Rosetta Stone ever was."

"Oh. What's a Rosetta Stone?"

Dr. Weatherbee's head turned to her. "You mean there's *something* you don't know?"

"That wasn't funny, Dr. Weatherbee. I don't claim to know as much as you or Michael. I never did."

"I know, I know, dear. But you have to admit, you certainly have given us some mighty big surprises since we've entered here."

"So I guess you can tell me about that Rosetta Stone later," she said, realizing their current interest took precedent.

"Well," Weatherbee said, "I'd be glad to tell you all about that when this is over." Then he addressed them both. "What's the consensus? Do we walk on or wait here?" He shined his light past the engraved wall where the corridor continued on.

"I'm game," Emmy admitted.

"You sure about that?" Theodore asked with a raised brow.

"I'm sure. How about you, Michael?"

He came up beside her, looked hard into her eyes, then took the lead again. "I'll be sure to tell the Ka this was all your idea."

"Coward," she spat back playfully. She grinned at the bantering and pushed him forward. "Lead on, Dr. Greystone."

The passageway angled right, then left. It twisted and turned. And, for great lengths of time it ran straight. The floor slanted downward the entire time. They were descending far below ground level. It became noticeably cooler.

"How far down do you think we are?" Emmy asked, pulling her sweater tighter around herself.

"Hard to say. . .quite a ways," the leader responded.

Silently the three descended for another forty minutes; then their lanterns reflected off a wall directly in front of them.

"Shit!" Michael spat.

"What do we do now?" Emmy groaned.

Dr. Weatherbee came up to the wall and examined it with a practiced eye. His fingers worked the crevices. His light played over the entire mass of stonework. "It would appear," he said, "that we've reached the end." He thoughtfully rubbed his chin. "Yet logic contradicts it. What do you think, Michael?"

The younger professor mulled the situation over. He, too, surveyed the dead-end wall. He turned to Emmy. "You didn't happen to notice any more of those tiny crawly passageways back there, did you?"

She shook her head with worry. "How can this be a dead end?"

"You're asking me?"

"I'm sorry."

He softened. "So am I. There's got to be an explanation for this. It just doesn't make sense that this is all there is to the place. If the papyrus belongs in here, where would it belong? There wasn't even a stone shelf or alcove anywhere." He then set to giving the stone his full attention again.

"Michael? Dr. Weatherbee?"

They both answered at the same time. "Yeah?" "Yes, dear?"

"What did the Ka mean about a Seal?"

The two men froze, then looked at her.

Michael responded first. "That's right!"

Just then, a great rumble thundered through the corridor. The three frantically looked around. Their yellow beams flashed back and forth like searching klieg lights.

A reverberation was felt in the stone corridor.

Emmy screamed in terror. "An earthquake!" And she lunged into Michael's protective arms.

Dust roiled up from the floor.

Dirt and pebbles of stone fell from above.

"Oh God," she cried, "please don't let us be buried down here."

The rumble thundered again.

More pebbles and stone dust fell around them.

They coughed in the thickening cloud that surrounded them.

Michael held the woman tight. "Emmy, we're not going to die down here." His voice was oddly calm. And he turned her around just in time to see the massive dead-end wall slide smoothly out of their way.

She clung to him in fear as they squinted into the blackness beyond. Her voice quivered with weakness. She voiced what the three had all been thinking.

"The *Seal!*"

Beyond the Opened Seal

The three stood transfixed as they watched the massive stone wall slide back.

When the deafening rumbling stopped and the billows of dust settled, they hesitantly leaned through the new opening to peer inside. Another corridor stretched out before them. This was far wider than the last. This one was expansive in height and breadth. The corridor was actually a long hall.

The trio cautiously stepped over the threshold to stand in the new passageway. Lantern light glanced off the walls—walls smooth as glass.

Frozen in speechless wonder, they stood in awe at what was before them. Down in the womb of the earth they had journeyed into a sacred realm unknown to humankind. Far beneath the Screaming, Burning Place Above rested a preserved testimonial to man's beginnings—as pristine as the ancient day it was created.

Black marble walls rose straight to the twenty-foot ceiling. Engraved on the walls were colossus figures etched with intricate detailing. The flooring was no longer uneven dirt, but was constructed of the same hard stone as the walls rising from it. There was no way to tell how far the new corridor went because the lights of their joined beams dissipated into the blackness of an opened archway that yawned at the distant end.

Michael looked to his companions. "Can you believe this?"

Emmy's eyes were wide with wonder. Her mouth opened to speak, yet no words issued forth as her eyes magnetically drew to the high walls that mirrored their reflections.

Dr. Weatherbee, in a similar state of amazement, haltingly stepped past the other two.

Dr. Greystone gently took Emmy's hand and guided her over

to one side. His voice whispered while his light traced an outline of a figure that was twenty feet tall. "Emmy, do you know who this figure represents?"

She was overcome with a profound reverence for the sacred aura the mystical surrounding was giving off. She felt diminutive standing at the feet of the huge figures before her. At her companion's question, all she could do was shake her head and watch the man's light trace over the engraved outline.

"This is Ra-Atum. He was a god of ancient Heliopolis who was believed to have created his physical form from his own free will. When he rose up out of the waters he brought land and light into the world. He's wearing a pschent—that's the double crown of the pharaohs. It's perfect, Em, the engraving is perfect in every detail."

The woman looked up at the figure. She then looked around the great hall to spy Dr. Weatherbee examining other figures. Then her gaze slowly came back to lock on the man before her. "But, Michael, what does it mean? What does all this mean?"

"I don't know, at least not yet," he smiled with excitement. "Maybe when we've recognized all the others represented here, Theo and I will be able to give you some kind of answer. If there's a pattern here that we can see, then maybe it won't be so hard to figure out why all these figures are here."

"But who made them?" she asked, gazing up in fascination. "How is it that Egyptian engravings are here beneath our desert?"

He exhaled a long breath. "Craziest damned thing I ever saw. In all my travels I've never seen anything remotely like this. Maybe we'll find out and maybe we won't. I've the feeling, though, that the Ka is allowing us to see all of this for a reason. Maybe we'll get our answers from him. I just don't know, Em. I just do not know." His fingers touched the cool stone. They followed the indentation of the engraved lines. He shook his head in utter confoundment. "Done just the way the ones uncovered in Egypt were. If I didn't know better I'd say these were done by the same ancient artisans, too."

"Michael!" Weatherbee whispered loudly from across the corridor. "I can't stop shaking! This is so unbelievable! Michael, my boy, I think this old coot has died and gone to Anthropologist Heaven!"

"Not yet, Theo, not yet. But it sure does feel like it, doesn't it."

There was no response from the elder man. He was already

consumed with studying another figure down the line.

The woman tugged on Dr. Greystone's sleeve. "Is this a pyramid within a mesa?"

Her whispered question sent an electrical jolt through him. Dumbfounded, he blankly stared back at her.

"Well is it?"

"It sure looks like it's turning out that way but, Jesus, Em," he sputtered, raking his fingers through his hair, "it's so incredible. . .almost too incredible to even imagine. The most imaginative writer couldn't create a scene this fantastic."

Ra-Atum towered above them. His etched-in-stone image was a touchable reality. It couldn't be denied. Regardless of the absurd impossibility. . .it existed here just the same.

The young researcher moved down the wide hall.

The woman followed close at his side. And their footfalls echoed with their movements. Then they stopped to gaze up at the wall again.

A lion-headed woman was depicted in fine detail.

"This one's Sekhmet. Theo!" he called out, "you see Sekhmet?"

"Yes! Yes! Isn't it wonderful!"

"Who's Sekhmet?" Emmy asked.

"She was the guardian and defender of Divine order, Em. The gods sent her forth as a great lioness so that, when people failed to honor the gods and keep to the natural order of things, she could chastise them."

Sekhmet held a long staff in one hand, an ankh in the other. The disc of Ra crowned her thick mane.

The two left Sekhmet in darkness as they moved on to raise their lanterns to illumine another figure.

"And here's the goddess Neith, the ancient Egyptian of the Earth Mother who was the source of all wisdom."

Emmy's lantern lingered on the goddess. "Yes," she agreed softly, "all wisdom is within the Earth Mother. They knew that way back then?"

"Oh yes. The ancient Egyptians possessed much spiritual knowledge. . .much of which is lost on us today, sorry to say."

"Why? What happened? Why didn't they preserve it as we do?"

The man shrugged. "Same old story, I suppose. Fads of new belief systems came and the old died away. Soon they're forgotten so completely they're only remembered and viewed as folk-tales. . .just stories."

"Our People have stories. But ours haven't changed—they remain pure—tradition demands they remain unchanged. Our stories tell of many ancient times too, but they are all true."

He gave her a warm smile of understanding. "That's why the native elders know things others don't."

She sighed with the thought of that.

Not wishing her to dwell further on the world's modern advancements into ignorance he stopped along the glistening floor. His beam shed light on an enormous bird with wings outstretched.

The woman sucked in her breath.

"You recognize this one?" Michael asked. "You know about Quetzalcoatl?"

Her brows furrowed. "Who?

"Quetzalcoatl. A god of the Toltecs and Aztecs."

"Michael, you need to get your mind off ancient history and bring it up to date. . .like today's belief systems. That," she said, pointing up to the detailed figure, "is not Egyptian, but it fits in with the others. Michael, that's the Great Phoenix!

"Centuries ago, the Old Ones say that the Bird People told of a day when the Great Phoenix would rise up out of the Earth Mother's womb. The rising of the Phoenix would coincide with catastrophic changes, both upon the surface of the land and within the hearts of humankind. Terrible things will happen then. Volcanos, devastating earthquakes, nuclear meltdowns, flooding, people going crazy. . ."

"Is this Phoenix an evil entity loosed in the world then? Is that what is believed?"

A sweet smile tipped up beneath softened eyes while she gazed respectfully up at the engraving of the immense bird. "Oh no, Michael, it represents a wonderful Being of Light. Like Sekhmet back there the Phoenix is also a Guardian and Defender of the Divine Order. He will come to chastise those whose ways are destroying the earth. He rises to cleanse and to bring a renewal that culminates in eternal peace for all living things. . .people included. Already the Indian People are hearing the mournful birth pangs of the Earth Mother. Already the Great Phoenix is stirring within her womb."

The man studied the expansive wingspan of the engraving. The bird's eyes were narrowed as if it were wisely perceiving its surroundings. The intricate feathers of the outstretched wings appeared to possess an acute awareness of themselves, as if they were poised, ready to lift off into the air and fly high over the land. It looked like it was one-minded and anxious to mete out its long-awaited justice and then bring its ultimate time of peace.

"I've never heard of that story. What tribe did it originate from?"

"The story was first given to the Bird People's descendants, the Spirit Clan of the Anasazi. This unique group was comprised of very wise people. This was over two thousand years ago and they were a strong spiritual force. They remained pure and kept the sacred laws. They were very wakan." She paused a moment to study the eyes of the Phoenix. When she began again there was a new solemnness in her voice. "It was those members of the Spirit Clan who the Bird People frequently visited with and taught. A precious few people today were once members of that ancient Clan."

"You're saying that some of the old Spirit Clan are back? Now?"

She simply nodded.

Dr. Greystone was thoughtful. "So far, from what we've seen, it appears that all these figures have something in common. They all represent basic truths that have remained unchanged since the beginning of time. I'm anxious to see who else is here in this great gathering." He took her arm and eased her forward. They shined their lights up on a man with the head of a falcon. Above the head rested a great disc. "Ra," he informed.

"The Sun God?"

"Yes, symbol of the Father of all gods."

One by one they examined the carvings as the anthropologist defined their names and purpose for his companion.

"Isis, symbol of Wisdom—another protector. Mayet, goddess who represented Justice and Truth. She was the daughter of Ra," he added.

Emmy looked up into the kohl-lined eyes of the beautiful Mayet. A headband was tied around the thick, flowing Egyptian hair. Through the narrow band an ostrich plume extended above her head. Emmy thought it reminded her of the way her own people often wore their feathers.

"Mayet guarded the realm between illusion and reality. She kept people's hearts pure with the truth," Michael explained.

"Just like the Storytellers of our People," she compared. "They preserve all the exact words of the stories' original events—never revising or changing interpretations, just repeating them as they were given long ago."

Michael aimed his light across the wide hall. The beam scanned the standing figure depicted there. Dr. Weatherbee was closely examining it. The figure was a man with a ram's head. Horns twisted out to each side. On the forehead was a disc, on the head was a tall crown sided by ostrich feathers. Dr. Greystone nudged his interested partner across the room. "Emmy, this is Khnemu. The name means 'molder.' He was believed to be the maker of the earth and the creator of mankind's environment."

The light moved as they advanced along the wall. Michael's knowledgeable litany continued.

"Reshpu, God of Eternity and Prince of Everlastingness. And here's Thoth," he said, illuminating the next figure of a man with the head of an ibis. "God of the Moon who spoke for Ra. He was known for many wonderful things. He reconciled time and the seasons, was judge of men's souls, devised the science of astronomy and also astrology. He was the God of Science and Wisdom."

"And this?" she asked. "What is this?" she repeated, lighting up an enormous single eye.

"Oh," he chuckled, "that's the Utchat."

"Utchat," she carefully repeated.

"That's right. It represents the Eye of Ra and symbolizes the fine balance of nature and physical laws. It was believed that when the Eye of Ra is lost, a great disturbance will occur in the natural order of the universe. And, when the Eye returns, so will the Natural Order—a far better one than before."

Curiously, Emmy stood before the thickly outlined Utchat and turned to shine her lantern directly across the room to the opposite wall.

The Phoenix illuminated to life.

"They're in the exact same position," she said. "Notice that? They both symbolize characters representing great disturbances and their resulting order are directly in line on each wall."

"You think that indicates something special?" Michael asked.

"Oh, I don't know. What would I know about all this? It is curious though," she mused. Then, advancing to the next engraving that'd been shrouded in darkness she raised her light. As the second beam rose to reinforce hers, the rays of light wavered from trembling hands.

"Oh shit!" Michael exclaimed. "Theo! You been over this way yet?"

The mumbling man across the room turned. "I'm busy here, Michael. I'll work my way around to you in a while."

"Theo, you'd better come see this. You're not going to believe this one."

"What are you talking about? This entire room is unbelievable. Oh all right," he gave in. "I'll come an' see what's so. . .Good GRIEF!" he spat, seeing what the two were shining their lights on.

Weatherbee quickly ran across the room to join the others. He looked up at the engraving. His mouth hung open.

Towering before them was the alien representation form of the Bird People. It wasn't unfamiliar to any of them. Emmy spoke first. "There are petroglyphs of these in Arizona. The Mayans also depicted these. The Bird People got around."

Dr. Weatherbee was incredulous. "Three cultures and peoples represented in one place! It's never happened before. Michael! This corridor was created in ancient times. Who knows how many others lay beneath these sands!"

Emmy joined in the excitement. "Our People say that beneath the paw of the Great Sphinx is another place such as this. We believe it holds great revealing truths that will negate much of what the world now believes, both spiritually and historically." She smiled up at the men's awe-struck faces. "This wasn't created yesterday."

Weatherbee had a question for her. "My dear, I realize your People know a great deal, but how in the blazes do they have stories about the Egyptian culture? I think you're getting carried away and stretching things a little, don't you?"

"Oh no, Dr. Weatherbee. You see, we have those stories because they originally came from our Starborn Brothers—our ancestors. And. . .*they* knew about *everybody*. They knew about people all over the earth."

The elder professor couldn't argue with the woman's logic. He nervously coughed. "Well, be that as it may." He paused. "After today I'd be the last to be called a skeptic. Maybe your grandfathers' grandfathers have their story straight after all. I guess only time will tell, my dear. I guess only time will tell," he said, glancing up at the alien figure.

Michael suddenly backed up to the center of the room and panned his light over all the engravings. "It's just like stepping back into another time and place, isn't it, Theo? Now I know how Howard Carter felt."

"Who?" Emmy asked.

Michael hadn't heard her. "Only this is so much more monumental! This proves out years of speculation and skepticism. This is going to shake the academic world to its very bones! This is such a discovery it's going to send shock waves through. . ." His words suddenly stopped as his head turned to the watching people. "It *won't* shock the world, will it."

They shook their heads with a painful pang of pity.

Everyone in the wondrous room knew the world could never find out about their spectacular find.

Michael sighed. "Ahhh. We're very much like them, you know," he whispered, looking up at the figures. "We're just like these silent Guardians who stand mute to what they know." He chuckled sardonically under his breath. "How bittersweet it is, how utterly bittersweet."

Dr. Weatherbee didn't agree. "Michael," he said softly while striding over to the younger man. "It's not bittersweet at all. It's the sweetest thing that could ever happen to you or me.

"Don't you see the beauty of it all, son? Look about you, Michael. Look! Here we stand in the center of the most amazing room in the entire world. Here we are, two anthropologists; one ending his professional days and one just beginning his, standing in the middle of the most incredible discovery ever made. What does that say, Michael? Mmmm? It says that, out of all the researchers in the scientific community, we two were chosen—chosen—to be granted this wondrous sight of sights!

"For me, Michael, I can now die a satisfied man. And for you, this should serve as a powerful impetus to carry the torch of enlightenment through the scientific community. Michael, don't you realize what this means for you?"

Dr. Greystone looked at his elder. "Mean?"

"Oh yes, man! Don't you even realize that this gives you your proof on a silver platter? Good God, I've had to struggle through my entire career battling with doubts, puzzle fragments, and *pieces* of ideas. I've never had any concrete proof of things to work from. But, Michael, you're just reaching your professional prime and look what you're presented with! Look! Look, Michael. . .the *proof!*"

And the young professor did look around him. His eyes rested on the most solid proof he'd ever have. He smiled then. "Yes, Theo, it is sweet, isn't it."

"That's my boy. That's the way to see it. It won't matter a whit if nobody else knows about it. We do. And, by God, that's enough."

"We're not alone, Michael," Emmy soothed. "There are others like us who know, yet do not speak of it. They too have held this secret in their hearts."

Visions of the high-flying nighthawk soared across his mind. "Yes, the old native man out there."

"And others," she added. "There are those others who know, who have also seen—the old medicine people, those of the Spirit Clan, the Dreamwalkers, and the true shamans. Yes," she said tenderly, "the wise ones know of these places around the world. Michael, we don't have to keep it hidden inside ourselves—we can *speak* of what we know, but only to those people who have the Knowing."

That realization appeared to help the young man who had been entertaining thoughts of how weighted this secret burden was going to be. He patted the glossy floor and Emmy folded herself down beside him. Weatherbee joined them and, together, the trio sat in awe-filled silence while gazing up at the magnificent figures.

"I just can't get over it," Michael expressed in a whisper. "I know I keep saying that but I don't have any other words for it. Right here—these figures right here—prove that the ancient Egyptians coexisted with the Native American people and other planetary intelligences. It really verifies it."

His statement didn't require a response from the other two.

Emmy's gaze followed the circlet of her companion's shining light. "Michael?"

"Yeah, honey."

"Why do most of the major Egyptian figures have animal heads or other body parts? Why'd they depict them that way?"

"Because the ancient artisans took great pride in their work. . .their exactness."

She frowned at that response. "But *why* were they depicted that way?"

He smiled. "I just told you. The skilled craftsmen took great pains to replicate their work right down to the finest detail." He gazed up into the face of Thoth. The long curved beak of its ibis head pointed down the unexplored end of the great corridor hall. "Thoth there, that's how he really looked."

She grinned with his suspected teasing. "Nahhh, you're pulling my leg," she laughed, shining the aura of her light in her companion's face.

The grave seriousness that now enveloped his expression sent an eerie chill rippling through her. "You are serious, aren't you." She turned to the other man. "Dr. Weatherbee, is he kidding me?"

The elder shook his head. "No, my dear, he speaks the truth."

Michael's eyes met hers. "Someday I'll tell you an interesting story of creation and how these characters here came to exist. It's quite fascinating stuff really." He shrugged. "Fact remains that all these wise ones really did live—just as you see them. Back then they were real living, breathing entities. Modern thinkers have lost the thread of their beautiful truth, so now they view these beings as mythological." He chuckled then. "Mythology wasn't even a word until people conveniently forgot what was real and then had to make up stories to explain the fragments of truth that were still remembered."

The woman understood that. "Our stories are based on truth too, but outsiders think they're just tales spun to pass the long winter nights. They don't see the symbolic connections that actually recount our history. They don't believe because their feet aren't on the ground. They're too busy seeking other things in life to have eyes and hearts for the spiritual part. They have eyes but are sightless. They have ears but cannot hear."

"It's always been that way, Em. Don't get yourself so worked up about it."

"But it's about to change, Michael. All of it is teetering on the very brink of change." She twisted around to aim her light on the massive Phoenix behind them. "He's preparing to rise and, when he's free and finally flying, *nothing* will ever be the same again."

The three gazed into the shrewd eyes of the Great Bird and a prolonged silence hung within the hall.

Michael's scalp suddenly crawled. He whispered. "Theo? Em? Do you feel it?"

Her wide eyes met his. "Yes," she admitted softly, "some part of them is here—now. I can almost hear them breathing."

Dr. Weatherbee glanced around with expectation pounding in his heart.

Their lanterns illumined the life-like faces that watched over and guarded the sacred catacomb. One by one, they looked into the staring eyes of the powerful ancient ones.

"I think the Ka is near," Emmy whispered.

The insistent tingling of their psyches persisted.

Michael moved his eyes around the darkened hall. "I don't think he's as near as you're thinking. I expect he's patiently waiting for us somewhere down there."

The other two turned to follow the yellow ray of light that Michael had directed down the corridor. The light was quickly eaten up by the blackness of the extended passageway that led into the unknown beyond.

"What do you think is down there?" Emmy asked.

"You kidding?" Michael said. "I couldn't begin to guess. At this point, I'd have to say that just about anything's possible. You agree, Theo?"

"Absolutely. I very much agree with that."

"Michael," Emmy began, "this may sound silly, but you're more knowledgeable than I am, and I already asked this, but. . ." she hesitated, "could this really be some sort of pyramid? A hidden one disguised by the mesa?"

"You want to handle that one, Theo?"

"Well, young lady," Weatherbee began, "the manner of passage layout certainly resembles some of those found in Egypt, but to say it's a bonafide pyramid may be reaching a bit more than we want to. Right now I think we should treat it as an ancient catacomb of some sort—one that was created about the same time as the pyramids, but for an entirely different purpose." The astute professor had anticipated her next question. He winked at her. "Let's hope the Ka sees his way clear to enlighten us on that purpose."

She smiled back at the kindly gentleman of knowledge. "Thank you, Dr. Weatherbee. Let's hope the Ka will feel like visitors."

And when the three began to go farther through the corridor their light rays glanced off the frozen stares of more ancient entities. All were expertly engraved on the smooth black marble. All were representative figures of Wisdom, Justice, Truth, Changes, and Peace. The depictions of the Bird People began to appear more frequently interspersed with the others. While walking the length of the massive hall, the anthropologists explained the names and purposes of each new figure they encountered until, finally, they no longer recognized any at all.

"Do you know this one?" Emmy asked, shedding illumination on a tall man in long flowing robes.

Michael shook his head. Then brought his beam down to the figure's bare feet. "Look, Theo, there's something here—like writing."

Dr. Weatherbee approached the cool wall. "It's a cartouche," he informed, excited to see the unexpected hieroglyphic.

"Do you know how to read it?" she asked.

The elder professor shook his head. "Sorry to say, Egyptology was not my forte. Michael? What about you?"

"I knew those figures back there only because Egyptology fascinated me in college. But it takes a good Egyptologist to decipher the actual hieroglyphs."

A little moan of disappointment escaped Emmy. "You sure you can't?"

"Well," Michael muttered, scratching his chin. "In college I had a roommate who was studying to be an Egyptologist and he used to try to teach me a little of this stuff."

"Oh please try," she pleaded.

"Give it a go," Weatherbee urged.

Looking up at the massive figure, Michael smiled wryly. "What's the deal? You two like this guy or something?"

Emmy didn't answer. And when he turned to look at her, she had a mesmerized expression as she stared up into the engraved face.

"Emmy? Em?"

Her eyes slowly lowered to look at him. "This was someone very important, Michael. I don't know how I know it—I just feel it. I'd like to know who he was."

"Okay, okay. Let me give it a whirl." Then he crouched near to the polished floor and began to mumble while tracing the symbols with his finger. Just when he thought he'd had it, he'd shake his head and attempt it again. After several more futile tries, he stood. "I guess I didn't pay close enough attention to my roommate. I thought I had part of it but the rest didn't fit."

Weatherbee just shrugged.

Emmy's disappointment was greater than he'd anticipated.

"I'm sorry, Em."

"Can you show me what you had?" she persisted.

He pulled her down and pointed to the cartouche. "This glyph here is the symbol for the sun. See the perfect disc?"

She nodded. "So, how does that interpret?"

"Ra. That's Ra."

"And this?" she asked, moving her finger down another notch.

He frowned. "That's Ta."

"And this last?"

"Men. That's Men."

She pointed over each outline in turn and said, "Ra-Ta-Men. Ra-Ta-Men. . .Ratamen."

"Well I know that's what it looks and sounds like," he said, "but as far as I can recall, there was no such person."

"You know all of them?"

"Well no, Em, like I said, I'm no Egyptologist, but. . ."

"Ratamen. . .Ratamen," she whispered.

The sound of the repeated syllables jarred his memory. He placed a hand on her shoulder. "Em! The last part was always a variable! It wasn't always used!" The blood drained from his face as he rose and stood back to view the figure. His voice was reverent.

"Ra-Ta!" Michael then turned to Dr. Weatherbee. "Ra-Ta!"

"Well I'll be," the elder said. "But how can you be sure?"

Emmy stood. Wildly curious at the man's peculiar behavior, she asked, "Ra-Ta? Who was Ra-Ta?"

"Oh Em, Theo, I don't believe this!"

"But who was he?" she persisted.

"He was one of the greatest wise men and teacher of ancient times. He had vision no one else had. And he was solely responsible for ending the bi-nature forms you saw on the walls back there."

"But how did he do that? Did he kill them all?"

Michael drew her to him and wrapped his arm about her waist while they looked up at the proud image of the robed Ra-Ta.

"No. He wouldn't do that. He established a wonderful place where the bi-natures were operated on to surgically correct their physical forms."

"*Surgically* correct them? But how could that be possible?"

"Back then much was possible. Even today we've got it all wrong regarding how the pyramids were truly built."

"We do?"

He kissed the top of her head. "We do. Honey, we can't even precisely duplicate mummification. Yeah," he said smiling, "back then they were privy to special secrets utilizing nature's natural forces, powerful gemstones, and spiritual laws. Crystals. Magnetic fields. The power of sound and color. Today those are all lost to us. This is the real Dark Ages."

"Did the Bird People help them learn those wakan things?"

He hugged her. "Your Bird People have been coming here for a long, long time. I wouldn't doubt they had a hand or two in helping out in Ra-Ta's time too." The man sighed. "God, Theo, isn't this amazing?"

The elder firmly agreed that it was.

"Michael?" Emmy said.

"Yes?"

"How can you be so sure this is the same Ra-Ta you think it is? Weren't there many people with names like that back then?"

"It has to be the one."

"But how can you be certain?"

He didn't answer, for he'd flashed his light up at a few of the figures that followed the one in question. Then he walked back a ways to retrace the way they'd come. All the while, checking the massive engravings on the walls.

Dr. Weatherbee had already come to the same conclusion as his younger peer and was greatly enjoying the sight of Michael's exuberance.

"What're you doing?" Emmy inquired.

"Taking inventory," he said, striding back to her side. A boyish grin covered his face and the sight of it made her smile.

"I bet you were a hideous child," she playfully commented.

"I had my moments."

"I bet you did," she snipped back, watching him quickly scan the wall ahead. "Michael! What are you doing? What are you up to?"

He put his finger to his lips and crooked his arm at her. "Come over here. I think I'm about to prove that that guy up there is who I think he is."

She frowned as he pulled her forward along the passageway

and eyed him as he kept the light beam fixed on the towering effigies as they quickly passed them.

Dr. Weatherbee stood back and watched the young man explode with the excitement of showing the woman his discovery.

"See him?" Michael asked Emmy as his light shone on a large figure.

"Yes."

"And her?"

"Uhuh."

"And him?"

She nodded with growing concern as they rushed past the figures.

Michael continued to pull her along. "See him?"

Finally she'd had enough of his private games and her heels dug in. She refused to be rushed any farther until she knew what was going on. "I saw them all, Michael. Now just what are you doing?"

"Tell me how many bi-natures you saw just now?"

"You really didn't give me much of a chance to see them very good."

"You saw good enough. How many?"

"Well. . .none."

"Uhuh. And how many did you see before the figure of Ra-Ta?"

Silence.

"See there? And I bet we won't see one more either because he was the one who changed all that." His shoulders dropped and his palms upturned. "Okay, okay, so it's not a very scientific way to prove out my theory, but you've got to admit it's an awfully convenient coincidence."

"Did I say you were wrong? Frankly, I'd have to agree with you. I would definitely say that that Ra-Ta is *your* Ra-Ta."

"Well? Now that that's all settled, what say we find out where this hall leads." He was concerned over her sudden worried expression. "Now what's the matter?"

"How much farther do you think we have to go?"

"Hell, I don't know." Michael looked over to Weatherbee who shrugged his shoulders. "Why, Em?"

She turned to look into the thick darkness of the arched opening, then she faced him. "What if we get lost down here?"

Weatherbee muffled a chuckle.

Michael grinned. "Emmy, we don't need to drop bread crumbs

to find our way out of here if that's what you're getting at. There's only been one way. Hey, all roads lead to Rome! Or Egypt. . .or to wherever it is we're supposed to be led to."

She gave him a half smile.

"Look," he said, "have there been a bunch of blind passageways?"

"No."

"Have there been lime pits to leap over or crocodile-infested rivers to cross?"

She grinned with the silliness that'd begun to make her feel childish for her former fear. "Stop that!"

"Well?" he grinned.

"All right. Let's go."

And after three more right angles that continued to slope downward, the wide marbled corridor abruptly led to a low and narrow passageway. Rather than the dirt or marbled floor, stone steps beckoned them downward around a smooth granite column.

"I don't like this," Emmy admitted in a shaky voice.

"I'm not nuts about it either. How about you, Theo?"

"I'm having a marvelous time! Why, I haven't had this much fun since I went on my first expedition! And now, look! A circular staircase! Down, down! Let's get down there!"

The two younger ones chuckled at Weatherbee's humor and it had served to ease the woman's trepidations about the descent they were about to make. Their advancement was slow as they went lower and lower, one step at a time around the circling steps. Where before, their lanterns illuminated an entire corridor or hall, now only three steps at a time were visible to them. The unknown that could be lurking right around the next bend sent chills down their spines. On the smooth column, their shadows loomed and cast a dervish dance behind them.

Suddenly the curving stairs ended. The new passageway was lower and considerably narrower. There wasn't enough room for them to walk side by side. The three explorers advanced with caution.

"I'm scared, Michael," Emmy admitted.

"No you're not. You probably suffer from claustrophobia and never knew it before now."

"That's not funny. We could be trapped down here real easy."

"Your imagination's having a field day, Em."

"Michael, I'm scared. What if something came up behind

us. . .it'd get Weatherbee, then I'd be next."

"Okay then," he said, halting suddenly and turning to face her. "You go first."

"No!"

"Well, in case you don't know it, you've got the safest spot in the line. You're monkey-in-the-middle. If you don't like that position maybe you'd like to lead or bring up the rear." He waited for her to decide which was worse.

She hesitantly looked beyond him, then back behind Weatherbee.

"I guess I'll stay where I am, thank you very much."

After another half hour of stooping beneath the low ceiling corridor they came out into a large room. It felt good to stand full up again. Their lanterns immediately went to work.

The vast height of the room gave them the feeling they could breathe better. An illusion of airiness filled their senses, but that wasn't all.

"What's that smell?" the woman asked, sniffing about.

"Got me. Maybe some kind of exotic incense or something?" Michael offered.

"Over here," Theo called from across the room where grey plumes rose from a golden dish.

They joined him to examine the object. "This was just lit," Theodore informed the little group.

With a single-mindedness they all spun around to search the room for the one who lit the incense.

No one was there except the towering statues stationed along the walls that sprung to life with the searcher's beams. Then Michael's lantern light settled on a large object in the back of the room. "Theo! A sarcophagus!"

"Yes, it would appear to be so,'" he said, moving forward to have a better look.

"Is it the Ka's?" Emmy asked.

"It'd be a good guess," Michael said as he made a move toward it.

Emmy yanked him back. "Where do you think you're going?"

"Over with Theo to take a look at that coffin."

Her eyes flared. "Burial places are sacred."

"You're here, aren't you?"

"But I had no way of knowing this was where I'd end up. Still, you shouldn't go near it."

He wanted to grin, but managed to smother it. "I want to have a look inside."

"*What?*"

This time he'd lost his control. He laughed and strode to the center of the burial chamber. When he was almost to it, he suddenly made a lightning about-face. "I thought you weren't going to come near this," he asked of the woman who'd followed on his heels.

"You're not leaving me standing all alone over there."

Then he softened. "I wasn't planning on really opening this thing up," he confessed. "I just wanted to see an undiscovered sarcophagus, that's all."

She released a sigh of relief as he raised his hand to gently touch the coldness of the outside coffin. "It's magnificent, isn't it, Theo?" he reverently whispered.

"To think it hasn't been touched by human hands is what has me under its spell," said the elder man while gliding his sensitive fingertips over the gold inlaid lid. "To think I'm actually touching an ancient sarcophagus is beyond comprehension." His eyes were almost glazed as they scanned the intricate carvings that adorned the gem encrusted lid. "Michael?"

"Yes, Theo."

"Our Ka was evidently a very great man." And he proceeded to show the younger the different symbols that proved it.

"Is he really in there?" Emmy asked with hesitation. "The Ka's body is in there?"

"I'm sure of it," Weatherbee said.

"So am I," agreed Michael.

Without moving her head her eyes furtively searched beyond the coffin. They rested momentarily on the glassy eyes of each of the facing statues that stood guard along the wall. "Where is the Ka then?"

"I don't know, but I do know he's not here right now," Michael replied.

Her voice had that scared tremble in it again. "Michael, then where is he? This is the end of the line. There's no more passageways, stairs, or doors."

The impact of her statement hit the two men hard when they realized she was right and, just to double check, they aimed their lights over the entire chamber. They looked over at the woman. Michael spoke first. "You didn't happen to notice any other. . ."

She was shaking her head. "No, Michael, there weren't any other passageways, tunnels or secret corridors along the way. This is it."

A worried frown creased his brow. He looked to Weatherbee. "That's odd, don't you think? You suppose he won't show? Maybe we're just supposed to leave the papyrus here and leave."

Dr. Weatherbee considered the idea while Emmy voiced hers. "That's the best idea I've heard all day."

Michael was deeply disappointed that it'd turned out the way it had. "Maybe we need to sit down and do that waiting thing we did with the Indian people. Maybe he's not ready for us yet."

An exasperated look met his gaze. "Michael," she warned, "give it up. He'd be here now if we were meant to communicate with him."

"What do you think, Theo? Think we ought to leave the papyrus here and go back up?"

"I was under the strong impression we'd be granted some type of personal communication when we got this far. But. . .if it's not to be then there's nothing left to do but leave it and return to the surface."

Michael looked around the room, then touched the stone lid.

He talked softly to the occupant. "We brought something of yours. We brought it back to you. Thanks for all you've allowed us to see. . .we'll remember it all our lives."

Then, very slowly, his hand came up to his jacket and fingers reluctantly curled around the zipper. He pulled it down and removed the envelope. Using extreme care, the delicate papyrus was extracted and set upon the sarcophagus.

The moment was intensely emotional and charged with high sensitivity, for it was then that the trio realized they wanted to stay. Their spirits were moved by the sacred aura of the Silent, Sacred Place Below.

Finally Emmy rested her fingers on the man's trembling hand. "We're done, Michael. We've done what we came here to do."

His head turned. Misted, soulful eyes met hers.

She caressed him in his sadness. "I know, honey. I know how you feel, but we've done what we promised and now we need to leave him to his peace."

Michael looked over to Theodore. The elder rubbed Michael's shoulders. "She's right, Michael. I know you feel a strong connection to this place and I know you expected to communicate with the Ka, but if this is what he wants, this is what we'll settle for. He's given us a gift more precious than gold. He's allowed us to be the only living people in the world to see his ancient realm."

Michael placed his palm over the man's hand. His other rested atop the papyrus on the coffin lid. "You're right, Theo. Let's go back up now."

And when the three turned their backs on the lonely sar-cophagus, they froze to the sound of a soft click behind them. They dared not turn.

But when the darkness of the burial chamber illuminated with the blinding brilliance of a sparkling white light, they were compelled to turn.

Slowly.

Slowly they turned.

One of the massive statues was silently sliding to the side. From the narrow opening that was quietly widening they saw that the cavernous room beyond glittered with ancient treasures. . .treasures that rivaled the combined discoveries of all the pharaohs' burial chambers put together.

Silently the three approached the sarcophagus.

Michael gently picked up the sacred papyrus and, together they crossed the threshold of the final Seal. . .together did they walk into the pulsing Soul of the Seventh Mesa.

The Ka

T he trio stood in petrified wonder at the staggering sight before them. Their eyes were overwhelmed with the dazzling splendor.

Michael swallowed hard. "Gold, everywhere the glint of gold," he uttered beneath his breath.

"W-What?" Emmy stuttered, not daring to take her own enrapt eyes from the mammoth hall of shimmering treasures.

Michael whispered, "That's what Howard Carter said the first time he set eyes on the riches he discovered down in Tutankhamen's tomb."

Dr. Weatherbee was frozen in place. His rapidly beating heart would not yet allow the strain of speech.

As the three were held in a paralyzing state of wonderment, their minds ached to rush forward and examine the trove of ancient treasures, but their legs were weak and their feet remained cemented in place. They were immobile and firmly rooted upon the top step, yet their eyes drank in the magnificence that filled the marbled hall like a museum storeroom.

Along the polished quartz walls, colossus statues of the gods lined two sides. Shoulder to shoulder, they towered to the height of the forty-foot ceiling. These gem-studded effigies were double the size of the ones in the corridor above. These made the others seem like miniatures, yet it was not only their massive size that made them different, these were forged of gold—pure gold glinted like reflected sunlight on sparkling midday waters. The Bird People, too, were there among the other sentinels that stood tall and straight, eyes wide with their stare fixed ahead. They appeared to be the powerful guardians of the riches that spread out at their feet like a banquet for the gods.

Countless ebony chests were strategically positioned about the marble floor. They appeared to create a purposeful symmetry of design. Though identical in construction and austerity, each possessed differing engravings on their arched lids. No two were the same. No two represented the same culture. The only color on the chests was the gold of the hinges and latches.

Still the three remained anchored to the stone steps, not because their limbs were still powerless, but because now the height of their vantagepoint gave them a better view of what the massive hall held.

Michael's trained mind, full of years of research experience, strained at the bit to take a closer look, yet he forcefully pulled in the reins of his impetuousness in order to fully absorb the import of all he was seeing. And, like a mainframe, his mind began to mentally catalogue all his bewildered eyes took in. As the list grew he was sure he'd soon reach the overload stage, for never before had such diverse cultural treasures ever been found in one location. There was just too much to absorb.

Emmy's impressions came not from the technicalities of the mind, but rather from her quickened spirit. Silently did she stand beside her stunned companions. Silently did she feel the great welling of her rapturous spirit. Here, within this grand and sacred hall, she had no rational explanation for the deep comfort she now felt. It was a "coming home" type of sensation that filled her breast with tranquility and sense of belonging. This place beneath the burning sands was made by an ancient people. All the extraordinary objects collected were placed here by the hands of an ancient group—select and wise. Her eyes sparkled with the reflections of myriad twinkling gemstones that winked and blinked like evening fireflies. From everywhere came the glimmer of gold and the shimmer of cut jewels.

Dr. Weatherbee's quick mind calculated all he saw before him. The impact of his conclusion was staggering. He lowered himself to sit on the step, the action affording the mind additional pause to absorb the hall's contents. His companions followed suit as they silently surveyed the collection of objects. And the three sat mute as each found and extracted the sensory information that was unique to each.

Long mahogany display tables stood waist high. Glass enclosed cases protected fragile parchments and papyri. Pendants, heavy with their golden chains, held jeweled amulets and precious stones. Egyptian collar necklaces, heavy with the weight of inlaid lapis lazuli and gemstones, were carefully arranged on velvet display stands. Ivory statuettes were interspersed with great alabaster statues along with silver cups and carved unguent jars. Tablets of hieroglyphics rested among fragments of redstone petroglyphs. Hundreds of scrolls were rolled and stored on their ends within large porcelain Chinese vases. Life-like statues stood to human scale about the hall.

Selket, Guardian and Protector of Tombs, stood at the bottom of the stairs. Her arms of gold outstretched to protect all that was before her. Forever did she stand as sentinel over the priceless treasures that spanned all time and all civilizations.

A great black marble statue of the falcon, Horus, perched among the rare objects. He towered taller than a man. Atop his feathered crown the golden disc of Ra sent glinting rays of reflected light throughout the room.

Great ostrich plumes wavered gently with the coming of fresh air from the opened seal. A dozen African lances stood in one corner. Jewelled copper boxes, untarnished and as beautiful as the day they were crafted, lay among delicate Chinese silks and the finest dynasty vases. Native American medicine pipes were set before a Mayan robe of brightly embroidered threads. A crooked staff rested across a table beside tattered leather sandals. All these things and more surrounded the luminous source of light that radiated out from a great crystal—a crystal that spired up from its pyramid shape in the center of the great hall. No generated sound emitted from it, just a brilliant glow, constant and eternal.

The visitors, upon sensing some silent signal, simultaneously stood. Slowly did they descend the seven stone steps that brought their feet in contact with the polished marble floor. Soundlessly they moved toward the strange source of light that swirled myriad prismatic colors within its illumined mass.

"What is this, Michael?" Emmy whispered.

"An aurora borealis crystal," he answered, gazing up to the tip that towered twenty feet above his head.

"How does it work? How does it give such light?"

"I don't know. I don't know."

"Where did it come from?"

He sighed heavily with so many unanswerable questions. He could only shake his head.

Dr. Weatherbee was captivated by the living crystal that pulsed with life. His quickened mind raced for answers to his own unspoken questions. He studied his way around the bright object, examining the base with particular interest. "Michael, this is set into the mesa. See here?"

The younger professor joined the elder. He gave his full attention to the floor where a break could be discerned. His excitement grew as he gave the entire perimeter a close inspection. In amazement, he looked over at Weatherbee. "Then what we see of it is only the *tip* of the crystal!" The ramification of that was staggering. "Theo, the rest of it must be buried deep below the ground!"

"Yes, it would appear that that's the case."

Michael peered up at the exposed portion. "This must be a monstrous crystal! How far down do you think it goes?"

The elder man hesitated. "Well. . .from my cursory calculations, I'd say that nine-tenth's of it is buried." The elder man gave the younger a curious look. "That bring anything to mind?"

"Right now my mind's in a spin. Give me a little time for it to slow down."

The two stood and walked around to Emmy.

Silence settled over the three while they watched the whorling colors. Reds. Purples. Greens and blues writhed and curled upon themselves within the stone.

"It almost looks alive," Emmy voiced.

"Mmmm," Weatherbee mumbled. "It certainly does."

The young woman spoke softly before the mysterious stone. "Our people have stories of a great stone that is said to live," she revealed. "They say one could nearly see through it except for the moving rainbow caught inside it. It was said to have belonged to the Bird People and that they gave one of these to two other races who used them wrongly and the Bird People took them back. There's more to the story but that's all I recall right now." She paused out of uncertainty before wondering aloud. "Could this be one of those two stones?"

"Could be, could be." Weatherbee responded. "The Atlantis people had such a crystal, too. They destroyed themselves by misusing its power. Perhaps this crystal once stood on the soil of Atlantis." The good doctor rubbed his chin. "I'm not usually prone to such outlandish suppositions; however, in light of the utterly *unbelievable* absurdities that we've seen to be believable this day,

I think our imaginations could reach as far as we wanted to stretch them and not end up off the mark. What we've seen proven out this day bears witness to mankind's shortsightedness and the stunted thinking of our scientific community." He locked eyes with Michael. "We've got a long way to go."

Dr. Greystone had nothing to add because the elder had said it all. He faced the crystal and held up his palms as though he were warming them by a cozy fire. "There's energy coming from it. Did you notice that, Theo? It's like a force field of some kind."

The others raised their palms in turn.

Emmy looked over to the men. "It feels like a gentle push on my fingers. What's causing that?"

Michael's brows furrowed. "I'm not sure but it might have something to do with its location. We're fairly far down and if this is a magnetic power point in the earth, the crystal is encapsulating the force by concentrating its powerful energy. It's its own power plant." He suddenly became pensive. "I wonder. . .?" he mused.

Emmy waited for the man to finish voicing his thoughts.

Dr. Weatherbee smiled to himself as he watched the young man's thoughts solidify.

Michael looked over to Theodore. Their eyes met and both men grinned. The younger then turned to the woman. "Em. Remember when we were talking about the Great Pyramid?"

She nodded.

"And remember when Theo asked me if his crystal reminded me of anything?"

Again she nodded.

"Well. . .did you know that the top of the pyramid is missing?"

"Yes, Michael. I remember reading about that. And the photographs of it make it look incomplete."

"Okay then. There are some very well-respected people who seem to believe that the Gizeh capstone was actually a huge crystal and that it had some valuable purpose as well as incredible power. They believe the capstone was much more than a simple pyramid top."

"What purpose would it have?"

"Ahhh," he mused with an impish grin, "that has been lost to us."

"Where is the crystal capstone then?"

His brow shot up in question. "Can't you guess?"

"I can't guess how something so enormous could be lost. There'd be no place to hide it. And besides," she added, "what kind of people would take such a. . ." Her wide eyes flared even wider. She looked from Michael to Weatherbee and back to Michael again. "The Bird People took it back!"

The two men smiled.

Michael spoke his thoughts. "That's what I was thinking," he said before kissing the tip of her nose. "My dear, you took the words right out of my mouth."

The woman turned to the elder man. "Do you think that's what happened, too?"

He shrugged. "At the moment I'd say that that's the most reasonable explanation we have. Who can say? There are so many enigmas about our past that we simple mortals don't yet know about. Who can say? But when you piece together all we've seen today it certainly is more than a possibility. . .it's the most probable explanation we have."

Michael beamed. "This is all so amazing. Who would've envisioned, even in their wildest dreams, that all this untouched treasure was buried beneath an Arizona mesa? It's truly inconceivable."

Dr. Weatherbee's brow rose in question.

Emmy's eyes playfully narrowed and twinkled. "I know someone who envisioned it in their dreams."

Michael glanced from one to the other. "Yeah, well."

Then the woman gazed beyond Michael to where the massive statues towered along the walls. "Michael?"

"What."

"Did you notice all the statues?" He and Weatherbee turned to face them. "What do you mean? Of course I noticed them, how could I not. . .they're colossal."

She pointed to them. "Did you notice anything special, I mean. See? Those lining those two opposite walls are replicas of the ones we saw upstairs, but those five along the back wall are different. Don't you think they're different?"

Immediately he realized what she was referring to. The five statues stood shoulder to shoulder and each represented one of the five races.

Curiously Michael approached the massive effigies. "To tell the truth, Em, I hadn't noticed the differentiation until you pointed it out. Did you notice it, Theo?"

The elder nodded and joined the others.

Their surveying gazes drifted from one statue to the next. All five were indeed different yet had been clearly crafted by the skillful hands of the same artisan who created all the others.

A Caucasian man in flowing robes looked out of round eyes. Sandals adorned his feet. A staff in hand.

An African chieftain with a leopard skin garment. Headdress billowed with ostrich plumes.

A Mandarin woman, hair coiled elaborately, stared out from beautiful almond eyes. She held a small gem-studded chest.

The native chief stood proud in skins bedecked with shells and beads. Trailing headdress of feathers fell gracefully down his back to the floor. Moccasins beaded in intricate designs adorned his feet.

The Egyptian was Ra-Ta—the only one they could name.

"They're the Teachers," Weatherbee informed. "They're five of the greatest Teachers that ever walked the earth. They represent the five earth races of creation."

Emmy's eyes revealed her shock. "All five were created at once?"

"Of course, my child," came the gentle voice from behind them.

The trio spun around.

The man in the long white robe made no reference to the sudden surprise in his visitors' eyes. Instead, he strolled slowly toward them as he spoke.

Emmy nudged closer to Michael who protectively wrapped his arm about her while they listened to the mellow new voice. "Surely you do not think your ancestors were mindless little amoeba aimlessly floating in the dark depths of the sea, do you?"

The woman's spine rippled and she trembled.

The man beside her tightened his grip around her.

Dr. Weatherbee beamed at the newcomer.

"No, no," the stranger soothed, "would a lonely Supreme Being create one-celled creatures for companions?" He smiled with warmth. "I think not." His eyes rose to gaze upon the five statues. "No, a God would create a being with a mind and give him *knowledge* and. . .a free will. He'd give him intelligence to use the gifts of knowledge and free will."

Michael had been closely observing every subtle movement of the stranger. He'd been keenly listening, sharpening his senses to every nuance of the man's voice. He gave special attention to the stranger's eyes. It was then that he realized this white-haired elder was no stranger to him. And convinced of his personal conviction, he wasn't reticent to voice it. "You're Ra-Ta."

Emmy sucked in her breath.

Weatherbee sighed when his companion voiced his own belief.

The man in white chuckled, then bent his head low. "Forgive me for being so unthinkably remiss in the social courtesies. It has been a long, long while since I've had visitors to entertain. Yes, once I was known as Ra-Ta during one of my many journeys. Your perception impresses me."

Michael nodded.

Emmy found her voice. It cracked as she spoke her mind. "We were expecting the Ka."

Michael's fingers quickly squeezed her arm in a hidden gesture of reprimand for her outspoken rudeness. Had she already forgotten about the masterful accomplishments he'd told her this man had succeeded in bringing about? Had she already forgotten how great was the entity who now stood before them?

The Elder suppressed a smile of genuine amusement. "The Ka? The Ka of whom?"

She nervously looked to her companions, eyes pleading each for assistance.

"Well?" Michael stammered, "we don't know," he admitted sheepishly, feeling much the fool in the Teacher's presence.

The stranger's light blue eyes twinkled with the gentle smile. "Well then, perhaps this Ka will show up later. In the meantime, allow me to be your host and show you around our Sacred Hall." He turned and motioned for his guests to follow.

Behind the man's back, Emmy tugged on Michael's arm and silently mouthed the question, "Our?"

"But of course, young lady," the Guide continued, "these precious treasures belong to everyone, do they not?" He didn't wait for a reply. "These are testimonials to all of humankind's fascinating histories since the dawn of time. Yes, all these," he said, stretching his arms as though he were lovingly holding them out to gather in his little children. "All these are so rare they are irreplaceable." And slowly he turned to face his visitors. Eyes lowered to rest on Michael's hand. . .what it held.

"Oh, I almost forgot. I'm. . .that is. . .we, are here to return this to the Ka."

The Teacher's hand rose from his side. The voluminous sleeve covered his arm and draped in long folds. "May I see that?"

Emmy tightened her grip on Michael's arm. It was a signal to beware.

Michael looked over to Weatherbee who nodded for the younger to go ahead and pass the papyrus over to their guide.

Emmy pinched Michael's arm in warning again.

Time froze for the four as Michael looked into the Elder's eyes that were barely four feet from the yellow ones of the huge Anubis statue behind him. Both pair of eyes watched his response as he frantically considered if they were being cleverly deceived by a sly impostor. He'd hesitated a moment too long.

The Teacher lowered his hand. His voice was soft and rich with admiration. "I understand, my friends. It would appear that the Ka has indeed chosen his emissaries well."

"It's not that we mistrust you, Ra-Ta, but we just. . ."

The Elder's hand came up to halt the words. "Please, that's so formal. Ra will do. . .just Ra."

"Well," Michael continued, "as I was saying, Ra, it's not that we mistrust you but we came here to return this to the Ka. We wouldn't feel right handing it to anyone else but him. We hope we haven't offended you."

The Man closed his eyes and nodded before opening them again. "No need to explain and no offense taken. If you're here to deliver it to the Ka himself, then it is only fitting that, into the Ka's hands it must be placed."

Emmy subliminally wondered if a Ka even had hands.

The Teacher then slid his perceptive gaze to her. "I'm sure he'll be most pleased to touch it again. That fragment is extremely important to him. . .it contains the complete personal history of his existences."

"Who is the Ka?" Emmy finally asked.

Dr. Weatherbee coughed at her boldness.

The Man smiled. "That is not for me to say. Perhaps later you will come into your own answer to that."

"Is he from here? Earth, I mean," she clarified. "Or was he of the Bird People?"

The Elder's brows arched in amusement. "An alien?"

"Yes," she underscored, not realizing the man found humor in her question.

The Elder stroked his chin and peered over at the three who anxiously awaited his answer. "As with all completed beings, the Ka was of all races. . .both from here and from other worlds."

Michael began to relax with the gentle man of wisdom. "That sarcophagus out there, it belongs to a great man. Would it be the Ka's?"

"The remains of the Ka's final form are resting within. Yes."

Michael boldly reached further. "And was this final form of *this* world?"

The Teacher smiled. "No, it was not."

The two professors eyed each other. Their heads spun with the confirmation that an alien was laid to rest in the burial chamber. They wanted to ask a thousand more questions but the researchers' minds were spinning. At the sound of Ra's voice, the matted tangle of thoughts were forgotten. "Would you like to examine some of these precious objects more closely?" he offered, spreading his arms out to the hall.

The trio exchanged glances. Never had they expected such a gracious offer. Never had they anticipated they'd be invited to walk about and look over the treasures at their leisure. This was too much to expect and none of them seemed to find their voice.

The Elder smiled in understanding.

Finally Dr. Weatherbee cleared his throat. "I think you've made us a very generous offer, Ra, and I'm sure each one of us is very anxious to look at everything here, but would you mind if we just talked for a while?"

The robed man turned his back on them and stepped away.

The guests flashed one another questioning looks.

Then, from across the hall, the Elder called. "We'll be more comfortable if we sit while we talk, don't you think? Here," he said, pointing to a pair of ancient Egyptian benches, "if you'll be so kind as to pull these out and clear them, you all can rest a while. I'm sure you're quite exhausted from your journey here."

The three advanced forward.

Michael and Weatherbee busied themselves with clearing off the fragile-looking benches. Arms full, they searched around for a secure place to set their valuable load.

Ra gave verbal assistance. "Set them anywhere, my friends. As long as they're here in the Hall, it matters not where."

The encumbered men found space on a large Persian chest.

As the two bent to carefully unload their burdens, each realized what he held.

Treasure. Ancient treasure.

And suddenly, they felt rather more like an ancient tomb grave robber standing there with armfuls of precious stones and heavy gold. . .the loot. Respectfully they took additional care to gently set down each priceless piece. When they turned, the Elder had been shrewdly observing them. "Now, if you'll just slide out these benches, you can rest and be more comfortable."

Emmy froze as she stared at the ancient wood.

Michael mirrored her thoughts. "They're very old, Ra."

"If you perhaps think they'll crumble you would be wrong. They are as sturdy today as the day they were made and brought here. Haven't you noticed that the alabaster is still pure white? That the copper remains shiny? And that all the silver is untarnished? Gold as lustrous as the day it was cast?" The Man laughed. "The crystal, my friends, the crystal takes care of the preservation here. Now, pull out those benches and see for yourselves."

They did as bid.

Emmy looked with concern to the Elder. "But there's only three here," she said, glancing about for another.

"Personally," Ra admitted, "I talk much better standing up. Pacing about helps me think."

"Oh."

And hesitantly, the three lowered themselves on ebony chairs handcrafted by Egyptian artisans who had died thousands of years ago.

The solid wood didn't even squeak, not even after Michael nonchalantly gave it a little more testing wriggle than needed.

"Now, what is it that you wish to talk about?" Ra asked, as he began a slow pace before them.

The seated ones looked to each other with sudden confoundment. There were so many questions it was difficult to untangle them. The main one seemed to be where to begin. And awareness of their dilemma brought sheepish grins to their faces.

Dr. Weatherbee was the first to find voice. "Why here?"

"Why not here? This is a very strong power point on this planet. And it's dry and usually warm. . .like Egypt. These wonderful mesas provided perfect cover. . .a natural shield, if you will. This was one of the chosen locations."

"They're more?" Theo inquired.

The Elder nodded. "Of course."

"In America?" Michael wanted to know.

"No. There are more around the world. This is the only location here in this country."

Emmy wanted to speak her question before the Ka appeared and they ran out of time. "Ra?"

"Yes, dear."

"Why do the Standing Stones speak?"

"Ahhh, yes, you've heard."

"Yes. But what makes them able to whisper?"

The Elder's hand rose to caution her. "Now you've asked not one, but two questions. Why? And how?"

The woman flushed. "I'm sorry," she meekly apologized. "I just wanted to know the real answers."

His brow rose. "Real? You don't believe the stories of your People?"

She felt duly chastised. "It's not that. I guess I just needed them verified."

Ra thought on that. "And what is it that your People say? What are the stories?"

"The stories tell of nature spirits who dwell in all things of nature. It is their voices who certain people can sometimes hear. The stories say these nature spirits are very powerful and want only to help humans realize their sacred bond with Grandmother Earth, so they sometimes speak in a way we can hear or feel."

"Yes?"

"Well. . .that's it." She waited.

"What more could I possibly add? Your people have kept the stories accurate."

She sighed with relief.

Michael was anxious for his turn again. "Who brought all this treasure here to the Seventh Mesa? Who did the collecting and transporting?"

"It was a joint effort. It was a joint effort by all the old Teachers of the time. From every country and land the Great ones gathered these things for the express purpose of maintaining a Legacy of Heritage—True Spirit Heritage—for all beings of intelligent life." The Elder then glanced casually around. "Articles belonging to all the Great Teachers are collected here in this Hall of Truth."

Michael's eyes had also scanned the valuables. They came to rest on the staff and tattered sandals. "All the Great Teachers?"

Ra read his mind, closed his eyes and nodded.

Michael thought on that. "But why, Ra? Why even do this wonderful thing if nobody even knows about it? Why the big secret?"

Ra smiled out of compassion. "Intelligence of earth is in its infancy still. Look how backward your scientific technology has fallen. You've created a nuclear monster that excretes deadly waste and you scratch your heads looking around for a toilet to dispose of it in.

"You rip open the earth's rich skin and contaminate its nourishing nutrients with the filth of the monster's waste matter. And you pour more of it into the fluid of the delicate veins—the life-giving waters.

"Tell me, an intelligence that does these heinous deeds and calls them energy advances, what would they do with all of this? Would you rest easy handing over these precious objects of truth to a people—a civilization—that calls interplanetary vehicles swamp gas?"

Michael blushed with the truth of it. He hung his head.

But Ra's compassion was great. "It will change. Already the Great Phoenix is stirring within the earth's womb. Already the native Peoples hear her labor cries. Yes, things will change soon and then the Truths will not be denied by the simple-minded doubters, the skeptics, and the self-deceivers. Until then, until mortals mature and open their eyes, ears, hearts, and minds, this place and others like it will remain protected by the Guardians who were charged with the task many centuries ago."

"Like the Ka of this one?" Emmy asked.

The Teacher nodded. "Yes, just like the Ka of this one."

Michael's voice became sorrowful. "I'm sorry we're such an ignorant lot."

Ra's head bent. "It's not your fault. Do not blame the blindness of entire civilizations on yourself. Each civilization and world population advances differently. Some go backwards a pace or two while others never make those errors of judgment. That's why the higher ones have been star traveling for centuries and the lower ones have just now made it to their moon.

"One day the higher ones will take compassion on their star

brothers and sisters. They will join to help them, but first the immature ones must grow more—into deeper wisdom and greater peace, harmony, and love. These things cannot be forced. They must evolve naturally in their own manner and order—in their own time."

Michael envisioned the earth people's time running out. It sickened him when he thought of the clever scientists and their miracle nuclear plants. Nuclear bombs in silos beneath peaceful and pastoral countryside. The primitiveness of bigotry. Materialism. Radioactive dump sites. Wanton pollution. The almighty dollar. Crime. Deceivers. Skepticism. All of them.

"Don't tear off more than you can handle, young man. One individual can't do it all."

"I know, but one man can start it. It has to begin with someone. It has to begin."

"And so it shall, so it shall."

A weighted silence hung in the room of treasure. A great stillness engulfed the Hall of Truth.

Dr. Weatherbee locked eyes with Ra. "Ra," he softly began, "do you foresee a time frame for the opening?"

"You refer to the discovery of this place. Yes, I do foresee the day, but a decade from now will still be too soon. Ten decades will be premature. The precise timing will depend upon many factors that only your people can bring about.

"Until materialism is replaced by spiritualism, until greed is dispelled and generosity takes its place, the discovery will not be manifested. Until the people of earth come to understand that they are a small but important part of a much greater Society of Beings, this place will remain hidden. Until the people of earth, as a whole, raise themselves to a more advanced level of thought, the Seventh Mesa will be protected from their prying eyes.

"My friends, this place will not be opened until those of earth deem it to be so by their own actions. . .their new thoughts. Only they can manifest their readiness. Only they can manifest the time for all this to be universally shared."

The three visitors felt weighted with the profound words of the Elder. What Ra spoke was true. Their hearts had recognized and validated the proof of it.

"Now," Ra said, "I know each of you have personal concerns and, if you so desire, I can give you each a small measure of time to privately consult with me on those."

The three looked at one another. They seemed to be in agreement with this latest suggestion.

Dr. Weatherbee verified the Elder's statement. "Yes, I do have a few personal questions for you. I appreciate your offer to discuss them with me."

The others admitted that they too would like a few moments alone with Ra if he could spare the time.

"Time is what I have most of," he said. Then, giving his attention to Emmy and Michael, he asked them if now would be a good time for them to have a better look around.

They understood and left Dr. Weatherbee with the Guardian. And as they moved about the Great Hall of Truth, they could hear the two engrossed in quiet discussion. . .one that was deep and highly meaningful for Dr. Weatherbee.

In turn, Emmy and then Michael spent time with the Elder, each resolving long-held concerns and receiving much-needed guidance that served to clarify their future paths. Between the three of them, the afternoon sped by and each sensed the time to depart.

A weighted silence hung in the Hall.

Michael was first to broach the subject. "Well? Guess the Ka got called away." He turned to his companions. "Ready?"

Weatherbee, with understanding, assented.

Emmy couldn't believe her ears. "But, Michael!" she whispered, "We have to wait and give. . ."

The young professor held out the papyrus to Ra. "Guess you get to deliver this for us after all."

Ra smiled in compassion for the enlightened man. He deeply empathized with him and understood his need to remove himself from the physical proof of the beautiful Truths his peers would remain too ignorant and arrogant to accept.

The Teacher raised his hand to the exit. "I'll show you out."

And Michael, still holding onto the fragile fragment, moved with his companions toward the opening.

Emmy, still confused but aware enough to perceive some nebulous communication passing between the three men, dropped her former objection.

The trio ascended the stairs and, without a last backward glance at the rich treasures or the swirling light of the crystal, stepped over the threshold and through to the burial antechamber.

Michael stopped beside the sarcophagus and turned to Ra who

remained just inside the Hall of Truth. "I'll just set this here," Michael said softly, resting the papyrus upon the lid.

"The Ka will like that very much. Tread gently though your world and, most of all, let compassion be your guide."

Click.

The towering statue silently slid back into place.

Blackness engulfed the three before they thought of the lanterns at their sides. The triple beams joined as one to rest on the papyrus.

"We were supposed to wait for the Ka!" Emmy cried, full of deep concern. "We were supposed to give it to him! Now we're all really in hot. . ."

Michael kissed her. "Who's burial chamber is this?"

"The Ka's."

"Who is this papyrus all about?"

"The Ka."

"And who were we talking with?"

Her shoulders slumped with impatience. "What is this? Fifty questions?"

He grinned. "Yes. Now just answer me. Humor me. Who were we talking with?"

She sighed. "Ra."

"And did you once, just once, ever see Ra *touch* anything? Sit down? Hold anything?"

She frowned. "No, not that I recall. Michael, for God's sake, will you stop beating around the bush and just come out with whatever it is you're trying to say?"

He smiled. "I'll do better than that. . .I'll show you."

He took her arm and guided her over to the paper fragment. He shined his light on a certain section. "Remember seeing *this* before?"

She leaned over the coffin lid to squint at the hieroglyph. And together, they sounded out the separate symbols within one of the Ka's many cartouches.

"Ra. . .Ta. . .Men."

The woman's scalp crawled. She looked up into Michael's sparkling eyes. She turned to see Weatherbee's smiling face. "Ra is the *Ka*? The Ka is Ra-Ta! We were *talking* with the Ka all along!"

The men nodded their heads.

She looked down at the papyrus. "So this tells his story." Her fingers traced along the engravings on the sarcophagus lid. "And this," she whispered reverently, "this is where his last body rests."

The truth of her words were felt by all. And each one, privately contemplating the message, reverently rested their hands on the Ka's coffin. . .the sarcophagus that held the alien essence of his final physical life.

The clear disc high above the desert sky cast an eerie aura of silver on the barren place below. In the ghostly mercurial light of the soft moonglow, three shadows silently moved across the spectral land. Together they walked away from the towering redstone Keeps. Away. Away they walked, never to return again.

A nighthawk glided overhead. With shimmering wings spread wide as it circled, it silently rode the drifting currents above the cooling desert. It veered over the rugged tops of the stone mesas that stood as eternal sentinels. It could hear their whispered words, their nocturnal chants, their singing. It heard their song to the ancient life that pulsed through the veins of the labyrinth below.

And it smiled.

Again the high-flyer veered off, away from the Standing Stones toward three shadows that slowly moved down below. Its head cocked. Keen sights eyed the quarry and it tilted to make its descent.

It was a night for whisperings.

The three walking shadows whispered.

And the nighthawk listened.

"Michael? Dr. Weatherbee? Are you sorry you can't reveal what's beneath the Seventh Mesa?"

"Sorry?" Weatherbee asked.

"Yes, because it represents a phenomenal discovery for you and Michael."

A bitter chuckle came from the elder man. "Would it be?"

She frowned.

Michael explained. "Emmy, don't you see that those precious treasures would have to be protected, cherished, and learned from if they were exposed? All those parchments and papyri and tablets and scrolls represent knowledge. Knowledge represents power. They'd have to be freely shared between countries, governments, peoples. The Truths that lay below could never be possessed by anyone—never owned, never tampered with."

Michael sighed with the heaviness of it as his misted eyes

looked up into the brightness of the silver orb that hung in the night sky. "Oh, Em, even if we could, who would we tell? Just who could we even tell?"

And again, the high-flying nighthawk smiled down.

The Silent, Sacred Place Below remained safe. It would continue to remain hidden beneath the Screaming, Burning Place Above until humankind raised itself up out of the darkness and walked tall into the Age of Light.

And the hawk veered away toward the distant adobe dwelling. It knew he could rest easy this night. . .and for many nights to come.

On the horizon, the stone mastabas stood tall in eternal relief against the sheer fabric of their delicate backdrop. The unyielding obelisks vaulted toward the heavens like mammoth markers in stark silhouette against the mystical blue moonlight. In classic symmetry did their long shadows stretch out across the gentle land below. In dignified silence did they proclaim themselves Sacred Sepulchers of the Knowledge of Causal Eminence that slumbered deep within. And the land shimmered in sublime consecration of their annointing stardust.

The Standing Stones softly whispered into the night but, this time, only the Wind Spirit was there to receive their sacred words.

THE KA'S
AFTERWORD

And so it is that the Sacred Articles and Treasures of the Timeless Wisdom remain forever protected from the greed of the immature civilizations.

So it has been written.

So it has been done.

Until Destiny's appointed Time—two measures beyond the outstretched wingspan of the Risen Phoenix—the Silent, Sacred Place Below will remain as a gentle heartbeat of Life Eternal beneath the funeral shroud of the Screaming, Burning Place Above.

For. . .I am.

I am the Sentinel. The Living Protector. The Guardian.

I am these because you are not.

And, until you are. . .I am.